Edward Everett Hale

# A Family Flight Around Home

Edward Everett Hale

**A Family Flight Around Home**

ISBN/EAN: 9783337192051

Printed in Europe, USA, Canada, Australia, Japan

Cover: Foto ©Andreas Hilbeck / pixelio.de

More available books at **www.hansebooks.com**

# AROUND HOME

BY

REV. E. E. HALE AND MISS SUSAN HALE

*Authors of "A Family Flight through France, Germany, Norway and Switzer-*
*land," "A Family Flight over Egypt and Syria," and*
*"A Family Flight through Spain."*

*FULLY ILLUSTRATED*

BOSTON
D. LOTHROP AND COMPANY
FRANKLIN AND HAWLEY STREETS

# CONTENTS.

# LIST OF ILLUSTRATIONS.

# A FAMILY FLIGHT AROUND HOME.

## CHAPTER I.

### BOSTON.

ON the second day of last April, a hack drove rapidly up to the warehouses of the Cunard Steamship Company, at East Boston, and stopped. A boy sprang out, opening the door himself, and was quickly followed by a gentleman about fifty years old.

"Is she in?" he demanded of the little crowd of loafers standing about.

"Just coming up now, sir," one of them replied.

"Ah! then we are not late. Come, Tom!"

"Your umbrella, sir," said the hackman.

"Oh, thank you, yes," replied the gentleman. "You must wait. Probably it will not be long now."

Mr. Horner and his son Thomas turned and walked as fast as they could through the long barren extent of solid sheds used for the reception and storing of freight by the Cunard Company. There was a little crowd setting in the same direction they were going, for the huge steamer was already coming up the bay, — close at hand, indeed, for they arrived at the end of the wharf just as ropes were thrown out and made fast to the stout posts prepared for them. As they hurried along, however, Tom, holding tight upon his father's arm, said:

"It must be rough outside. I am afraid the voyage has been pretty bad all the way."

He had to hold his hat on firmly, for the wind was blowing

hard. Against the wharf waves were dashing, and the small boats fastened there were bumping each other and bobbing up and down, while out at sea white sails were scudding fast in the breeze.

"A fine day to come up the harbor," said Mr. Horner. "Nothing prettier than the approach to Boston on a day like this."

Tom Horner was now fifteen. His features were not regular;

BOSTON HARBOR.

his mouth, when he laughed, which was often, might be said to stretch from ear to ear, but his eyes were bright, and his expression always was so animated that it did you good to look at him.

"Here we are!" he cried, "and here she is," referring to the steamer, swarming with passengers, stewards, and sailors, all in a hurry to leave the ship; "and there is Hubert," he added, with more excitement, running forward, shouting and waving at some one he had thus quickly discovered leaning over the rail of the upper deck.

It was Hubert Vaughan, much grown since the Horners had left him, but slight still; for some time, he did not find these friends in search of whom he was anxiously scanning the group of people on the wharf, but after a while his face lighted up as he caught sight of Tom's frantic hat-waving. Mr. Horner was behind, not having made so much headway as his son, but soon they managed to come together close under the place where Hubert was, and with some difficulty, on account of the roaring sound of escaping steam, and all the din and confusion of such a scene, they managed to make themselves heard.

"Can — you — come — down — to us?" bellowed Tom.

"Yes; I think so, IN A LITTLE WHILE!" shouted Hubert at the top of his lungs. "The gangway is too crowded now."

Then they all smiled upon each other longingly, and every one had so much to say, that no one could think of anything suitable for this shouting distance. Hubert, however, leaned over and said something which the others did not catch.

"What?" asked both the Horners.

Hubert repeated it with no better success.

"We don't hear what you say!" called Tom.

Hubert then made a mighty effort, and speaking through his hands, like a trumpet, said:

"No matter! I only said 'How do you do'!"

After this futile effort at communication, it seemed best for all to rest their lungs; very soon Hubert saw a chance of reaching the gangway, and, with his shawl-strap, he pushed for himself a passage, while his friends below watched his progress and followed in the same direction, in order to meet him as soon as he could leave the ship. They saw him stop several times to shake hands with fellow-passengers; and once he stopped to kiss a pretty little girl, about six years old, who seemed sorry to part with him.

At last, Tom could stand it no longer, and swinging himself along the outside of the passage plank, by holding fast to the rail, he alighted on the deck of the steamer close to Hubert's shoulder, in the middle of the crowding passengers who were somewhat disturbed and displeased for a moment.

The boys were so glad to meet, that a close grasp of the hand was hardly enough to express their delight. They would both of them been pleased to embrace, after the continental fashion, with a good, cordial kiss, but of course this would not do, between two staid young gentlemen of English descent.

"I'm so glad to see you, old fellow," said Tom; "here, let me take your bag."

"No; I can manage it," said Hubert, and by this time they were on the wharf, and Mr. Horner was looking kindly into Hubert's face, which brought back to him the sorrowful little fellow left fretting in the hotel at Madrid.

"We must come and see about your baggage at once. It is *baggage*, Hubert, here in America. Have you much?"

"No; only one rather big box, and my cabin things."

Thanks to the friendliness of the Custom House officials, a friendliness made active by Mr. Horner in a manner we need not describe, there was not much delay in finding and passing Hubert's modest possessions.

The driver strapped the trunk on the carriage, the three friends entered it, Mr. Horner banged the door, and called out:

"Now to the Vendôme!" and they were off.

"I am afraid, sir, it was inconvenient for you that I came in a Boston steamer," said Hubert. "My father put me in charge of the Hungerfords, and their passage was engaged for the *Samaria* already."

"That was all right," replied Mr. Horner, "it is perfectly easy

THE VENDÔME, ON COMMONWEALTH AVENUE.

for us to run on to Boston, and Tom here was glad of the chance."

"Are any of the rest here?" asked Hubert. "I want to see Bessie tremendously."

"No; we left them all at home; Bessie is very anxious to see you, and there was some little talk of her coming with us, but that plan fell through."

"But Miss Lejeune is in Boston!" said Tom.

"Is she?" cried Hubert, with a little start of delight. "Oh! I am so glad!"

"She is staying here with some of her numerous Boston

FANEUIL HALL.

friends," said Mr. Horner. "I sent her a telegram inviting her to meet us at the hotel, so I hope we shall see her in the course of the day."

It was now about lunch time.

"How jolly!" said both the boys; then Tom exclaimed:

"See. Hubert, that is Faneuil Hall, the 'cradle of American liberty'!"

"Faneuil Hall," repeated Hubert, and looking at the ancient building with some curiosity but more indifference.

"Hubert does not know yet enough of our history to be interested in its landmarks," said Mr. Horner. "We must give him some idea of the way by which America has grown to be" —

He paused, to see why their carriage was stopping, and Tom finished his sentence grandiloquently with the words —

"—a great and glorious nation."

The stop was caused only by a block in Washington street, close by the Old South Church. Huge drays, street cars, herdics, were tangled together in what seemed to be a hopeless dead-lock.

"What a funny cab," said Hubert, "with a door at the back!"

"Those are herdics," said Mr. Horner, "a sort of street conveyance lately introduced and much in use in Boston. They are not half so nice as hansoms."

"But have you no hansoms?" exclaimed Hubert.

"Very few," answered Mr. Horner. "In our American cities, and especially in Boston, the streets are so taken up with the rails of the street cars that it would be almost impossible for hansoms to dash about as they do in London."

OLD SOUTH CHURCH.

They were now disentangled, and soon were driving along by the Common, and afterwards the Public Garden, large open spaces pleasantly laid out with trees, but still dreary looking, without the first sign of spring. Patches of dirty snow still lingered on the north side of the streets.

Hubert was much surprised. When he left England, a fortnight before, the plum-trees were in blossom, crocuses and wall-flowers were profuse in gardens, and the grass green everywhere.

# CHAPTER II.



AS Mr. Horner, followed by the two boys, passed through the large vestibule of the Hotel Vendôme, a servant stepped forward and handed him a visiting card, upon a tray.

"The lady is waiting, sir," he said, "in the drawing-room."

Mr. Horner, smiling, showed the card to Hubert, who read upon it the name:

Miss Augusta Lejeune.

Miss Lejeune had been for some time in the handsomely furnished parlor of the hotel, inspecting the very good engravings on the walls. The furniture was new and handsome. The carpet was soft, and of quiet tones. A few books were scattered upon the centre-table, an open fire burned in the grate. A melancholy, solitary woman, travelling by herself from Nova Scotia to Manitoba, sat in a window, holding a book, but not even pretending to read. She was looking out upon the street, but the prospect was as dreary outside as in, large flakes of snow falling, accompanied by a drizzling rain, the sidewalks wet, and only a few pedestrians passing. A hand-organ was droning away in Commonwealth Avenue.

Miss Lejeune turned to put a damp foot upon the fender, and continued to study the apartment in the large mirror over the mantelpiece before her

"Every hotel," she reflected, "should employ a decayed gentlewoman to come in and out of the parlors at intervals, with work in her hand, and an air of being at home. She might put down a newspaper on the table, and then go away again. It would not cost much to pay her, besides her room and board, and would be an excellent enjoyment for some deserving" —

Her philanthropic scheme was disturbed by the sound of voices, and she saw Tom and Hubert and Mr. Horner coming from the hall.

"Hubert! Hubert Vaughan! What's this?" exclaimed Miss Lejeune. "Is it really you? Where did you come from?"

She placed her hands on his shoulders and looked earnestly in his face. Then the recollection of their sad parting at Gibraltar overcame her, filling her eyes with tears. She stooped and kissed him, for Hubert was not yet quite so tall as Miss Lejeune, though Tom was well above her in height.

Mr. Horner stood by enjoying her surprise. He had purposely, in his telegram to her, omitted all explanations, and she had no idea why he came to Boston at this time.

"Time enough for explanations later," he said cheerily, as he shook hands with her. "Augusta, you look younger than ever. Boston agrees with you."

"This climate does not," she replied. "Look at this weather. It has been just like this for six weeks. It does nothing but snow."

"Come and lunch with us," said Mr. Horner, "for we are as hungry as bears, are we not, boys?"

After a good lunch, during which they all talked at once, recalling Madrid memories, and the delights of Toledo, the boys were sent off to explore Boston by themselves, for Hubert pro-

ENLIVENING AN APRIL MORNING.

tested he was up to it. He had borne the voyage very well, with only a few days' sickness at first, and felt now perfectly well, with the exception of a little giddy feeling in his head, for which walking would be the best cure. He had had a fairly good passage, up to the last, when the steamer was greeted by a rough reception off our coast.

"And now let me hear what this means," said Miss Lejeune, when she and Mr. Horner were cosily seated, in a small private parlor, before a cannel-coal fire, little cups of black coffee beside them.

"May I have my cigar?" he asked.

"By all means, but begin."

"Well," he said, with half a laugh. "history repeats itself, you know. Not longer ago than yesterday, I received a letter from Colonel Vaughan. The boys, you know, exchange letters regularly."

"I think," interrupted Miss Lejeune, "that the Colonel has acquired the impression that you are responsible for Hubert for the rest of his life."

Mr. Horner shrugged his shoulders, and went on.

"He is ordered to India again, whatever that means, and it has occurred to him that Hubert would nowhere be so happy as with us; suddenly finding that certain friends were to sail at once for Boston, on this *Samaria*, he pops Hubert into the steamer with them, pops a letter in the box for me, saying he has done so, *et voilà tout !* "

"Well, well," said Miss Augusta, using her favorite means of comment. "But he must say something else: what does he want, does he mean the boy to be hanging upon you always?"

"There's always plenty of money, you know," said Mr. Horner. "Colonel Vaughan makes that clear in the letter. He simply says in addition, that he would like Hubert — to gain some knowledge of America and American history, a subject which at present more than ever interests or should interest Englishmen while it is one upon which in general they are singularly ignorant.'"

Mr. Horner as he talked had pulled the letter of Colonel Vaughan from his pocket, and he now read the last sentence from it.

"Very true," remarked Miss Augusta. "Now what are you going to do about it?"

"That's what we expect you to say," replied Mr. Horner. "You see we received this letter only yesterday, and that by good luck, as it came in a fast steamer, while the *Samaria* is slow."

"Is not she, though!" commented Miss Lejeune.

"I read the letter at dinner last evening," continued Mr. Horner. "There was not much time for consultation. Tom and I took the night train; breakfasted here; were told the *Samaria* would be up about ten o'clock; we drove to East Boston, and just arrived in the nick of time. Meanwhile, I have been revolving schemes in my head, as we came in the train, and only want to consult you about some good summer plan for these boys. Have you one of your ideas, Augusta?"

"Not yet," she replied musingly, "but I feel that there is a glimmer of one in the back of my head."

"There's no hurry," said Mr. Horner, "let it work. What I am thinking of is no new plan, but one which Hubert's coming develops and helps, that is, that my own children are better informed upon the history of any other country than their own; and that a summer might be spent very profitably as well as pleasantly by Tom, and even Bessie, in looking about them a little here in New England."

"Quite so," assented Miss Lejeune. "Take Boston now, Tom is showing Hubert the lions, but does he know the lions, and how to make them growl?"

"I doubt," replied Mr. Horner with a smile; "we shall see, however, what they report."

"Let us go to the theatre this evening," said Miss Lejeune. "And now tell me what you hear from the Herveys."

"Perfectly happy," replied Mr. Horner, "and I judge, from the letters, that Mary is perfectly well. The winter at Pau was just the thing for her, and I am glad she escaped our trying one here. I hoped they might be coming home this spring; but Hervey writes to urge our coming to them."

"And do you think"—asked Miss Augusta.

"Not for a moment," said Mr. Horner, holding up his hands to prevent even the mention of another foreign tour. "My wife is so happy in her own house, that she will not listen to anything but a New England summer, and as we can hardly stay in New York through the hot weather, you see we must invent some plan."

BUNKER HILL MONUMENT.

While they were thus talking, the boys returned, in good spirits, but tired and glad to rest, as indeed they might be, for with the courage of youth, they had walked over to Charlestown, to inspect Bunker Hill Monument.

"Why, Tom, we do not consider it the height of politeness to take an Englishman there the first thing."

"I know," said Tom, "but I could not think of anything else to show him, and we wanted a good long walk. They invited us to go to the top, but as there would be no view in this weather, we decided to follow aunt Dut's practice, and stay below."

Hubert asked a question which showed that he still knew but little of what every child in America is familiar with,—the story of the famous Battle (on June 17, 1775, of Bunker Hill.

"I believe, sir, I understand it now, only I do not think I quite know whom Tom means by the British."

The rest tried not to laugh, but it was not a successful effort. When Hubert saw this, he blushed furiously, but Mr. Horner said:

"Always own up your ignorance, my boy, and you will soon get over it. 'British' means subjects of Great Britain; when the quarrel began between the American colony and the government at home, the word British was generally used. So we keep to it now, in referring to that time, though not much otherwise."

After which Mr. Horner added:

"Tom, I dare say, is not well grounded in his country's early history; we must try to work it up."

## CHAPTER III.

### IN THE TRAIN.

"BOSTON and Lowell!" shouted the conductor of a street car, rattling the sliding door as he opened it with a bang. Out swarmed the passengers,—an old woman with a basket, a stout man with a bundle, a lawyer with his blue bag. Last of all, with shawl-straps and travelling bags, came Mr. Horner, Miss Lejeune, Tom and Hubert. All these persons passed into the large and handsome hall belonging to the station of the Boston and Lowell railroad.

It was cold and chilly, but not raining or snowing now.

"I believe you will have lovely weather," said Miss Lejeune.

"Change your mind, Augusta, and come with us," said Mr. Horner, coming back to the group with a handful of tickets for Wells River Junction and beyond.

"Oh, do, aunt Dut, come with us!" said Tom, and Hubert looked it.

"My dear, I have a lunch and a dinner to-day, both made for me, and am knee-deep in engagements all the week. It was only by Special Providence that I could give you yesterday."

"And by Special Heroism that you came to see us off so early," said Mr. Horner.

"I had to see the last of you," she replied cheerfully. "I shall try to break off here in order to be at home before you are, and learn the result of your pioneer expedition."

"Come, papa, they are all going to the train," said Tom.

They left Miss Lejeune hastily, who did not follow them to

the cold, bleak platform where a long row of cars was standing.

"Be sure and come to New York to meet us!" called Hubert, as he ran after the other two.

"You have no umbrellas!" exclaimed Miss Lejeune at the last moment.

Mr. Horner stopped, dismayed.

"Mine is at the hotel!" cried he.

"Never mind," was her ready answer. "I will find it. Go on!"

BOSTON AND LOWELL RAILROAD.

And so she did; but it would have been better placed during the next few days in the hands of its owner.

This was Hubert's first experience of American cars. He thought it very funny to enter at the end of a long passage-way, with a series of double seats on each side, instead of the short

SIGNS OF SPRING.

one, at right angles with the track, of most European compartments.

"How do you like it?" asked Tom, as they settled themselves by turning over the back of one seat, so that all of them could be together, and heaping their possessions in the vacant corner.

"Very much," said Hubert, "for Miss Lejeune has just been reminding me that I must like things as they are, and not think ill of them, because they are different to what I am accustomed."

"That is her favorite philosophy," said Mr. Horner.

"And all because Hubert said a hansom was better than a horse-car!" cried Tom.

"It is jolly," he added, "to have you with us, Hubert, for it makes us look at this from a travelling point of view."

They passed out over one of the long bridges which enclose Boston like a network on its water sides. It was a pretty, animated scene; the sun trying to break through the clouds lighted the water and tinted the smoke and steam from numerous tall chimneys. The monument on Bunker Hill looked more dignified at a distance than close under it, the boys thought. Many trains were darting in and out of their several stations. It seemed as if they must dash into each other; the engines shrieked as if in fear of collisions, but no such thing happened. Theirs was an express train and very soon was sweeping through the open country, freed from suburban streets, and cheap, squalid-looking houses, past fields, rusty and sere, with here and there a trace of spring. As they went farther north, there was more snow on the ground; only a few catkins of willow and alder were visible.

Tom's grandmother lived in Keene, N. H., and there he, as a little boy, had passed many a happy week in her house. This was his maternal grandmother. Mr. Horner's people came from Vermont; and he had spent his earliest years in the little town of Utopia, far away in the northern part of the State. The family home there, however, had long been broken up, and its members scattered. Nobody dared to say how many years it was since Mr. Horner had visited the place, although he had it always on his mind to do so, until now, when he was moved to take the boys on a little trip to survey the ground, hoping to find some pleasant resting-place for the summer, where all the family, or a part of them, might settle down. It was rather vague, for Hubert had suddenly come upon his American friends before they had begun to think of summer plans.

As the train swept through Lowell and Lawrence, busy manufacturing cities on the Merrimac, and afterwards Manchester, in the lower part of New Hampshire, Mr. Horner reminded the boys that the wonderful evidence of civilized industry they saw was the growth of but one century.

One hundred years ago, no manufacturing villages were to be found in all New England. Beavers built their dams unmolested along the banks of streams since crowded with mills and factories, each one of which finds work now for more men and women than, until the end of the eighteenth century, made up the population of the largest country town in America.

One hundred years ago Lawrence was a mere handful of houses; Manchester was no better. When the census was taken in 1820, the country around Lowell was a wilderness where sportsmen shot game. The falls which now furnish power to innumerable looms were all unused, and the two hundred sole inhabitants of the town found their support in the sturgeon and alewives taken from the waters of the Concord and the Merrimac.

At that time no manufactories could be said to exist with the exception of a few mills for making paper, scarce so good in quality as that grocers are now accustomed to wrap around pounds of sugar and tea; a foundry or two where iron was melted into rude pigs, or beaten into bars of iron; or a factory where cocked-hats and felts were made.

As for cotton manufacture, the first cotton mill was not erected in New England at the time the Constitution was formed. The place now held by cotton fabrics was filled by linen spun at every farmer's hearth. To spin well was then esteemed an accomplish-

THE SMALL WHEEL.

ment, like playing on the piano, or painting china at present, and every damsel of the old time was proud to excel in it. The "spinning bee" was once the fashion among the rich; it continued in vogue in many country towns when the ladies of the great

cities had deserted the wheel for the harpsichord and the spinet.
The bee was generally held in the town hall; but if the village
was not prosperous enough to contain such a building, the house
of some minister was chosen. Thither the women went with their
spinning-wheels and flax, and as they spun were brought cake and
wine by the fine gentlemen of the town.

All this spinning is done away with by the introduction of
machinery, and flax and linen have yielded for most household
purposes to cotton and cotton goods.

"Did you ever see a spinning-wheel?" Mr. Horner asked of
Hubert. Hubert was doubtful.

"Aunt Augusta has one," answered Tom, "in a corner of her
parlor, all tied up in blue ribbon like a pet dog."

"I fancy she would be puzzled to know how to use it. That
used to be called the small wheel."

"Oh! I know," cried Hubert. "I have seen them on the stage
in 'Martha,' the opera, I mean."

Mr. Horner said, "I remember another kind with a much larger
wheel, not uncommon when I was a boy; at which the pretty
spinner had to stand instead of sitting. We must try to find one
in Vermont."

"Was the spinner always pretty, sir?" asked Tom. "I imagined
them old women."

"As the fashion grew old, the spinners did, I suppose," replied
his father. "The young ladies would not learn, but the old ones
did not give it up. Lately, the fashion of collecting old things
has been so general, that garrets and barns all through New England have been pretty thoroughly ransacked, and, as you say, small
spinning-wheels have come out of their cobwebby corners to be
ornaments to modern drawing-rooms."

More and more snow covered the landscape as our travellers
went farther north; and when they came to Lake Winnepesaukee
horses and sleighs were driving merrily across the lake on the

ice. Hubert could not believe it. "On the ice!" he cried. "It looks like all the rest of the country."

He had never seen so much snow in his life; and as the ice of the lake was covered with a white enfolding sheet of it, no one could have distinguished between underlying land and water, except that here and there men were fishing through holes cut in the ice, below which was revealed the black water of the lake.

At noon they reached Wells River Junction, and after that crossed the Connecticut River, and leaving New Hampshire, passed into the State of Vermont. The country was very beautiful, even at that barren season; certainly it was at least to the eyes of Tom and his father, familiar with the roughness of American scenery. To Hubert's unspoken judgment, the heaped-up stone-walls, ragged root fences, small wooden houses, wide, desolate tracks of burnt-over land, little fulfilled the boast of progress and civilization of which Mr. Horner had been speaking.

# CHAPTER IV.



THE Indian names of places were puzzling to Hubert, and he entirely declined trying to remember how Winnepesaukee was spelt. Tom assured him that there were much worse ones down in Maine, such as "Pamedemcook Lake" and "Ambajem-ackomas Carry." Hubert asked if they were likely to see any Indians upon this journey.

"Not one," replied Mr. Horner. "You must travel much farther West or North to find any of them. Pretty much the only trace of them here is to be found in the names they gave to lake and mountain, and arrow-heads which are still dug up occasionally. Specimens of their weapons are preserved in historical collections. Yet until the first white colonists settled in America, the Indians had the whole of the country to themselves, roaming about, living upon game of which the forests were full, for the arrows of the Indians made no such wholesale destruction of animals as our modern weapons."

"What fun to have been here then!" cried Hubert; "just fancy an Indian all war-paint, behind that tree, for instance!"

"Brrrr!" said Tom, shivering, "I'm glad he is not, though!"

Time and absence from the early Indian have softened so much the general impression of his character, novels and legends have invested it with so much romance, that he has become an ideal sort of creature of romantic and attractive qualities. We are no longer in danger of being tomahawked in New Eng-land. An Indian in his paint and feathers is a rarer show than a white elephant. We are therefore more disposed to pity than to hate. But one hundred years ago, there were few men who had no reason to hate the Indians, and there were thousands whose cattle had been driven off, whose homes had been laid in ashes by the braves of the Six Nations, who had fought with them from behind rocks and trees, whose women had fled at the

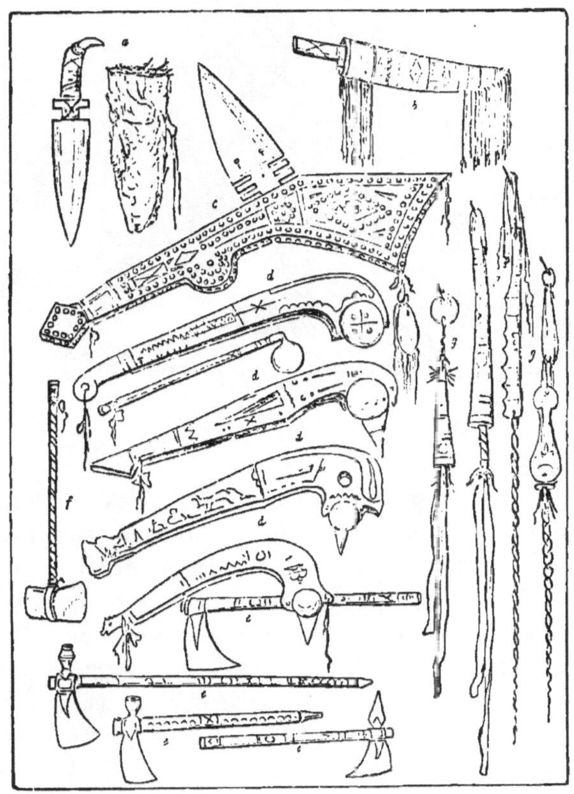

INDIAN WEAPONS.

dead of night from cabins set on fire by these relentless enemies.

Before the arrival of white people in America, the Indians, without fire-arms, and without whiskey, which had a fatal influence upon the disposition of the race, possessed, doubtless, many interesting traits of character.

The Indian was essentially a child of nature. His life was one long struggle, for his daily food depended on the skill with which

SQUAWS BUILDING A WIGWAM.

he used his bow, on the courage with which he fought fierce beasts, on the quickness with which he tracked, and the cunning with which he outwitted the timid, keen-scented animals of the forest. The clearness of his vision, and the sharpness of his hearing were wonderful by which he followed an obscure trail over difficult ground; with a cat-like tread, over beds of fallen leaves and heaps of dried twigs, walking close up to the grazing deer. Courage and fortitude in bodily suffering he possessed to a high degree; yet he was given to the dark and crooked ways which belong to the weak and cowardly. His favorite method of warfare was to rouse his sleeping enemies at dead of night with an unearthly yell, to massacre them by the light of their burning homes. Cool and brave men who have heard that whoop, have testified that no number of repetitions could strip it of its terror; that at the sound of it the blood curdled, the heart ceased to beat, and a sort of paralysis seized upon the body. Roused, and on the war-path, the savage was all activity. He would march all day through the snow, heedless of intense cold, and at night, rolled in buffalo robes, go hungry to sleep. But when the war was done, he liked to sleep all day in a wigwam of painted skins, blackened with smoke, decorated with scalps, and hung with tomahawks and arrows, singing, laughing and dancing at night in the moonlight. He made his squaw do all the work. It was Starlight or Cooing Dove that brought the wood for his fire and the water for his drink; that ploughed the field, and sowed the maize, and adorned his moccasins with bright embroidery and beadwork. When he travelled, she trudged along behind with the pappoose on her back.

The minds of the Indians were as crude as their characters, with strong imaginations, and but little reasoning power. They were full of superstitions, and the simplest things that happened, were to them fraught with meaning. If they were sick, some enemy had caused the malady, and the medicine man came and cured it by pretending to take out of the patient a toad, or a bright stone. Gay colors pleased them greatly, and the early settlers could barter with a handful of glittering beads, or a bright blanket, for a bundle of skins many times more valuable, or a hundred bushels of corn.

It was natural that the Indians should resist the encroachments of a civilization so different from their own as that of the whites; but their mode of warfare, with which, doubtless, they had dealt with each other for generations, was most horrible, and a grave impediment in the way of the early settlers of New England.

In the beginning, the colonists meant to keep on the right side of the Indians, though it is very likely that injustice was often done. There were men among the Puritans who were always trying to do good to them, and to secure peace by gentle methods. "The Apostle" Eliot, as he was called, devoted himself to making a translation of the Bible into their language. But after fighting had begun, the only course for the white settlers was one of self-defence, and for long years the struggle continued.

When first visited by Europeans, the Indians were said to be already decreasing in numbers, through their wars among themselves, and through diseases they were too ignorant to check. They have been diminishing ever since, although to this day settlements of the United States, in the far West, still live in constant fear of attacks from Indian tribes. But there are many children in New England who have never seen a real Indian, and none have heard the dreadful war whoop.

About noon, the conductor came to Mr. Horner to say that the train would shortly after stop over half an hour at Ellville, and that there, as he expressed it, "would be as good a chance as any to get some dinner." This was a joyful sound to the boys, who had breakfasted early; they were already on the platform when the engine stopped, and jumped out with alacrity, to find themselves facing the broad street of a considerable town, with brick sidewalks, blocks of houses and shops. The conductor showed them about forty rods off the sign "HOTEL," placed over a doorway, assuring them there would be ample time for dinner, besides going and returning. It was snowing fast, and the mud was miles deep, according to Tom's description.

"Now would be the time for your umbrella, papa," said he.

"Alas, yes," replied Mr. Horner; "Hubert, how comes it that you, an English boy, are without an umbrella?"

"They are not much in use in Gibraltar, sir," he promptly replied.

By this time they were wading through the mud, crossing the

INDIAN WARFARE.

street; a few planks placed for passengers, were sunk deep in
the mire, but gave a clue to the right direction, and on landing
on the opposite side, they found themselves directly in front of
the hotel, where a waiter was ringing a clamorous bell of invitation. They ran up-stairs, and entered a large, clean dining-room,

BARRICADE AGAINST THE INDIANS.

where several people, passengers in the same train with themselves,
were bolting their food, having already finished their soup.

"How in the world did they get here so quickly," murmured
Tom, as his party seated themselves, and shook out their napkins. A plate of hot soup was promptly placed before each, by
a pretty girl with "banged" hair who pronounced at the same time
the following sentence, or single word, for it sounded like only
one :

" Roastbeefdinnerpiechickenandporktripe."

" Say it again, please," said Tom, "and a little slower."
When she had repeated it, he said: " Bring it all except the
tripe."

The food was excellent, and well-cooked. Hubert was puzzled by
the little tubs set around his plate containing all kinds of vegetables,
tomato and apple-sauce; but he was warned to waste no time.
This course was followed by a choice of several kinds of pie.

By the time they had finished, with all possible expedition,
every one but themselves had left the place. The pretty waitress,
though she said there was plenty of time, looked anxiously at
the clock.

"Come, boys," said Mr. Horner, taking his hat. " I will go
first and pay, but do not delay!"

Fifty cents apiece was expected for the dinner, which was fully
worthy of that price.

They hurried back to their seats in the train, and had just five
minutes to spare before it started.

"So that's an American Fonda!" cried Hubert, whose spirits
were now rising to their usual level. Poor boy, the novelty of
the scene, the fatigue of the voyage, and the sense of being a
stranger in a strange land, were indeed enough to make him
reserved and silent; but the kindness of the Horners was irresisti-
ble, and he was beginning to feel the relief of being among true
friends after the comparative solitude of the last ten days on the
steamer.

" Yes," cried Tom, "shall you ever forget the time we all
tumbled out in the night, and bought knives?"

" It does not look much like Spain outside," said Mr. Horner.
The snow was falling more thickly than ever, and the sky was
dark and lowering. After a few hours they reached East Utopia,
their destination for that day, and went at once to the hotel
opposite the station.

# CHAPTER V.

## PROFESSOR BRUCE.

THE hotel at East Utopia was a modern affair, built of wood, and painted white. The public parlor, into which our friends were shown, up one flight, was a square room, containing a stove, a piano, a marble-topped centre-table, a sofa as hard as the Rock of Dundas, and two good rocking-chairs. The carpet on the floor was gaudy with huge roses; the paper shades in the windows were decorated with festoons of flowers, coarsely painted. On some bookshelves in a corner were several odd volumes of Congressional Documents, and a Bible. The paint was clean and fresh; everything looked neat, new, but stern and uncompromising. The days have gone by of old, large, hospitable fireplaces with commodious chimney corners. The tall clocks of colonial times have been first relegated to garrets, then removed to bric-à-brac shops, and now, burnished and polished, stand in halls of modern houses, which, by a freak of fashion, represent better the life of two centuries ago, than any really old interior. Even if the old house be standing, its huge, square chimney has been torn down, to give way to smaller flues, more economical of fuel. Andirons, roasting-jacks and cranes have gone up with the chimneys. A real old-fashioned kitchen would be hard to find in New England to-day. The best way to get an idea of such relics is through pictures and reproductions.

So the room of the new hotel seemed bare and forlorn; but a man came in with short logs which he popped into the stove, and in a few moments a crackling, snapping sound came from them, which was by no means cheerless; a bright glow shone through the little isinglass-covered openings of the stove door, and

OLD CLOCK.

a genial heat spread itself about in an incredibly short space of time.

"These Yankees know what they are about," said Mr. Horner, as he warmed his hands; "an old-fashioned fireplace consumed twice the amount of wood without warming half the space."

A cheery voice was heard below, and then somewhat heavy steps on the stairs; the door opened, and a gentleman, whom the boys considered old, entered.

"Ha! Horner, is this you? Well, I'm afraid I should not have known you."

"Mr. Bruce, this is very kind of you, to come over in such weather. I should know you anywhere, sir. You look younger than you did twenty years ago."

"Come, Horner, none of your jokes. I'm an old man, sir, yes, an old man. But here are the young ones; which is yours?"

"Tom," said the father, "this is my old schoolmaster, Professor Bruce. The first time he saw me, I was about your age."

"Why, Thomas, how are you?" said the old man, shaking hands cordially. And from that time ever afterwards he called him nothing but Thomas.

"And this is Hubert Vaughan, a young English friend of

ours, who has come over to learn something about America."

"You thought you would give him a lesson in climate, first, hey?" asked Mr. Bruce. "This weather is rather rough, even for us, but it can't last, — it can't last."

He sat down and rubbed his hands before the stove, kicked off his India rubbers, and loosened the knit comforter from his neck.

Mr. Horner sat down near him, and then between the two, to the amusement of Hubert and the amazement of Tom, there began a series of questions and answers about old friends, companions of Mr. Horner's youth, of whom Tom had never heard in his life up to this moment.

"Well, Horner, your mother is dead, and your father, too. Let's see, how long is it since you were here?"

"Seventeen years, sir. You know, after my father's death, my mother came down and lived with us; and so many of the old folks were gone from here, there has been no real object in a visit to the old place."

"Abraham is living, you know, and your aunt Jersey's second husband, he is still residing here."

"How is Susan?" asked Mr. Horner.

"Let's see, she is your father's niece; Susan Jones; why, she's married and living in Minnesota."

And so on, and so on, till the boys grew weary of the catalogue, and slipped away. It seemed to them as if nearly everybody were dead, or married and gone West.

"I wonder who is alive in the place!" exclaimed Tom, as he and

ANDIRONS AND CRANES.

Hubert wandered off to explore the house, and to inspect the weather, in case there were a chance of going out. Thick mud in the village street, encrusted in a kind of frosting of new snow like wedding-cake, forbade this scheme. Meanwhile the gentlemen talked on, never weary of old reminiscences.

Mr. Horner had been fitted for college at Montpelier, Vt.,

THE OLD PLACE.

by Professor Bruce, in his charge, and boarding in his family. This life of several years made them intimate, and a friendship was formed of the lasting sort, which comes from true respect and gratitude on the part of the younger man, and affectionate approbation on the older one's side. The difference in years was not excessive: for Mr. Bruce was but a young man just graduated when he began his career as a schoolmaster. He was now somewhat over sixty. He married, in early life, a Utopia girl, a cousin in fact of the Horners, and as on the death of her parents she inherited a comfortable little property, Mr. Bruce then bought the whole Horner estate, with its old-fashioned house, large barns, and ample farms; and thus it came about that he was now occupying the homestead where Mr. Horner was born, and where he and his brothers and sisters passed the happy days of their youth.

Mrs. Bruce never had any children; Mr. Horner remembered her as a delightful little woman. As soon as he thought of the plan of coming into Vermont with the boys, he wrote to Mr. Bruce to inform him of it; and the genial old gentleman harnessed up in spite of the weather, and drove into town from the farm, which was three miles distant from East Utopia, the nearest station on the railway.

Mr. Bruce stayed to the early "meat-tea" of the hotel, an ample meal of nice beefsteak, baked potatoes, real cream and sweet, fresh butter. Then he drove away in his buggy with the old white mare, Lucy.

"Get up, Lucy! get up!" said he, as he took the reins and shook them on her back. "Cl'k! cl'k!"

The leisurely starting of the excellent animal gave him ample time to say, as he poked his head out of the side of the buggy:

"Seems like better sleighing than wheeling, Horner. Guess you'd better tell them to send you over on runners!"

It was snowing more vigorously than ever. It had been agreed between the gentlemen that it was best for the Horner party to spend the night at the hotel, where they were, and to drive next morning to Utopia, about three miles "over the mountain," as the natives called it. A beautiful road which Mr. Horner well remembered.

The boys of course longed to go on runners, and were delighted next morning with the verdict of the master of horses, that there was "about as much sleddin' as wheelin' anyway, and always plenty of snow on the mountain."

The sun, for a wonder, seemed trying to break through the clouds as they all emerged from the house, well buttoned up in great coats ready for an early start. Their driver, the owner of the team, composed of two stout black horses, was encased in a warm coat of coarse yellow fur. Thick leather boots were drawn up over his trousers, and he had a fur cap on his head.

Mr. Horner and Hubert were packed in on the back seat of a

FALLS BY THE ROAD.

wide sleigh, with a buffalo robe to sit on, and a buffalo robe over their knees, tucked in closely about them. Tom was stowed away on the front seat next the driver; two huge umbrellas were placed in the vehicle, one for each seat; the small travelling effects of the party were underneath.

And so with cheerful good-bys to the host and several assistants who were by to see them off, the team started.

At the very outset, a steep ascent was to be made, and this was more mud than snow. About half-way up, the sleigh was stuck fast, and for a moment it seemed doubtful if they could get on.

"I don't know but we shall have to give it up!" said Brick, the driver; but he jumped out into the mud, and by coaxing the horses, and pulling at their mouths, he persuaded them to a part of the hill where the ruts were not so deep. Once at the top, they found themselves better off, and soon were gliding over almost unbroken snow, in a lovely wood road. On each side tall trees rose, and behind them huge rocks. Streams rippled along down the hillsides, wetting ferns, which, evergreen the winter through,

OLD-FASHIONED FIREPLACE.

overhung their borders; birds were singing, the air was soft, and seemed to promise spring, though spring had not arrived.

"How lovely it must be here in summer!" cried Tom. "It is like the road under West Mountain, at Keene, papa!"

"There used to be a crow's nest in the top of that tree," said his father, "and here is where I fell off the rock once, twenty feet down." He was full of reminiscences of his boyhood, which all came back to him vividly, on returning to the spot where they were enacted.

VERMONT IN APRIL.

## CHAPTER VI.

### THE PILGRIMS.

IT was but three miles to their destination, and where the sleigh-ing was good in the woods, they slipped rapidly over the ground. Soon after passing some lovely falls and rapids, they began to approach the little village of Utopia.

Mr. Horner exclaimed:

"There's the house! there's my old home! Do you see it, boys?"

It was conspicuously placed on high land, which fell off rapidly behind the house to the level of the Connecticut. This river here flowed through a broad valley, in a shallow bed, now encumbered not only with ice, but logs, which had floated on the water from some place higher up.

Mr. Bruce was awaiting them on the broad flat doorstep, as the party drove up. They all stopped to look at the wide view down the Connecticut valley.

"So that is New Hampshire!" said Tom.

"Yes; we are just on the boundary," said the old gentleman; "but come in, come in! Mrs. Bruce is waiting for you, and it is cold outside."

Good Mr. Brick, dismissed with a friendly good-by, and a suitable sum in his pocket, now drove off down the hill.

The others entered the house, where Mrs. Bruce was standing at the door of a large room. She was a little bit of a woman, with gray hair that had once been yellow, smoothly put away under a cap; she was wrapped up in a knit shawl, and she shivered as she urged them to come in. The room was nice and warm from the heat of the inevitable wood stove.

Every one sat down for a few minutes; but Mr. Horner, with all the impatience of a boy, wanted to see the old house; and with Mrs. Bruce's permission, they went all over it from garret to kitchen, pausing to look at the extensive views from every window, which, fine even at that season, promised to be beautiful in summer.

The hope of the early morning, that pleasant weather was coming, failed; before noon snow began to fall, and when the mid-day din-

EARLY NEW ENGLAND SCHOOLMASTER.

STILL SNOWING.

of our city friends, was an open fire of logs. The walls of the room were lined on all sides with shelves, crammed with books, books, books; old, modern, shabby, some few splendid in calf and gold.

"This looks natural," said Mr. Horner, as he walked up to the shelf of dictionaries and pulled out a battered Latin Lexicon. "Nothing so familiar as a well-worn old friend of this sort." He turned at once to a certain leaf on which he expected to find, and did, his own initials scribbled on the margin and decorated with the American flag, drawn in a flourishing style.

"Here is History," said Mr. Bruce, turning to the boys, pointing out one large division of shelves, "and all this is American History; or ought to be," he added with a smile. "My books are arranged according to a system, but it is not so unerring as the Solar one; my planets often wander from their orbits." As he spoke, he took a volume of Palfrey's New England from among the dictionaries and placed it in its own gap on the New England shelf.

"You had better amuse yourselves," he continued, "with the books, while your father and I are talking matters over." The two elder gentlemen settled themselves before the fire, the professor with a well-browned pipe, and Mr. Horner with a cigar, while the younger pair took down various books relating to American History, and compared notes as to their ignorance or knowledge of the subject. Tom, of course, had the familiarity of an average boy, not especially fond of reading, with the past of New England, but he soon found Hubert's questions were too much for him, and after a time, and as it grew towards dusk, the boys came to the fireside, and by their remarks, led Mr. Bruce into some rather rambling talk on his favorite hobby, the early life of New England.

It came out that the aggregate stock of the combined knowledge of the two boys amounted pretty much to this: that Columbus discovered America; that his voyage was not the same as that of the *Mayflower*, though Hubert was not clear on this point, on account of the general resemblance, in pictures, between that vessel and the caravels of the discoverer.

CARAVELS OF COLUMBUS.

They also knew that the Puritans left England for more freedom in religion than they could have at home; that they went through all sorts of sufferings from the hardships of the climate, and the lack of the comforts of civilization, also on account of the Indians, with whom they could not keep peace.

By and by, the boys supposed, the colonies became prosperous, and all went on well until they quarrelled with the mother country, resisted the control of rulers and laws sent out to them from England, and began, with Lexington and Bunker Hill, the struggle for independence, which ended in the famous Declaration of July 4, 1776.

"And since then," said Tom, "we have just had a Republic, with Presidents, beginning with Washington, you know, Hubert, and going on straight along down to our own times."

On a Saturday noon, near the close of autumn (November 11, 1620), the *Mayflower* dropped her anchor in the harbor of what is Provincetown, Cape Cod. This was the beginning of the Colony of Plymouth. When four years had passed, the village consisted of only thirty-two cabins, inhabited by a hundred and eighty persons. Six years later it numbered three hundred persons, and at the end of its life of seventy years, its population had probably not come to exceed eight thousand. It is on account of the virtue displayed in its institution and management, and of the great consequences to which it ultimately led, that the Colony of Plymouth

FIRST NEW ENGLAND WASHING DAY.

claims its importance. Its early records describe the building of log houses, turning sand heaps into corn fields, dealings with stupid Indians, anxious struggles to get a living, and the sufferings of men, women and children, wasting under cold, sickness and famine; it is the heroism and courage, moved by the noble impulse of a sense of religious obligation, which give interest to the details of the first days of this settlement.

Having kept their Sabbath quietly, the men began the labors of the week by landing a shallop from the ship and hauling it up on the beach for repairs, while the women went on shore to wash clothes. While some of the men were at work on the boat, sixteen others set off on foot to explore the country. On this expedition they saw five or six savages, who ran away from them.

Such is the simple account of the first week-day of these pilgrims in a strange land. The time of year was most unfavorable. December was upon them, and the severity of the cold was extreme.

THE MAYFLOWER.

After some exploration, by land and water, it was on the twenty-second of December that they decided upon a place "as they supposed fit for situation." Trustworthy tradition has preserved the knowledge of the landing-place. It was PLYMOUTH ROCK.

No time was now lost. By the end of the week, the *Mayflower* had brought her company to keep their Sabbath by their future home. Their first favorable impressions of the spot they had chosen were improved by further exploration. There was a convenient harbor, "compassed with a goodly land." The country was well-wooded; the sea and beach promised abundance of fish and fowl, and four or five small running brooks brought a supply of "very sweet fresh water." After prayer for further divine guidance, they fixed upon a spot for the erection of their dwellings; a storm came to interrupt their proceedings, very naturally, on the sixteenth of December. Then they set to work to fell timber and set up their houses. It was agreed that every man should build his own house. The frost and bad weather hindered them much. Seldom could they work half the week.

Yet they persevered through far worse troubles; sickness from exposure and want of proper food carried off nearly half their number during the terrible first winter. But courage and fidelity never gave out. The well carried out the dead through cold and snow, and then hastened back from the burial to wait on the sick; and as the sick began to recover, they took the places of those whose strength was exhausted. There was no time, and no inclination, to despond. The lesson was not forgotten, that "all great and honorable actions are accompanied with great difficulties, and must be both enterprised and overcome with answerable courage." The dead had died in a good service, and the fit way for survivors to honor and lament them was to be true to one another, and to work together bravely for the cause to which dead and living had alike been consecrated.

"Warm and fair weather" came at length, says their record, "and the birds sang in the woods most pleasantly." Never was spring more welcome. It began, fortunately for them, to show itself in early March, a full month earlier than the year when the Horners, on a day near the middle of April, were sitting before a comfortable fire. Snow fell thick without, while Mr. Bruce was reading or repeating the above, from Palfrey's History of New England.

# CHAPTER VII.

## IN BED.

THE delicious country tea provided by Mrs. Bruce's hospitality failed to tempt Hubert's appetite. He refused muffins, and even hot brown waffles, to be eaten with maple syrup; and finally asked to be excused, saying he felt a little faint.

He was advised to go to bed, and Tom went up with him to the large room at the top of the house which had been assigned to the two boys. Mrs. Bruce, a little anxious, followed them a little later, and on her return, reported Hubert as feverish. She made him as comfortable as she could, and left him, hoping a good night's rest would set him right; but the next morning he was quite ill, and kind old Doctor Goodkin was sent for. He pronounced it fever, though not alarming; the consequence, probably, of over fatigue, not an unnatural effect of the voyage, and prescribed staying in bed for the present.

This was awkward, for Mr. Horner's business compelled him to be back in New York by Saturday night, and for this it was necessary to leave Utopia at noon, that day.

Hubert knew this, and begged Mr. Horner to leave him with the Bruces, who would, he said, be just as good as possible to him. Mr. Horner hesitated, then said, at first, that he would leave Tom with Hubert; but after all due delicacy, it was decided that Hubert only should remain, while Tom and his father went on to Burlington for that night, and home to New York the next day, through Rutland and Albany.

Thus it happened that Hubert began at once his Vermont life, and did not go to New York, for the present. Tom went back to school, which was important, as he was finishing his last year. It was arranged that Mr. Bruce should take the two boys for the summer, to board and teach, beginning at once with Hubert, on a regular course of study and reading.

"Good-by, old fellow," said Tom, standing at the bedside of his friend ; "it seems rather rough to leave you in this way."

"Don't you worry," returned Hubert with a smile ; he was really not very ill, only not quite up to travelling. "I shall be out and all over the country directly, while you are grinding away at school."

"Be sure," said Mr. Horner, "to write us if you feel lonely, and we will send Bessie up to you, or somebody."

"That would be a temptation to make believe I was lonely," replied Hubert gayly ; "for I long to see Bessie. But I think there are people here I shall make friends with. Tom, did not you see a pretty girl in the snow storm yesterday, just as we were arriving ? "

"Was she pretty ? I did not look at her, but her dog. I hope she is, for your sake."

"Come ! " called Mr. Bruce from the foot of the stairs, and the parting was hastened.

Tom and his father again packed into a sleigh, went back over the mountain to the station, while Hubert turned on his pillow with a sigh, more disheartened, now that he was really left, than he had allowed to appear. Poor fellow, he had a stout heart, and had already in life met with sad experiences.

Before long, Mrs. Bruce came to him, and put a soft hand on his head.

"If you feel equal to it," she said, "I want you to slip on my husband's dressing-gown and come down-stairs one flight. You will be more comfortable there, and we can look after you more easily."

The change to the Blue Room was very pleasant. It was a small chamber opening from Mrs. Bruce's own room, — a sort of boudoir in fact, though she would have been amazed at such a name. It contained some old-fashioned things, — an old easy chair with high sides, to rest the cheek against, a work-table with drawers and a bag beneath, and a nice little bed, just put up on purpose for the invalid, with a delightful patchwork quilt made of bits of very old prints, — cocks and hens, gaudy flowers, men and beasts, sewed together in diamonds and squares.

THE RED SCHOOLHOUSE.

The room was on the sunny side of the house, and the sun, for a wonder, was streaming in at the window; the warmth of a large stove in the adjoining chamber penetrated it pleasantly. Here Hubert was installed, and here, by and by, Mrs. Bruce came and sat by him, knitting a stocking. Her fingers flew fast, and she chatted cheerfully, about all manner of things. That first day Hubert was too languid to talk much himself. He slept a good deal, and the rest of the time liked to lie looking at the patterns of his bedquilt.

Mrs. Bruce had lived all her life in the country, where her parents and grandparents were born and died, true representatives of the New England type. She remembered herself a primitive sort of life, and she could repeat also a thousand traditions of olden times.

"My grandfather," she said, "was a schoolmaster, just as Mr. Bruce has always been, but things were very different in old times. No such comforts as we enjoy fell to his lot, and yet he raised a large family. He kept school in the little red schoolhouse

THE COLONIAL SCHOOLMASTER.

I will show you, the first time we drive out. It is standing yet; but you will see also, some day, what a fine Academy there is over at East Utopia.

"School was held for two months in the winter, by a man, and for two months in summer by a woman. The boys went in winter, the girls in the summer.

"My grandfather," she said, "was scarce out of his teens when he began teaching, and some of his boys were bigger than he was. He did think of studying for the pulpit, but he kept straight along teaching all his life. His pay was small, but he did not have to lay out any of it on his keep, that is, not till after he was married, for the district paid for his board with whatever farmer would board and lodge him the longest time for the amount.

"In some districts this was far too expensive a method, and the master was expected to live with the parents of his pupils, regulating the length of his stay by the number of the boys in the family who went to his school. So it happened that in the course of his teaching, he became an inmate of all the houses in the district, and not seldom had to walk five miles, in the worst of weather over the worst of roads, to his school. But he was always a welcome and honored guest. He slept in the best room, sat in the warmest nook by the fire, and had the best food set before him at the table. In the long winter evenings, he helped the boys with their lessons, held yarn for the daughters, and escorted them to spinning matches and quiltings."

"What are quiltings?" asked Hubert feebly.

"Why, that quilt that you are lying under was made at a quilting bee," said Mrs. Bruce; "it was when Grandfather Horner was courting his wife."

"What! My Horners?"

"To be sure. Tom's great-grandfather was this same schoolmaster. We have quilting matches now once in a while, up here in the country. When you get well, I will show you the great quilting-frame in the garret."

When Mr. Bruce came in to see Hubert after dinner, and heard what they had been talking about, he added some of his own reminiscences, as a schoolboy, when manners were but little changed from those of a hundred years ago. They used to sit eight hours a day on hard benches, poring over Cheever's Accidence, puzzling

out long words in Dilworth's Speller; they had to read long chap-
ters in the Bible, and learn by heart Doctor Watts' Hymns for
Children; to be drilled in the Assembly Catechism; to go to bed
at sundown, get up at sunrise, and live on brown bread and pork,
porridge and beans. When Sunday came round, or, as they called
it, the Sabbath, they found it anything but a day of rest. There
were long prayers in the morning by the master, and commenta-
ries on some Scripture text to be got by rote before meeting,
to which, dressed in their best, they marched off, with ink-pot and
paper, to take down the heads of the sermon, in order to give
what account of it they could at evening prayers. Between morning and afternoon meeting they were indulged with a cold
dinner.

"The master did not, in old days, consider it his duty to explain
anything to his school. His business was to stand, rod in hand,
while his pupils pondered hopelessly over lessons which ten words
would have made clear. There were no modern appliances to help
the eye and mind, such as maps and charts, blackboards, globes and
models."

"Oh, dear," sighed Hubert, "I'm glad I was not there!"

The early colonial schoolboy had more trouble with his arithmetic
than those of the present day, on account of the confusion caused
by the different kinds of coin. Our easy table —

<blockquote>

10 mills make a cent  
10 cents make a dime, etc.,

</blockquote>

would have seemed to him but a trifle. Until after the framing
of the Constitution, there was no national currency based upon a
universally recognized unit. The English pound and the Spanish
milled dollar were equally current, the pound being divided into
shillings and pence, while the Spanish dollar was divided into shillings, Spanish bits or pistareens, half-bits or half-pistareens, coppers
or pennies, while these varied in value in different States. The

schoolboy therefore was expected to convert with readiness pounds and shillings into dollars and bits, and to know whether a pistareen, New York money, was worth more or less than a pistareen, New England money. Not that he was allowed to spend himself many of either.

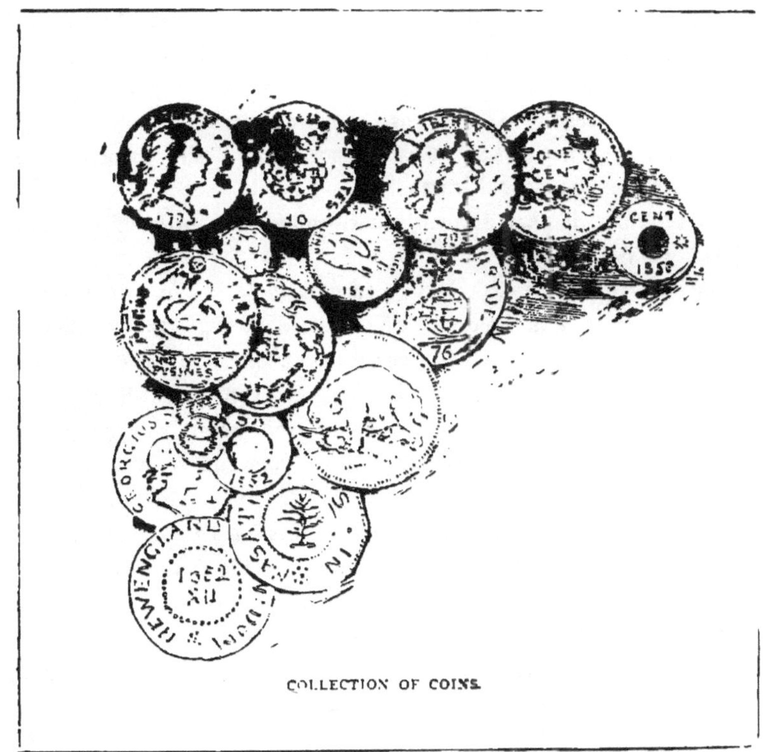

COLLECTION OF COINS.

# CHAPTER VIII.

### REGULAR LESSONS.

HUBERT'S illness was hardly anything more than the over fatigue of his voyage. The rest in the quiet country house where he now found himself, the gentle care of Mrs. Bruce, and her husband's pleasant manner to him, were all comforting and salutary. In a few days he was anxious to be up and out, especially as there began to be signs of spring weather.

One morning he asked Mrs. Bruce, when she came in as usual, after her household cares:

"Whose voice is that I heard down-stairs? A little girl's voice, I should think."

"That is Alice," replied Mrs. Bruce with a smile, "my niece, who lives over in that house." She pointed through the window at a house not very far distant. "She has been here once or twice to hear how you are, and she wants to see you. See, here are a few May-flowers! By the time you are well, there will be plenty in the woods, and she wants to go with you and show you where to find them."

Hubert had never seen the pretty flowers of the *Epigæa repens*, trailing arbutus, or May-flower. It bears all these names, the first being its true botanical one, the second given to it, in various places where it grows, for no imaginable reason, and the last a tribute to the welcome it gave, the first spring flower they saw, to the Pilgrims at Plymouth, after the dreary winter of 1620.

That afternoon, when Hubert had been established in the old easy chair, and partaken of a juicy bit of beefsteak, Alice Martin was allowed to come up and make him a visit. As soon as he saw her, he recognized the pretty girl in the snow storm, whom he had noticed the day he arrived.

She looked about his own age, and she was very pretty. At first, she was shy, and so was Hubert. Neither of them thought of anything to say, after the first few sentences.

"Are you Tom Horner's cousin?" asked Hubert, at length.

"Sixth or seventh only, I believe," said Alice, "and you know I have never seen any of the Horners. They have never been here, and I have never been in New York. I suppose they are rather stuck up, they have been abroad so much."

Alice had been boarding at East Utopia, to "attend the Academy," for two years, from which she had returned feeling herself somewhat superior to ordinary beings, which accounts, perhaps, for ascribing to others the condition called "stuck-up."

"Oh, no, they are not in the least!" cried Hubert, prompt to defend his friends, "although I don't know

MAY-FLOWERS.

at all what you mean, only something unpleasant."

"Oh, I didn't mean anything unpleasant," hurriedly replied the

GOING AFTER MAY-FLOWERS.

girl, as she buried her face in the sweet-smelling May-flowers. "Are they not sweet?" she continued, to change the subject. "We are going to have a party to gather them, as soon as they are plenty. Won't you come?"

"With pleasure," replied Hubert, "only if it is a large party I shall be afraid."

"You stick close to me," said Alice with a smile, "and you will be safe enough."

Not many days afterwards, the party came off, — several children of the place, with Alice and Hubert, and Professor Bruce, as young and active as any of them.

Going after May-flowers has not the ideal charm of going a-Maying as described by the poets. Hubert knew nothing of an English May, as his life had been chiefly passed away from home; but he fancied there must be a difference. The day was bright. The road was muddy; after they had turned from it into a wild cart path through the woods, they walked on damp, dead leaves of the year before.

By and by they came to a sort of opening, where the sun

EARLY SETTLERS.

streamed in and made it warmer. Tall pine-trees surrounded the spot, and the ground was red with the fallen pine tassels.

"Here it is! Mine is the first!" cried Alice.

Hubert had seen nothing, though he was walking by her side:

but now, as she stooped, he perceived she had found a bunch of
the pretty, starry flowers, poking their heads up from the leaves
and pine tassels. To his surprise, as she pulled the stem, a long
string of the plant came up, with plenty of flowers attached to
the strong stems. The leaves were of the year before, which,
under the warm covering of fallen pine, had passed the winter

A RUDE BEGINNING.

comfortably, the incipient buds hidden in their axils, all ready
with the first breath of spring, to push up and open.

After this they found plenty, and their baskets were rapidly
filled. A kind of mania seized every one to find the pinkest
blossoms. There was every shade, from pale pure white to deep-
ening rose color.

Mr. Bruce wandered off, searching for botanical specimens, but
there was nothing yet to be found. The May-flower precedes
everything else. Evergreen ferns, left from the autumn, and bright

green moss, in the wet places, were the only variety of color upon the gray and reddish tints of bare branches, and the yellow leaves still clinging to birches and some oaks.

As they came home by a roundabout road, Hubert saw, for the first time, maple-trees ready for sugaring. Each tree had a hole bored in its trunk, and a pail hanging on a peg below the opening, waiting for the sap to run. All the pails were empty.

"The sap don't run worth a cent this year," said Mr. Brick, the day he drove them over; "we don't seem to have the right kind of nights. Real cold, and then the sun out bright afterwards. That's what makes it come. I ain't sure as there'll be 'ny more sugar."

Somehow or other there was sugar and very delicious maple syrup, to be eaten on griddle cakes and waffles.

Meantime, Hubert's trunks had arrived; and he had returned to the up-stairs room, where he installed himself with all his possessions.

A corner of the library was also allotted to him, and regular lessons began. Mr. Bruce found him on the whole, better grounded than Mr. Horner had led him to hope; the boy's training had been so desultory, there was little reason to expect much in the way of results. He wrote a good hand. His spelling was rather wide of the mark, bearing traces of the different languages he had made acquaintance with. As yet, he had no settled habits of study; but he was willing to apply himself, and on the whole, did not waste much of the three hours, daily devoted to study, in scribbling over pieces of paper, and practising styles of handwriting.

He read aloud every day, for Mr. Bruce believed that daily practice alone makes perfect in an accomplishment so well worth having as a good style of reading and enunciation, not elocutionary, but simple and distinct.

Hubert was surprised to find how much ground he went over

by such steady reading aloud for two hours every day. It seemed much slower than reading to himself, and yet the pages of Palfrey's New England melted like snow beneath the sun; and he found, moreover, that what he read in this way he understood and enjoyed more thoroughly than what he read to himself, in the skimming, skipping fashion which may suit a story book, but is bad as a habit.

The Plymouth Colony was the first of the early settlements of New England. It was followed by others, and in 1692, united with that of Massachusetts Bay, under the name of Massachusetts, which, being thus first settled, was in a manner the parent of the later colonies.

Maine was one of the earliest parts of the country visited and explored by Europeans. An English colony tried to establish itself there, and a French colony soon after. But in the end, during the colonial period, Maine was reckoned as a part of Massachusetts.

New Hampshire was visited very early, and Portsmouth and Dover were settled in 1623. These settlements were chiefly on the coast for fishing; the colony extended very slowly, and it was long before the northern and interior townships were filled up; in many cases, by people coming from Scotland and Ireland. By the time of the American Revolution, New Hampshire was a strong and independent colony, taking its name from Hampshire in England, whence came some of its early settlers.

Vermont was first explored in 1609; but had no European settlers for more than a century after that. Down to the time of the Revolution it was not recognized as a separate colony, but went by the name of the "New Hampshire Grants," as if that State had the control of its land. New York, however, also laid claim to these same "Grants;" it was a long time before the Green Mountain Boys, as they called themselves, became independent of the other colonies. The name Vermont means only Green Mountain.

During all this time the different colonies were under rulers appointed from England, and had no thought of a separate government. The first planting of the soil, and foundation of settlements, from the very beginning, as we have seen of the seventeenth century up to the period of the Revolution, were under the auspices of the English government. The wars were English wars, the troops were British troops, who fought against the enemies of the English crown, whether French or Indian.

Up, therefore, to the time of the separation, the interests of the American colonies and of the Home Government were the same; and the colonists became involved in the quarrels between England and France. Thus the war known in American History as "King William's War," in which Indians fighting for the French, perpetrated horrid barbarities upon the settlements of the colonies, was in fact between England and France, or rather between Catholic France and the Protestant countries of Europe. It lasted for nine years, during which Louis the Fourteenth of France won many battles; but at the end of which he was willing to make peace, at Ryswick, just before 1700.

LARCH CONES.

# CHAPTER IX.

AN ADVENTURE.

A LICE and Hubert became, perforce, constant companions; not so much from any great congeniality, as by strength of circumstances. Hubert felt himself greatly superior to the country girl, who, in spite of certain airs and graces acquired at school, was lacking in polish, and whose pronunciation of some words was a constant surprise to him. Alice, on the other hand, while she stood in awe of Hubert's fine manners, and somewhat dainty ways, held her own very well. She had no idea of being patronized, and if on any occasion there seemed danger of his getting the better of her, in points of etiquette or good grammar, she readily turned the tables on him by exposing his utter ignorance concerning all country things. The science of the barn, the hen-coop, and the farm was one in which she was well versed, while he had not even studied its rudiments.

Mr. Martin, the father of Alice, owned a large farm, and with the help of many men, took care of it himself. As the spring opened, Hubert spent most of the time over at Alice's, where the attractions for the two children were greater than at the professor's.

Hubert loved animals, and he delighted in the long barn, where the long row of cows and a yoke of oxen were at home in their stalls, six of them, sticking out their great friendly heads, and giving steamy puffs of breath that smelt like hay. He was, to tell the truth, a little afraid of them, and never learned to venture so near them as Alice did. Hens wandered freely about the place, and took familiar liberty with the good-natured cattle, and little birds flew in at the door to peck the scattered corn upon the ground. Over the horse-stalls was the loft, reached by a somewhat shaky set of steps, where feats of climbing could be performed by means of

THE OLD BARN.

the bars, stretching from one stall to another. Alice was well versed in these feats, although at fifteen she considered them beneath her dignity; she rather despised Hubert for his awkwardness in getting about over beams and down cribs; it was an awkwardness caused by ignorance rather than want of courage, and at last a little adventure redeemed him in her eyes from a suspicion of cowardice.

Above one part of the barn was a large barn-chamber, so called, which ran the whole length of the building. It was approached by a steep flight of stairs, directly at the top of which was the door opening outwards with an old-fashioned latch, and secured from swinging by a stout hook on the outside. The great room had been used for all sorts of things,— threshing on the floor, drying corn, and the like, but now was nearly empty, with the exception of a pile of old barrels, broken rakes, and the remains of a decrepit sleigh which were heaped up in one corner. The place was lighted at each end by a small window with a number of small panes, covered with the dust of ages, and plenty of cobwebs. Hubert took a sort of fancy to the long, low, dingy apartment, and he proposed to himself, when Tom came, to make it the scene for some tournament, wrestling match or theatricals.

One afternoon, Hubert came over as usual; it was a windy day, and not very attractive outdoors, and learning that Alice was not at home, he established

FAMILIARITY.

himself alone, in the sitting-room, and soon became absorbed in a book which he found there.

By and by Alice came in, full of high spirits after a walk in the wind and sun.

Hubert looked up, but did not otherwise notice her, going on with his book. This was not unusual, for the two were so much together, scant ceremony was used between them. Now, however, Alice unfortunately wanted to talk.

"Hubert, there are cowslips down in the brook. I wanted to get them, but I had on my good boots and I was afraid of wetting them."

"Ah?" said Hubert, reading on.

"But if you will go, I will put on my old boots. Do you have cowslips in England, Hubert?"

"Yes, plenty. Just let me finish this."

"What, that *Wide Awake?* It is an old one. I read it long ago, and guessed all the riddles."

Hubert grunted, and shook himself as he would to drive off an impertinent fly. This roused Alice, and she laid hold of the book to pull it away from him, whereat he sprang up in deep displeasure, and exclaiming, half in fun,

"Alice, you are a nuisance," he dashed off out of the open front door, with his *Wide Awake* still in his hand. Alice followed, and an active chase ensued, round the house, in and out of the garden, which suited her very well, as she considered it all fun. Hubert, however, was in earnest, and really wanted to get out of the way. As she fell behind a corner of the barn, he darted into it without her seeing him, and up the stairs to the barn chamber, unhooked the hasp, let himself in, and hastened to hide himself behind the sleigh. The door swung to in the wind. As Hubert heard no sound of Alice following, he ventured to peep out of the window, and saw her in full career running away from the barn toward the house, where, luckily for him, at that moment, her mother appeared, calling her.

With a sigh of relief, Hubert slid down upon the floor and finished his story; then went on to consider the rest of the number.

It was perhaps an hour after that he got up, stretched himself, and thought of looking up Alice, to make peace with her. He went to the door, lifted the latch, and found it would not open. Shaking it did no good, neither did kicking it, though he tried both, and though it was a loose old door, on rusty hinges; but of course he did not care to break it down.

A very slight inspection showed that it was hooked on the outside. At first he was very angry, suspecting a trick played upon him by Alice, but when he came to think about it, — and he had

THE BARN FLOOR.

plenty of time to think, — he was convinced that the great hook on the outside had fallen over of itself into its hasp when the door was blown to; and this must have been the case.

Hubert resolved to be philosophical, and he returned to his *Wide Awake*. But the number had lost its charm; interested as he had been at the first in its contents, he was indifferent to reading it over so soon a second time. Moreover, he was hungry.

So Hubert set about looking for means of deliverance. He tried the nearest window, the one which looked toward the house. It stuck fast, and he soon perceived that the sash was kept down by stout nails. After giving the door one more futile shake, he crossed to the other end of the chamber, and tried the window there.

That too was fastened, but more loosely, the woodwork of the old window-pane was rotten, and the nail which held it gave way, so that he could pull it out. To his great joy, he pushed up the little sash, and looked forth.

There was barely room for his head and shoulders to push through, and when he looked down, the prospect was not promising of escape.

The ground was some fifteen feet below, and the nature of it not attractive, the pigpen being placed directly under this part of the barn. Two immense great hogs were grunting in a good old-fashioned sty; they turned their emotional noses upward at the unusual sound over their heads, caused by the opening of the window, and gazed feebly at Hubert with their small blinking eyes.

"Pig! pig!" called Hubert, and flattered them by imitating their noise, "how shall I get out of this window?"

There was nothing to keep the sash open when it was not resting on the back of his neck. Hubert continued his inspection of the outside for a few moments, and at last determined on a somewhat precarious plan.

Meanwhile, teatime arrived.

"Is Hubert going to stay to tea?" asked Mrs. Martin of her daughter.

"I don't know," replied Alice crossly. "He is a tiresome, hateful boy. I don't care what becomes of him. I dare say he has gone home, and I hope he will never come back!"

"Why, what's the matter?" exclaimed her mother, surprised. She was a thin, nervous woman, given to worrying. "He cannot have gone home, for here's his hat on the chair."

"Probably it's the English fashion to go home without your hat," said Alice, "especially when you take French leave."

"Now don't be silly," said her mother, with a plaintive tone. "You must look him up, Alice; he is not used to the place, and if he should get lost, and a foreigner at that"—

Mrs. Martin looked as if she thought the diplomatic harmony between America and England might be disturbed by the loss of Hubert. Alice replied:

"The great baby! Can't he take care of himself?"

She saw her mother was seriously angry; and besides she felt a little anxious herself. As she suspected Hubert was still lurking in the barn, she turned her steps in that direction, looked into it, went through it, but was too proud to call to him. As she came out at the further end, she was just in time to see Hubert in mid air, one leg still within the barn, the other placed upon a precarious wooden spout, or gutter, which slanted along below the window.

Alice gasped, afraid to scream. Her anger was changed to genuine alarm.

Two steps along the spout, still grasping the window-sill with his hands, brought Hubert to an upright gutter-way which ran up and down the barn, slightly projecting from it. He clasped it, prepared to slide down. The whole thing gave way, and he was precipitated into — the pigsty!

AT HOME.

# CHAPTER X.

## MOLLY STARK'S BONNET.

HUBERT'S landing-place, though not attractive, was a very lucky one, for he fell without coming to the slightest hurt. Alice's scream brought old Jacob from the barn; the pigs, astonished at the arrival of their headlong guest, left him the field. He was soon picked out of the mire in a sorry plight, so ridiculous that he had to laugh, in which Alice joined him, half-crying, at the same time.

This was the end of the adventure. The old gutter was never put up again, having served its last good purpose in promoting Hubert's escape. Peace was made, in few words, between the two young people, and Hubert secretly became a hero in Alice's eyes, though the older folks reproved his heedless rashness. After this, Alice learned to leave Hubert alone when he was absorbed in reading, while Hubert also resumed a little of his early politeness to her, feeling that he had been at fault.

The farm of Mr. Martin was a very prosperous one, carried on with all the modern improvements; Hubert saw all sorts of machines, of which, during the summer, he came to know the use; such as were little thought of in the early colonial days. Threshing and mowing machines, drills, potato-diggers, hay-rakes, corn-cutters, were all unknown a hundred years ago.

The Massachusetts farmer who witnessed the Revolution, ploughed his land with the wooden bull-plough, sowed his grain broadcast, and when it was ripe, cut it with a scythe and threshed it with a flail, on the floor of such a barn-chamber as was the scene of

A PURITAN DAUGHTER.

Hubert's imprisonment. Very simple, too, were the circumstances of his life, and his daily habits.

His food was of the plainest kind, served upon coarse crockery, and eaten with the knife chiefly, for silver forks were unknown. Split-spoons, these were called by the country folk, when first introduced, but this was later.

Beef and pork, salt fish, dried apples and vegetables made up the daily fare from one year's end to the other.

In these early days of New England, wheaten bread was not so common as that made of Indian corn. A mixture of two parts of Indian meal, with one of rye, has continued far into the present century, to furnish the bread of the great body of people. Hubert liked it very well, good brown bread, especially as buttered toast, which on Sunday morning, with baked beans, was still the regular breakfast provided by Mrs. Bruce. In old times,

the minister had white bread, for brown bread gave him the heart-
burn, and he could not preach upon it, according to the idea of
the day; but brown bread is now universally considered very
healthy, and a useful change upon too much white.

OLD DAYS AND WAYS.

If the food of the farmer was plain, so were his clothes, which
would, to his descendants, be thought to furnish a wardrobe scanty
in the extreme.

For going to meeting on the Sabbath, and for state occasions
during the week, he had a suit of broadcloth, or corduroy, which
lasted him a lifetime, and was at length bequeathed, little the
worse for wear, with his cattle and his farm, to his son. The
suit in which his neighbors commonly saw him, the one in which

he followed the plough, tended the cattle and dozed in the chimney-corner, was of cloth spun and woven at home.

The New England farmer, we may suppose, had no great regard for the fashions, as he took whatever was supplied to him in whatever form it came. It is interesting to see how the steeple-crowned hat of the Puritan, with jerkin, small clothes and ruff, gave way to the cocked hat, straight coat, with large cuffs and square-toed shoes, introduced in the reign of William and Mary. These have been followed in the course of the century by gradual changes. Breeches have grown to trousers, jerkins have become cutaways, and the steeple crown has turned into a bean-pot.

To us, a rough country boy driving a sled through the woods

OLD STYLE.

in a three-cornered hat and breeches, seems like a masquerade; but to him it was as natural as a wide-awake and ulster. Such was the dress of the farmer. A man of fashion or means in the last century, with clothes based on the same models, was far more splendid. He wore a three-cornered cocked hat heavily laced. His hair was done up in a queue, and profusely powdered. His coat was light-colored, very long in the back, with silver buttons engraved with the letters of his name. His small clothes came scarce to his knees, his shoes were adorned with huge buckles:

HOME MANUFACTURE.

his vest had flap-pockets, his cuffs were loaded with lead to keep them in place.

Thus it seems that the fashions of men are as changeful and fantastic as those of women. The simple costume of the Puritan maiden, with her modest cap, gave way to cumbrous hoops and huge bonnets, even in the country where gorgeous brocades, tall feathers and high-heeled shoes were not likely to be seen.

In the garret of the Bruce house was an immense collection of bonnets of all ages; and in a period of rainy days, Hubert and

Alice found some amusement in rummaging these specimens of head gear.

Mrs. Bruce promised to come up and give the history of some of these things.

"For I dare say," she said to Hubert, "I can find the bonnet I wore to Mrs. Horner's wedding. It was considered a gorgeous thing; sent for to New York on purpose for the occasion."

Alice and Hubert pleased themselves by trying to discover in

MOLLY STARK'S BONNET

the collection which was the one that had appeared at the wedding of Tom's father and mother.

"Let us take it down-stairs, and when Bessie comes she can wear it," said Hubert.

"You talk a great deal about Bessie," said Alice, with a little impatience, "is she so very wonderful?"

"She is not so very wonderful," replied Hubert, who was

sitting in an old swing, which, strange to say, was suspended from a beam of the old garret. "She is simply the nicest girl that ever was."

"Oh," said Alice.

"But then, she is older than you," added Hubert consolingly, as if to imply that Alice had time for improvement.

"Do you believe they will really come up here?" asked Alice.

"What! the Horners? Of course, Tom certainly, and I do hope Bessie will come. But let us see about the bonnets."

After a good deal of disagreement, they settled on one bonnet which had an air of faded style about it, they both thought: so they brought it down to Mrs. Bruce, whom, after some search, they found in the very kitchen from which a delicious odor, and an equally alluring sound, issued. She was frying doughnuts; a dish piled up with hot brown rings was on a table near the stove, on which the rest of the batch were hissing and sputtering in the hot fat.

The doughnuts at once turned the thoughts of the young people, and, for a few moments, they discussed with tooth and tongue, two favorable specimens, fresh from the fire; but afterward Hubert said:

"See, Mrs. Bruce, is this the wedding bonnet?"

"That — no, indeed; why, that bonnet belonged to Molly Stark!"

But who was Molly Stark? Such ignorance was punished by the banishment of the offenders from the kitchen, where indeed they were in the way, while the batch of doughnuts was much in danger from their presence, and Hubert betook himself to the library, with the intention of looking up Molly Stark.

His attention was again diverted, however; for on the library table a letter was lying for him.

It was from Bessie Horner herself, and when Alice was allowed to read it, she was forced to acknowledge it was a very good letter. The excellence of it lay chiefly in the good news that the Horner house in New York was to be shut up at once, and that

Mrs. Horner and Bessie herself would come for a while, at least, to Utopia, on the first of June. May was now drawing near its end, so there would not be long to wait.

Tom was still busy at school, but he and his father were to shift for themselves, like many other unfortunate New Yorkers detained in town after the dust and heat have driven away their families.

"But just imagine where they are to be!" added Bessie. "Miss Lejeune will of course be away in June, and papa and Tom are to live in her apartments, and have dinner and all, if they like, sent in from the restaurant below, just as she does."

"I wonder where Miss Lejeune is going?" said Hubert to himself.

"Is she splendid also?" demanded Alice.

"It would do you a great deal of good to know her," replied Hubert, with a smile.

Bennington is a town in the southwestern part of Vermont, noted as the place in which one of the early battles of the Revolution was fought. In 1777 the British army of General Burgoyne,

THE BENNINGTON TRUNK.

marching to the South from Canada, created great commotion in New England, since Boston was supposed to be its point of destination. General Stark, who chanced to be at Bennington, hastily collected the continental forces in the neighborhood, and after a hot action of two hours, forced the enemy to retreat. The battle was renewed, but the British were obliged to retire, leaving behind their baggage and ammunition.

This was on the morning of August 16, 1777. As he led the men to the attack, Stark cried out to them:

"See there, men! there are the red coats! Before night they

are ours, or Molly Stark is a widow." So much Hubert learned.

"Mrs. Bruce," said he, pausing to attract her attention, still concentrated on the doughnuts.

"Well?"

"I don't believe that was Molly Stark's bonnet at all!"

"Why not? You are a daring boy, to doubt the traditions of the family!"

"Why, because I don't see how it came in your garret!"

"That was because my grandmother used to spend a great deal of her time at Bennington."

"But the Starks did not belong in Bennington," said Alice, who had been looking up the subject with Hubert, "they were New Hampshire folks."

"You young people are getting far too learned for me," replied Mrs. Bruce; "all I know is, that amongst my grandmother's things there was a trunk called the Bennington trunk. It was an old hair trunk, with the hair all worn off of it; and this bonnet came out of that trunk, and it was always said to be Molly Stark's bonnet."

MORE OLD BONNETS.

## CHAPTER XI.

### WILD FLOWERS.

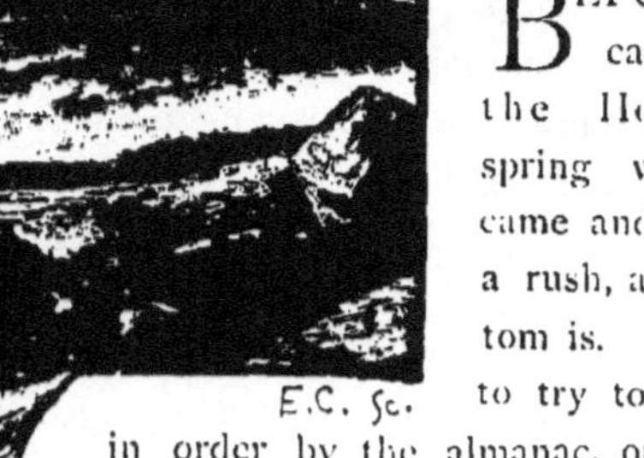


JACK-IN-THE-PULPIT

BEFORE June came, bringing the Horners, the spring wild flowers came and went, with a rush, as their custom is. It is in vain to try to keep them in order by the almanac, or reminding them when they are due, according to Gray's Botany. They insist upon waiting, past their dates, if necessary, until the inevitable warm breezes and hot suns summon them, after which they burst forth all together, and are gone. He who would see and gather specimens of all kinds of wild flowers, has to lead an active life when they have once appeared.

Professor Bruce was an enthusiastic botanist, who every year devoted himself at the right season, to the early wild flowers. He knew their homes, and where to watch for them, and was often the first to find the little blue hepatica, hiding behind its stout old last year's leaf, which acts as a waterproof cloak to shield it until it is ready to show itself. He knew that on the willow road, close by the edge of a flooded meadow, the overflow of the river at this season, there was sure pretty soon to be known, by a deep pink flush all over the bushes, the flowering of the rhodora, whose blossoms come out before the leaves appear. He knew that any time about then it was well to scan closely wet swamps among the bushes, for the sake of finding an early jack-in-the-pulpit poking up its head between huge light-green leaves of skunk cabbage, splendid in color and luxuriance.

As for cowslips, no search was needed to find them, for they spread themselves abroad over the meadows in great yellow patches, as good as sunshine on a cloudy day.

Hubert declared they were not real cowslips, and so they are not, from the English point of view, but Alice refused to call them anything else, or to believe that the English cowslip was any prettier than the American one.

Our cowslip, commonly so called, is a caltha, botanically speaking, a flower nearly allied to the buttercup. In fact, it is a stout buxom buttercup, with thick stems, broad leaves and good, honest, bright yellow flowers, rather coarse to examine, but with plenty of sunshine in them. The proper popular name for it is marsh marigold, but as it is no more like a garden marigold, than it is like an English cowslip, it may as well keep the prettier name.

The English cowslip is a primrose, and is much like the pink primroses easily raised here in pots, but where it grows wild it seeks the open pasture, while primroses hide themselves in hedges, or in the shade and shelter of the woods. Cowslips. as well as primroses, are favorites of the poets.

Milton calls them

Cowslips wan that hang the pensive head;

a description full of truth, for the English cowslip is essentially a pale hanging flower, unlike our sturdy marigold, which keeps its head well up to the sun.

Hubert was a little persistent in defence of his own cowslip,

THE WILLOW ROAD.

while these, he said, were called nothing but *mare-blobs* at home, where they grew in plenty.

Mr. Bruce came to the rescue when the quarrel was growing dangerous.

"Shakespeare's name for the marsh marigold is the prettiest. Doubtless he means your mare-blob in the lines —

> Winking mary-buds begin
> To ope their golden eyes!"

Compromises are never agreeable, but the discussion was silenced. It took place in the middle of a wet meadow, where Alice and

RHODORA AND FRINGED POLYGALA.

Hubert were both gathering big bunches of the flowers in question. They turned away from them to pull up long-stemmed, pale violets, which grew also in the wet, very different from the little darker blue violets, scattered everywhere close to the ground hidden in their leaves. Here again Hubert was critical, for the wild violets in England are sweet-smelling, while ours, alas! with the exception of the little white violet, have no perfume.

"Come, friends," said Mr. Bruce at last, "I think I shall leave you and go home, unless you can find some better way to regard the flowers than squabbling about them. The true way is to enjoy what you have got, and not to be comparing it with things which you might, could, would or should have had at some past indefinite time."

He spoke lightly, but with decision. He was, in fact, becoming a little wearied with the want of harmony between Alice and Hubert, which increased as the time went on. The solitude in which Hubert found himself away from boys of his own age, was having a bad effect upon him, and Alice had not sufficient character to counteract it. However, the time would not be long before Tom Horner's arrival, which would, it was to be hoped, set everything to rights.

"Let us come on, now," said Mr. Bruce; "if we go back through the woods, we shall find anemones and perhaps columbines."

The anemone (*nemoroso*) of New England is a delicate little flower, hanging its head among the dead oak leaves in the woods, of every variety of 'rose-tint, from pure white to deep pink. In other parts of the world, a flower, similar in construction, which bears the same name, is large and brilliant, sometimes bright red, like the field poppy, sometimes purple, again yellow. It is more showy, but not so delicate as the pretty little wind-flower, as ours is sometimes called.

Not far off, in a cleft of rock, they spied the first columbine, holding itself up proudly, though its red head hung down with the weight of its tubes filled with honey. Against this flower, Hubert had nothing to say. A little ashamed of his former mood, he burst into loud approbation of it, and after this he called it always his favorite.

The next time they went for it the ground was red with its bright bells, and a slanting ledge of gray rock was covered with them. The columbine loves little crevices in rocks where a scanty measure of soil and moss is enough for its foothold.

Not far off, but avoiding the rocks, grew the dog-tooth-violet, not a violet at all by the way, as it belongs to the lily tribe. It is said to have its name because the large bulb at its base bears a mark as if it were bitten by a dog's tooth. It is a graceful, pretty yellow flower, with long leaves shaped like those of the lily of the valley, spotted with brown.

The trees at this time, the end of May, were still without their leaves, with the exception of a shimmer of green on the birches. The maples were red with their feathery blossoms appearing before the leaves, and all the woods in the distance were spread with a marvellous sheen of faint, delicate tints, green, pink, yellow, the most lovely effect of the whole year, and the most difficult to catch in a picture.

Town people who do not reach the country before the middle of June or later, lose all this: it is a little early for comfort, for roads are bad, the weather is capricious, and the cities are still attractive. It is, though, a pity not to know the tender richness of the early spring foliage, as exquisite as the autumn tints are brilliant.

Through the many tinted branches, Hubert spied a mass of white, as if a flock of white pigeons had alighted upon a tree.

"Ah," cried Mr. Bruce, "that is giant cornel, as we call it. Is it possible that is in blossom already!"

The tree was twenty feet or more high, and, still bare of leaves, was covered with large white blossoms, an inch or more across, showy and decorative in the extreme.

Hubert scrambled up on a rock from which he could reach the blossoms, and broke off large branches of them.

When they reached the house, they were laden with their treasures, the most conspicuous of which were the great white cornels.

Mrs. Bruce was in gardening trim, her skirt turned up, old gloves on her hands, holding a trowel, with which she was turning up the soil of the beds before the house. Crocuses were there, but already going out of blossom. tulips, hyacinths, and daffodils were just coming on, and a great bed of lilies of the valley was crowded with buds. This was at the end of a long, warm day. The robins were singing. the air was all full of golden light. Hubert and Alice sat down on the door-steps, laying their great bunches of flowers aside; Mr. Bruce wiped his brow, for the last part of their walk had been fast. He was warm and tired.

The children were

COLUMBINES AND DOG-TOOTH-VIOLET.

tired. but it was a good comfortable tired. and it seemed delightful to sit and rest. and watch the changing lights.

"I do believe," said Hubert, "that spring is just the loveliest season of the year. It is such fun to go off and find these flowers, and then to think that the whole long summer is coming."

"Yes," said Alice. "Autumn is all very well, but then the days are short, and you know that winter is coming, with lessons, and cold weather, and India rubber boots."

Mr. Bruce had gone to his library, and Mrs. Bruce had taken trowel, basket and gloves round the house to put them away in the tool house.

"Alice," said Hubert suddenly, "I think I have been very disagreeable to you lately. I mean to turn over a new leaf from this very time."

"Do you?" said she simply; "well, then, I will too."

GIANT CORNEL.

# CHAPTER XII.



IT was Saturday, the very last day of May, and Hubert was growing restless, because no absolute tidings came of the plans of the Horners. He had been studying diligently all the morning, and as the clock struck one, he shut up his books, stretched himself, and went to the front door to look about and draw a breath of fresh air.

The village was quiet, as usual, but slowly coming up the steep hill before the house, he saw the singular phenomenon of a horse and buggy, and as it drew near, he recognized the now familiar face of Mr. Brick, who drove him over to East Utopia, with the Horners, on the first day of his life in Vermont. It seemed already an age ago. At East Utopia was the nearest railway station, and thus the nearest communication with the world which the Utopians had at command, was by means of the three-mile drive over the mountain. Such communication was not frequent, but Mr. Brick had been over twice once to bring Hubert's trunk, and once, a few weeks later, upon his own affairs. The mail carrier drove through three times a week from East Utopia to Burnett and back.

"Hallo! Mr. Brick," called Hubert, "what brings you over the mountain?"

"Telegram, Mr. Hubert," was the brief reply, as Mr. Brick jumped out. He handed him a pale yellow envelope, and looked away, pretending to busy himself with the check-rein at his horse's head.

In the country the very outside of the yellow envelope means misfortune, as it is generally the bearer of tidings of illness or death.

Hubert turned pale as he tore open the cover. He was not only relieved, but delighted at the contents.

Meet us at Burlington, Van Ness House, Monday evening.—THOMAS HORNER.

His whoop of joy caused Mr. Brick to turn round.

"Nawthing serious, I expect?"

"It is serious, Mr. Brick," cried Hubert.

The good news spread through the house. Mr. Brick was engaged

HEAD OF LAKE GEORGE.

to come on Monday, to take Hubert to the necessary train at a preternaturally early hour of the morning.

Sunday was passed in a pleasing state of wonderment as to what the plan was, who "us" meant, whom he was to meet at Burlington, and where they might be going afterward.

"At any rate, I know it's something nice, for that's the way the Horners do things."

"I wish I were going," said Alice, with a sigh.

"So do I," said Hubert, as the vague thought passed through his mind that he would like to have her

Monday came, and with the mail came letters to Mr. Bruce, explaining the intentions of the Horner family; but these arrived after Hubert was off, and he took his solitary journey still in doubt and speculation on what was to happen next

This was Hubert's first essay at travelling alone in America. He had to change cars for Montpelier at Wells River Junction, where many engines were snorting upon their respective tracks, bound for many different destinations. But he managed to find the right train, when the time came, after waiting upon the platform for fifteen minutes, and even to advise a woman, who had lost her head, to stick close to the conductor of her line.

The train he took passed through Montpelier, the capital of Vermont, and then on to Burlington.

It was dark when he arrived, but he could guess that Burlington was a large city, from the bustle and importance of the station. An omnibus was in waiting to take him to the hotel, and after the delay of waiting for baggage, it started. The city seemed to be all up hill. It reminded him of arriving at Madrid, and he half-expected to see a custom house official poke his head into the omnibus, demanding to examine the small baggage, but no such thing occurred.

They stopped before the door of a large hotel, gaslight streaming from its many windows. The passengers groped out of the vehicle, and stood dazed in the bright light of a small office upon the street.

"Hubert!" said a voice, and Tom Horner seized him by the hand. In a moment, he was hustled up a broad flight of stairs to a large parlor, where he found, to his delight, several friends

Mr. Horner was waiting for him in the doorway. Instantly Bessie advanced, and greeted him cordially He had not time to take in how tall she was, how grown up, what a mature kind of hat she was wearing, for Miss Lejeune's cheery voice was heard, saying:

"Come and be introduced to Mrs. Horner, Hubert;" and to her, "My dear, this is Hubert Vaughan."

There was no stiffness in the introduction, for they all regarded

THE COLD HEIGHTS OF THE ALPS.

Hubert as one of the family; and although he felt awkward for a moment, Mrs. Horner's kind and easy manner put him at his ease at once. He really felt more stiff with Bessie than any of the rest.

Not much was told him that night about plans; only that they were to stay the next day and see Burlington, "the Queen City of Vermont."

It is beautifully situated on a long, sloping hill, on the east shore of Lake Champlain. It is the largest city in the State, having a large business in lumber, which is brought from the Canadian forests, sorted and planed in Burlington, after which it is sent by rail to Boston and other Eastern cities.

Burlington is an academic city, containing the University of Vermont, beautifully placed on the summit of the hill on which the

CROWN POINT.

town is built, a mile from the lake, and more than three hundred feet above it. There are besides several fine schools, a Seminary and an Institute.

The town was settled about 1775, and named in honor of the Burling family of New York.

Tom and Hubert shared a room in the hotel which overlooked not only streets and houses, built upon the sloping hill, but the broad expanse below of the lake itself. As soon as they were awake they were at the windows, admiring the lovely view. Putting their heads out, they perceived Bessie's stretched from her window on the opposite side of the entry; all three exchanged expressions of praise.

From the dome of the University the same view is seen, only more extended, and therefore to better advantage.

Lake Champlain is to be seen from below Crown Point on the south, to Plattsburg on the north, dotted with many wooded islands. Beyond the lake the Adirondacks fill the horizon, over sixty peaks being visible on a clear day, among them Marcy, the highest between the White Mountains and the Alleghanies. The lake is ten miles wide at this part. In the opposite direction, looking toward the east from the University, are the Green Mountains, the *verts monts* for which the State is named.

It was a lovely June day, and the Horners employed it in visiting some hospitable friends, who were proud to do the honors of their beautiful town by driving them to the different points of interest.

The sunset across the lake, with the dark outlines sharp against the glowing light, was wonderful. As they sat enjoying it, in the garden of one of their friends, the travelled Horners willingly acknowledged it to be fully as beautiful as similar scenes among the lakes of Switzerland, with the addition of a certain charm of wildness which, to Americans, American scenery alone possesses.

"The only thing is," said Bessie, "that, after all, these mountains seem low. I should like it better if they did not call them mountains."

"Mount Marcy," said the host, "is about five thousand four hundred feet above the level of the sea. The Indian name, Ta-ha-was, means 'he splits the sky.'" He added, "You must not be

LOGGING IN THE WOODS.

too critical. Marcy is the highest to be had east of the Mississippi, except the White Mountains, and the Black Mountains of North Carolina."

"For my part," said Miss Lejeune, "I like it all much better than if the hills were higher. The Alps are all very well, but they weary me with their cold heights. I am always wishing to get away from them. Here, where we look across the broad expanse of water, these hills compose themselves in exactly the right way to suit the exigencies of the landscape."

"Miss Lejeune is celebrated," said Mr. Horner, in explanation to the host, "for always liking best the 'best that is to be had,' as you have expressed it."

The Adirondack chain proper is the backbone of the five ranges of the wilderness, dividing the waters that flow northerly into the St. Lawrence, from those that run south into the Hudson. These five separate chains constitute a great mountain belt full of the most varied scenery, much resorted to now in summer by pleasure travellers. The whole great wilderness was once an old Indian hunting-ground, which has come to be called by an Indian name, Adirondack, a term of derision given by one family of Indians to another tribe of despised enemies who, during the long Canadian winters, when their game grew scarce, lived, driven by hunger, for many weeks together, upon the buds and bark, and sometimes even upon the wood of forest trees. Ad-i-ron-dacks means *tree-eaters*.

This great wild region of Northern New York is almost everywhere as high at least as two thousand feet above sea level. It contains more than a thousand lakes, and from its heights run countless rivers and streams in every direction, while over all is spread a primeval forest, broken here and there only by a few small settlements. It will long remain under the uncontested dominion of nature.

## CHAPTER XIII.

### A LITTLE HISTORY.

WHILE English Colonists were settling upon the shores of Maine and Massachusetts, the French were making explorations farther North in Canada.

Early in the sixteenth century, Jacques Cartier had sailed up the St. Lawrence; and in 1603, Samuel de Champlain sailed from France, to found a settlement in North America, with the permission of his king, Henry the Fourth (the hero of Ivry and Navarre), who gave him the title of General Lieutenant of Canada.

Champlain founded a colony at Quebec, upon the site of an old Indian hamlet which Jacques Cartier had seen seventy years before; and there, or during his hunting excursions with the Indians, sitting around their wild camp-fires, he heard from them marvellous stories of a great inland sea filled with islands, lying far to the southward of the St. Lawrence river. His curiosity was excited, and as soon as the snow melted in the spring, he set out upon a voyage of discovery, with only two companions besides his Indian escort of sixty warriors, with twenty-four canoes. These Indians were of the Algonquin nation, and they were about to penetrate into regions inhabited and controlled by their hereditary enemies, the fierce Iroquois, called "Mohawks" by the New England Colonists. After a toilsome passage up the rapids, they came to the lake to which Champlain has given his name, the far-famed "wilderness sea of the Iroquois." It was studded with islands clothed in the early summer verdure. From the thickly wooded shores on either side rose ranges of mountains, the highest peaks still white

with patches of snow. Over all hung a soft blue haze that seemed
to temper the sunlight and to shade off the landscape into spec-
tral forms of vague beauty.

One morning, after paddling as usual all night, they retired to
the western shore of the lake to take their daily rest. The savages were soon stretched along the ground in their slumbers, and

JACQUES CARTIER.

Champlain, after a short walk in the woods, laid himself down to
sleep upon his bed of fragrant hemlock boughs. He dreamed that
he saw a band of Iroquois warriors drowning in the lake. Upon
his attempting to save them, the Algonquins told him that "they
were of no consequence,—nothing but Iroquois."

His Indian friends were constantly besetting him to tell his
dreams, and this was the first one he had remembered since the
beginning of his voyage. It was considered by his allies as a

most auspicious vision, and its relation filled them with joy. Perhaps in telling it, Champlain colored the recital a little, as we are all apt to do in repeating our dreams.

At nightfall they set out again in their canoes, flushed with a hope of an easy victory. About ten in the evening, near what is now Crown Point, not many miles from the southern end of the lake, they saw dark, moving objects on the lake before them. It was a flotilla of Iroquois canoes. In a moment more each party of savages saw the other, and their hideous war-cries mingling, pealed along the lonely shores.

Thus Champlain, and through him the whole French nation, became involved upon one side of an hereditary quarrel between two sets of Indian tribes. The consequences of this first encounter extended down through all the subsequent struggles between the contending powers on the continent; for the Algonquins remained allied to the French, while the powerful Iroquois, their inveterate enemies, became from that moment hostile to the French and pledged to the opposite cause, that of the English colonists.

In this first forest encounter Champlain and his Algonquins had the advantage. The sight of Champlain, clad in the metallic armor of the time, struck amazement and terror to the hearts of the Iroquois warriors; one shot from his arquebuse made one of their chiefs fall. Panic-stricken at the strange appearance of a white man in glittering steel, sending forth from his weapons fire, smoke, thunder, and leaden hail, they broke and fled in uncontrollable terror toward their homes on the Mohawk, leaving everything behind them

In 1620, the year the Pilgrims arrived at Plymouth, Champlain was made Governor-General of Canada, and brought his wife to Quebec. She was then very young, having married when she was only twelve years old. The Indians were struck with her frail and gentle beauty, and made her the object of their adoration. Champlain died in Quebec, in 1635. His wife returned later to France and founded there a convent, we are told, where she died in the year 1654.

The lake to which he gave his name has since been the scene of long campaigns and desperate battles in the course of the history of the settlement of this part of America.

It is a large and picturesque sheet of water more than one

TICONDEROGA AT SUNSET.

hundred miles long, containing large islands with populous towns upon them.

In the same summer that Champlain discovered his lake, Henry Hudson discovered and entered the mouth of the Hudson, now since called by his name, and ascended it as far as the Mohawk, one of its branches.

This same Hudson was an Englishman, but he was employed at that time in the service of a Dutch company. Thus, while the

French were exploring the upper region of New York, the English were establishing their right to the lower part of it; and out of these conflicting claims arose the series of bloody conflicts between the two nations and their respective Indian allies.

After leaving Burlington, the Horners found themselves on the deck of one of the large and commodious lake steamers, on their way to Ticonderoga, at the southern end of Lake Champlain. The day was lovely, and the scenery interesting; the little party sat together at the stern of the boat. It was the first time really that there was a chance for what might be termed family talk, for the day at Burlington had been taken up with sight-seeing, and the attentions of their hospitable friends.

Tom and Hubert were leaning over the rail talking to each other apart, when Tom turned to the rest of the party, and said:

"Hubert wants to know what we are here for, and where we are going, if you do not mind."

"I did not say any such thing!" said Hubert, coloring; "I only wondered" —

Mr. Horner laughed, and so did the others.

"I believe nobody has taken pains to tell you our plans, Hubert. The telegram we sent you was short, but we thought you would ship for the voyage, wherever bound."

"Why, Hubert," said Miss Lejeune, "we thought we would do a little sight-seeing in our own land, without crossing the Atlantic, and we began at the wrong end, by coming up first to Burlington, for the sake of having you with us."

"Does it not seem," said Bessie, while Hubert was expressing his pleasure, "as if we were all on the Rhine or some foreign lake?"

It did indeed, for they were surrounded with the usual travelling paraphernalia. Even the red guide-book, on the seat by the side of Miss Lejeune, was got up to resemble Baedeker, which they always had at hand in Europe. It was Osgood's *New England* a valuable companion.

"We are going to Ticonderoga," said Mr. Horner, "and thence across Lake George, after that we shall see. This is only a little trip, Hubert, before settling down for the summer."

The rush of travel sets in later,—not till July has begun,—after which railways, steamboats and hotels, all over the picturesque

ON THE LAKE SHORE

the summer, are clean and empty, landlords, maids and waiters are fresh and attentive; above all, the fly, that pest of a New England summer, has not made his appearance.

They began to ask Hubert about his life at Utopia, and Mr. Horner made some inquiry into his progress in lessons and reading. He found by the intelligent answers he received, that the boy was really interested in the subjects he had been going over, and fully ready to understand what they were to see of historic interest in the scenes of battle-fields and early events.

"I should not wonder, Bessie," said her father, "if Hubert could give you points in American history already."

"I am afraid he can, papa," she replied, "for I have not been cramming, you know."

"I have not been cramming either," said Hubert. "But I have a few more ideas in my head than the day I landed, Tom. Then I hardly knew the difference between Bunker Hill and Plymouth Rock."

Hubert was beginning now to see clearly how it was that New England became settled; how a century or more, after 1620, was occupied in contesting discovered territory with the French, the founding of towns and States, all under the name of colonies of England; how the battles were the quarrels of England, embittered, of course, by the personal antagonism between the Indians and all white settlers.

These difficulties were scarcely over, in the middle of the eighteenth century, when the greater one arose, of disagreement with the mother country. The growing colonies were become too strong to submit to home rule. Then came the Revolution, the war for the sake of freedom of the colonies, which resulted in the Declaration of Independence, in 1776. This, though the close of one struggle, was but the beginning of an effort for separate existence, for it was long before the United States became firmly established.

# CHAPTER XIV

TICONDEROGA is particularly remarkable for the prominent place held in American History by its fortifications.

As early as 1731, a century after its discovery by Champlain, the French built Fort St. Frederick, and occupied it, at Crown Point, and then, after a careful survey of the lake, advanced to Ticonderoga and began a fortification there in order to command the passage of the lake. This fort they called "The Carillon," or chime of bells, on account of the music of the falls near it.

Soon after, the commander of the English and colonial army, Sir William Johnson, intended to attack the two French fortresses, but as the French re-enforced them largely, he contented himself with fortifying Fort William Henry at the southern extremity of Lake George, as he now called it for the first time, in honor of the English king, and in token of his empire over it. The French name for the smaller lake was St. Sacrament.

This was the beginning of the last French and Indian War, which lasted from 1755 to 1759, and resulted in the loss by the French of their control over the region of Lake Champlain and the St. Lawrence.

Fort Carillon remained in the possession of the French nearly all this time, but in 1759 it was invested by the English forces, and fell into their hands. Crown Point also was soon after abandoned. These events were closely followed by the final victory at Quebec, by General Wolfe over Montcalm, which closed the war. In 1763 peace was declared between France and England, which was a cause for great joy among the war-worn inhabitants of the northern valley.

The name of Fort Carillon was now changed to Ticonderoga, which means *chiming waters*, and it became an English fort. As the times were peaceful it was allowed to fall into decay, and was held by so small a force that it fell easily into the hands of Ethan Allen, one of the boldest leaders of the rebellious colonists, who, upon the receipt of the news of the battle of Lexington, surprised the fort, on the tenth of May, 1775, and captured the little garrison of fifty men, with their artillery and munitions of war.

THE CHIMING WATERS.

Later the English regained possession of it, and it continued in their hands until the end of the Revolutionary War, when its English garrison retreated down Lake Champlain, dismantling the fort. After this war, it was suffered to fall into ruins; these are large enough in extent to give evidence to all its old importance.

The ruins of the fort crown a rocky promontory close to the steamboat wharf. Near them rises a forest-covered mountain, beyond which the lake narrows to a river. Between the promontory and the mountains a stream issues from the woods and falls into the

INDIAN DIFFICULTIES.

lake, making the fall which Champlain heard, but did not see, which has given both the French and Indian names to the locality.

Here the little party of Horners established themselves in the pleasant hotel, an old-fashioned mansion-house near the lake and

PINK AZALEA.

landing. It was interesting to scramble about the ruins of the fort, which though less extensive than those of Heidelberg, and less glowing than the Alhambra, have their own claim to the interest of Americans, while the views of the lake, and the mountains across it, are very lovely.

There were pleasant expeditions to be made to Crown Point, along the lake, and to the top of Mt. Defiance, across the widenings of the outlet of Lake George. The summit is eight hundred feet above the level of the lake, and the view is very fine.

The last excursion was accomplished by Bessie and the two boys, along the nearly vanished military road constructed by General Burgoyne. The elder portion of the party were content to stay at home, and to receive the merry accounts of the returned climbers, and to put in water the branches of wild cherry-blossoms, pink azalea and the like, they brought back.

There were good boats to be had, and often after tea the family went out to row on the lake. Tom, of course, pulled a good oar, and Bessie did fairly well for a girl. As for Hubert, he disgraced himself, and caught many a crab, having no knowledge of the art. He secretly resolved to remedy this deficiency.

There was one boat large enough to contain the whole party, and in this family excursions were often made, not altogether popular with Tom and Bessie, who had to do the rowing on such trips, but pleasant occasions for general talk. Mrs. Horner took her place always in the stern, under the vague impression that she could steer. Indeed she could, if she set her mind to it, but in the ardor of conversation she was apt to let the rudder stray at its own sweet will. This was of no great consequence, as the party were seldom going anywhere in particular. There were seats enough also for Miss Lejeune and Mr. Horner, in the stern. Mr. Horner always offered his services at the oars, but Bessie and Tom preferred to pull for themselves. Hubert, meanwhile, stretched himself out in the pointed bow of the boat, enduring, as best he might, the slurs of laziness which were put upon him. He would have gladly taken his turn in rowing, but was too clumsy, as yet, to be tolerated.

One late afternoon, as they were floating about, rather than rowing, among the shady nooks of a narrow part of the lake, Mrs. Horner exclaimed,

"Augusta! we have never told you about the Stuyvesants!"

"What about them?" asked Miss Lejeune.

"They have left Paris and come home to live."

"Impossible!" she replied. "Leave their beloved Avenue Joséphine! I can't believe it."

"Nevertheless I have seen them," replied Mrs. Horner. "They are at the Fifth Avenue Hotel; all their furniture is stored somewhere. Miss Stuyvesant is to come out in New York next winter; they mean to spend the summer in Newport, and they are looking about for a place for the twins."

"Well, well!" ejaculated Miss Lejeune.

"Mamma thinks," called out Tom from his oar, "that I had best take the boys to Utopia for the summer."

"And you do not approve of her plan?" said Miss Lejeune, inquiringly.

"The boys are nothing but a couple of monkeys," grumbled

HUBERT'S PRIVATE PRACTICE.

Tom, "and if they are in my charge, I had best engage a hand-organ at once, to go with them."

"They may have improved," suggested Miss Augusta; "how old are they now?"

"Two years younger than I am," said Tom. "Come, Bessie, pull all you can, and let us try, if we can, to turn the corner in time to see the sun go down."

While they were both silent, putting all their forces into their rowing, the grown-up people at their end of the boat went on discussing the Stuyvesants.

"Mr. Horner thinks," said his wife, "that their investments are down, and so they want to retrench."

"The worst thing they can do, then, is to try and live in New York and Newport."

"Yes; but their establishment at Paris was very extravagant; if they give up their horses and their apartment there, they can manage more simply for a year or two, and then if their income improves, they can go back again."

"*Reculer pour mieux sauter*," remarked Miss Lejeune; then suddenly changing her tone, exclaimed, with every one else in the boat,

"Oh, how lovely!"

Vigorous pulls of the rowers had brought the boat round a wooded corner to an open space, where the shores receded and lay flat before them, just in time to see the sun go down in a cloudless sky, a ball of living fire.

Tom and Bessie, panting, rested upon their oars. The little party watched the sun setting until the last rim had disappeared.

"We ought to go home now," remarked Mrs. Horner; "it will be growing cool directly."

"Who are these Stuyvesants?" called out Hubert from the end of the boat.

"They are some boys who were with us on the Nile," replied Tom; "they were small, ill-bred creatures, who had not the faintest idea of minding what anybody told them, least of all their father; as for their mother, she had no idea of telling them anything."

"Tom! Tom!" called his father in a warning voice.

"You are hard on them, really, Tom," said Bessie. "One of them was rather nice, though I do not recollect which; but Mary could manage them."

"I say," began Hubert, "let us have them come to Utopia, Tom;

FLOATING.

you've no idea how dull it is there without any fellows, only a girl to talk with all day long."

"Only a girl! thank you!" said Bessie.

"There are girls *and* girls, you know, Bessie," quickly replied Hubert. "Alice Martin is all very well, but "--

"Tell us all about her," said Bessie; and Hubert, sitting up in his end of the boat, began an account, lively for him, of his acquaintance with Alice Martin, his adventure in the barn, and other tales of his life in Utopia.

"I think," said Bessie condescendingly, "that Alice must be a nice girl."

"But if there were other boys, we could have all sorts of good excursions, and build huts in the woods, and that," pursued Hubert; "especially little boys whom we could make mind."

"You wait and see if you can make these boys mind," grumbled Tom.

However, he did not vigorously oppose the scheme. Mr. Horner knew the Bruces wanted to fill up their house with boys for the summer, and he thought the chances were more in favor of two boys they already knew something about, than entire strangers. It was decided that he might as well talk to Mr. Stuyvesant about it, who was a sensible man.

## CHAPTER XV.

### FRENCH AND ENGLISH CAMPAIGNS.

THE English were not disposed to allow their French enemies the control of the two lakes, and Colonel Johnson was already making preparations to attack Crown Point when he learned that the French had firmly established themselves at Ticonderoga. The French general, Baron Dieskau, sent to defend Crown Point, determined to advance upon the English, at their encampment upon Lake George. In this encounter the French were driven off, and Dieskau was mortally wounded. Johnson did not pursue them, or at that time make any attempt upon their works at Lake Champlain. The rest of the campaign of 1755 was spent by the English in erecting a fort at the south end of Lake George, which was called William Henry, after the Duke of Cumberland. Up to this time, their nearest stronghold was Fort Edward, at the southern end of Lake George.

At this time, the French side had the advantage of being controlled by a man of great heroism and courage. Louis Joseph de St. Véran, Marquis de Montcalm, was born in France in 1712. He entered the army when fourteen years old, and had served bravely in several campaigns, when, in 1756, being then a brigadier-general, he was appointed to command the French troops in Canada.

As soon as he arrived, he began operations against the English with great activity and success, making the field of his exertions the southern end of Lake Champlain. For this purpose, he collected at Crown Point and Ticonderoga all his forces, consisting of regular troops, Canadians and Indians. As early as the twentieth of March, 1757, he attacked Fort William Henry, but his object was defeated by the bravery of the garrison there, which Colonel Monroe was then sent to reinforce. The day after his arrival, the French and Indians, under Montcalm, again appeared upon the lake, effected a landing with but little opposition, and immediately laid siege to the fort. Montcalm at the same time sent a letter to Monroe, stating that he felt himself bound in humanity to urge the English commander to surrender before any of the Indians were slain and their savage temper further inflamed

DEATH OF GENERAL WOLFE.

by a resistance which would be unavailing. Monroe replied that as the fortress had been entrusted to him, both his honor and his duty required him to defend it to the last extremity.

The garrison, amounting to only twenty-five hundred men, made a gallant defence, while Monroe, aware of his danger, sent frequent expresses for succor to Fort Edward, farther south, the head quarters at that time of the English commander, General Webb. But Webb remained inactive and apparently indifferent during these alarming transactions. On the eighth or ninth day of the siege General Johnson was permitted to set out for Fort William Henry with some troops; but he had proceeded only three miles when he received orders from Webb for his immediate return, Webb at the same time advising Munroe to surrender on the best terms he could obtain.

Munroe and his garrison had defended themselves with much spirit, in hourly expectation of relief from Fort Edward, till the ninth of August, when all their hopes were blasted by the reception of Webb's letter, which Montcalm had intercepted, and now sent in with further proposals of a surrender of the fort.

Articles of capitulation were therefore signed, and no further trouble was apprehended. But the Indians belonging to the French army attached no importance to the pledge made by their general for the safety of the conquered enemy. The garrison had no sooner marched out of the fort than they fell upon the defenceless soldiers, plundering and murdering all who came in their way. On this fatal day more than half the English were either murdered by the savages, or carried by them into captivity, never to return. The fort was entirely demolished; the barracks, out-houses and building were a heap of ruins; the cannons, stores, boats and vessels were all carried away.

The French, satisfied with their success, retired to their works at Ticonderoga and Crown Point; and for that year nothing more was done either by French or English in this quarter. The English had suffered much in loss of life and property, and had gained nothing. This want of success was chiefly owing to the inefficiency and ignorance of the British ministry in relation to American affairs, which led as a natural result, to want of ability and energy in the generals to whom the prosecution of the war was entrusted, a deficiency made conspicuous by the talent and boldness of Montcalm.

The next year, however, the tables were turned. The repeated failure of the British arms in America created so much dissatisfaction both at home and in the colonies, that a change was found indispensable in the conduct of affairs, which began to assume a more favorable aspect. Instead of defeat and disgrace, victory and triumph now usually attended the English arms.

On the other hand, the personal bravery of Montcalm, although it raised his popularity with his soldiers, could not redeem the want of energy of the French government. There was dissension in the councils of the governor of Canada and the commander. Even in the midst of victory, Montcalm predicted that in the end the English would be masters of the French colonies in America. Resolved, however, to struggle to the last, and as he himself said, to find his grave under the ruins of the colony, he actively carried on the campaign.

The English determined that the French settlements should be attacked at several points at once; one of these was the stronghold at Ticonderoga. The fort was favorably situated for defence, as can still be easily seen. It was surrounded on three sides by water, and about half the other side was protected by a deep swamp, while the line of defence was completed by the erection of a breastwork nine feet high. The ground before this breastwork was covered with felled trees and bushes, to impede the approach of the enemy.

The English general, Abercrombie, believing that this place might be attacked with a fair prospect of success, marched forward, undismayed by the heavy fire from the French, till they became entangled and stopped by the timber. For four hours they strove with their swords to cut their way to the breastwork, through branches and bushes, but the attempt was futile. At last they retreated, with severe loss, and were forced to hasten back to their encampment at Lake George.

Everywhere else the British troops had been successful, and in spite of the unlucky defeat at Ticonderoga, the confidence of the colonists began to revive, and that of the French to languish.

The next year the French, dreading an attack which was in preparation, abandoned the fortress at Ticonderoga, and repaired to Crown Point. This also they relinquished later in the summer, without destroying their works.

While this was taking place on Lake Champlain, the brave Montcalm was concentrating his forces at Quebec, where General Wolfe, with a large army, presented himself. The success of the conquest of Canada depended upon the taking of that city.

The battle on the Heights of Abraham, which decided the contest, took place September 13, 1759. Both generals were determined to conquer or die; both fell at the head of their respective armies. The English carried the day, and the French were defeated, dispersed or made prisoners.

Montcalm, having received one musket ball early in the action, was mortally wounded while attempting to rally some fugitive Canadians. On being told his death was near, he said, "So much the better; I shall not live to see the surrender of Quebec."

He died the next morning, and his death was followed by the loss to France of Canada.

"I should like to go to Quebec," said Miss Lejeune, adding, "do you mean to visit all the battle-fields of American history?" with a smile, as she addressed Mr. Horner.

"I am afraid we shall not hold out to do that," he replied. "There are many other places of equal interest to Ticonderoga, merely looking at the story of these French and English contests for territory. It seems as if one place might serve as a sort of specimen for all. If we become interested in the scene of a part of the struggle, and study carefully the actual ground over which the contending parties came and went, we shall acquire a living knowledge of the whole. Of course it is to be remembered that this spot was but one point in the struggle going on all along the line. The

PAUL REVERE'S RIDE.

story of Braddock's defeat, at Fort Du Quesne, and the subsequent taking of it, is just as interesting as that of the events we are now looking at ; the fact that Washington was there engaged makes it perhaps more so. But," he added, "I doubt if the neighborhood is so picturesque."

On the site of Fort Du Quesne, in the western part of Pennsylvania, the city of Pittsburg now stands, and blackens the neighborhood with the smoke of its many chimneys. It was a post contested, like Ticonderoga, between French and English. Washington, then a young man, selected the spot for an English fort. The French drove away the workmen employed upon it, and finished the fort themselves, calling it Fort Du Quesne. A veteran English army was sent there under General Braddock, with Washington as a staff officer, but the General was defeated, and mortally wounded. This took place July 9, 1755.

GEN. BRADDOCK.

Three years after, Washington was again sent to Fort Du Quesne, and took it at last. These events had great consequences among the colonists. They taught them that the red coats were not invincible, and in the training of battle, they themselves were preparing for the greater struggle against the same generals who were now their commanders.

General Wolfe, the English commander at Quebec, displayed as much bravery as his French opponent. Hubert and Bessie had a quarrel over their respective merits, Hubert taking the side of the English hero, Bessie teasing him with her preference for the French.

"Oh, come along, Hubert!" cried Tom, "what do you care for either of them ? Come down to the lake for a row."

# CHAPTER XVI.



NOTHING induced Tom to take an interest in these historical discussions. He was tall, strong and active, with a fine appetite, and thorough enjoyment of muscular exercises. He had never been known to devote himself to books, and was the only Horner without a decided aptitude for foreign languages. On the other hand, he was of a most genial, sociable disposition, and was a general favorite wherever he went, among schoolfellows, young ladies, and especially matrons, to whom he had naturally an attractive, gratifying manner of addressing himself.

Bessie was extremely pleased with Hubert's lately developed taste for her favorite pursuit of history, and if she loved to disagree with him, it was to discover how well he could defend his own side of the question.

"Hubert," she said, "how did you come upon all this knowledge about Wolfe and the Heights of Abraham?"

"Why, I have been reading about it, with Professor Bruce. You will like him, Bessie; he is just loaded to the muzzle with facts."

After a charming week at Ticonderoga, our party left that place, and crossed Lake George, one afternoon, to Caldwell, at the head, or southern end, of that lake. Here they established themselves at the huge Fort William Henry Hotel, built actually on the site of the old fort, with a fine view down the lake.

They found Lake George even more picturesque than its far larger companion, and plentifully supplied with points of historic interest of which the stories are, with time, becoming legends, like those of the Old World.

"The only difficulty with our early history," said Miss Lejeune, "is that we still have to see it too near. It is like these hills

LAKE GEORGE.

in this clear atmosphere. They were intended to 'carry' for a long distance, and we come close up to them, like an amateur critic in a picture gallery."

"Time is remedying that, Augusta, as fast as it can; it is already two centuries and a half since the first white man saw Lake George," said Mr. Horner.

This was a Jesuit priest, Father Jogues, who was brought hither as a prisoner by Iroquois, in 1642, thirty-three years after Champlain had terrified the savages so that they fled in terror from his murderous weapons, to their home on the Mohawk. Since then they themselves had been supplied with firearms, and learned the use of them, and now their turn of revenge was come. They took the war-path and infested the forests all over the country like ravening wolves. It was one of these hostile bands that had attacked Father Jogues and his companions as he was returning with supplies from Quebec to a far-off mission where he was doing his best to give to Indians the faith and benefit of civilized life.

Having seized these captives, the savages returned with them, inflicting horrid tortures to their home on the Mohawk, and thus they came, after passing "the chiming waters" at Ticonderoga, to the shores of the beautiful lake sleeping in the depths of the limited forest, the fairest gem of the wilderness.

Jogues remained among the Mohawks for nearly a year, a captive; in the midst of his sufferings, he lost no opportunity to convert his tormentors to Christianity. In a lonely spot in the forest he cut bark from a large tree into the form of a cross, before which, half-clad in furs, he used to kneel in prayer upon the frozen ground.

One of his companions they adopted into one of their families; the other they killed. At last, after a year of suffering, Jogues managed to escape, and was secreted by the Dutch at Fort Orange, near Albany. These kind-hearted people paid a large ransom for him, and gave him a free passage home to France. He arrived in Brittany, his native place, one Christmas day, and was received by his friends, who had heard of his captivity, as one risen from the dead. He was treated everywhere with mingled reverence and curiosity, and was summoned to court, where the Queen Anne of Austria kissed the poor mutilated hands of the slave of the Mohawks.

He returned to Canada, and twice revisited the country of the Mohawks; the second time was the last, for he was treacherously slain by the savages, for whom he had done so much. He was struck on the head with a tomahawk as he entered a wigwam

SHELVING ROCK, — LAKE GEORGE.

where he had been invited to supper. His head was cut off and displayed upon one of the palisades that surrounded the village. His body they threw into the river.

Lake George is thirty-six miles long, but so narrow that it seems everywhere like a river. The shores are steep and rocky in some places; as at the spot called Rogers Slide, where Major Robert Rogers was chased to the edge of the cliff by Indians, in the winter of 1758. Hidden from them for a few moments, he managed to turn round upon his snow-shoes, and retreated from the edge of the cliff, so that his tracks, being reversed, made it appear as if he had cast him self over it. He slid down the ravine close at hand, and when the Indians came up a few minutes later, they saw him skimming away over the ice towards Fort William Henry, and attributed his escape to the protection of the Great Spirit.

Lake George is now quiet and still, but for the daily steamboats which in summer ply across it from end to end; but it was the scene of imposing spectacles during the contests of French and English. In 1758, the English army advanced up the lake with sixteen thousand men, in large bateaux, convoyed by gunboats, all brilliant with rich uniforms and waving banners, while the music of the regimental bands echoed among the hills. A few days later the scattered and defeated army passed back up the lake, having left half their number dead and dying under the walls of Fort Carillon; this was the time of the unsuccessful attack among the bushes and timber. The next year another martial procession crossed the lake, and this march was soon followed by the Conquest of Canada.

Cooper's novel, "The Last of the Mohicans," has for its plot and situation the campaign at Fort William Henry. The story is very exciting, and though highly colored, adheres closely to the facts. The Red Indian as depicted by Cooper is a more romantic, emotional being than it is possible to consider him after reading Parkman's description of his characteristics; but the painted figure seems better for a romance than the cold reality.

The description of Fort William Henry in the novel is faithful to the scene.

"Directly on the shore of the lake, and nearer to its western than its eastern margin, lay the extensive earthen ramparts and low buildings of the Fort. Two of the sweeping bastions appeared to rest on the water, which washed their base, while a deep ditch and extensive morasses guarded its other sides and angles. The land had been cleared of wood for a reasonable distance around the work, but every other part of the scene lay in the green

PUTNAM SAVING FORT EDWARD

livery of nature, except where the limpid water mellowed the view, or the bold rocks thrust their black and naked heads above the undulating outlines of the mountain ranges. In front, numerous islands rested on the bosom of the lake, some low and sunken, as if imbedded in the waters, others appearing to hover over it in little hillocks of green velvet."

If Montcalm were responsible for the massacre by his Indians which followed upon the surrender of Fort William Henry, it would be a dark blot upon his reputation as a hero. There is reason to believe, however, that the conduct of these savages was beyond his control.

This was a subject upon which Bessie and Hubert could never agree, Bessie defending her general because he was French, and Hubert taking the view of Cooper, that the event left a stain upon the reputation of Montcalm, not erased by his early and glorious death.

Fort Edward, built in 1755, was a post of military importance as the point on the Hudson where troops and stores were landed to pass to Lake Champlain, a distance of only twenty-five miles, which, however, in those early days, was a difficult passage, beset with savages. It was built of logs and earth, and surrounded by a deep ditch.

The whole neighborhood which the Horners were now visiting is as interesting for scenes in the Revolutionary War as for the earlier ones described; but Hubert did not yet care so much for the later events, having, as he said, not come to them yet.

"Well, Hubert," said Bessie, "when you have studied up the Revolutionary War, we will come again, and see all the places we have overlooked now, or neglected."

"I think Hubert will find it more interesting to read about the struggle of independence, now that he knows who the men were, and what material they were made of, that entered into it, and carried it through to the end."

"Yes, Hubert, you read all about it, and tell me anything you think may really improve my mind," said Tom, as he stretched himself out on the hard sofa of the hotel parlor, with a bundle of shawls under his head.

They had come in from a long excursion on which there had been too much talking of old battle-fields, too much standing round, and too little straight-ahead, steady exercise to suit Tom, and he professed himself entirely used up. Tom was a good sleeper, and equally good for a ten-mile walk or a three hours' nap.

In about five minutes he was fast asleep. His mother carefully threw something over him to protect him from an open window near, and they all left him to his slumbers.

# CHAPTER XVII.

## SCHROON LAKE.

AMONG the many pleasant excursions which the Horners made about Lake George was one especially desired by Bessie, on account of its name.

Schroon Lake lies at the foot of one of the mountain ranges of the Adirondack region, and Schroon river winds through its deep valleys. This name was given to the lake and river by the early French settlers at Crown Point, in honor of Madame Scarron, wife of the celebrated French dramatist, Paul Scarron, and afterwards herself celebrated as Madame de Maintenon.

Bessie was delighted when she found that Schroon was a contraction of Scarron. Doubtless some admirer of the poet, or of his young and beautiful wife, who had frequented their beautiful salons in Paris, named the stream and river in their honor, which he found in lonely wanderings in the wilds of a new world. On the old maps, the name is always written Scarron.

Françoise d' Aubigné was born in prison, where her father, a worthless baron, passed many years. He died afterwards in poverty, and Françoise became a mere drudge in the service of a countess, her godmother, minding poultry in the farmyard in a peasant's dress and wooden shoes.

In the same street lived the poet Scarron, a paralytic and cripple. Becoming interested in the poor girl, he fell in love with her, and offered himself in marriage. She was seventeen, and he more than twice her age, but she accepted him. The house of Scarron became the resort of the best intellects of Paris.

After the death of her husband, Madame Scarron, as governess of the children of Louis the Fourteenth, so captivated that king,

BLUE FLAG.

that after the death of his queen, Maria Theresa, he married her in secret. Thus she became the Queen of France, in fact, though not in name. The king settled upon her the large estate of Maintenon, and made her Marquise de Maintenon. For thirty years she exercised a remarkable influence over the destinies of France.

In many ways the advice she gave the king was good and useful: she made him think more about religion than he had ever done before, but she encouraged his dislike to the Huguenots, and it was in harmony with her inclinations that he revoked the Edict of Nantes, by which these French Protestants had hitherto been protected.

It was such severity towards the Protestants which made enemies for Louis in all the countries of Europe, amongst them William of Orange, who had become king of England.

"In short, Bessie," said her father, "we may consider that the lady who gave her name to this lake was the cause of all the bloodshed in its neighborhood for the last two hundred years."

"That is putting it rather strong, papa," she answered, "for the French and English would have quarrelled about the land anyhow, and the Indians would have taken different sides."

The war between England and France, known as King William's War, which lasted from 1689 to 1697, involved the American colonies. It was during this war that some of the Indians became the allies of the French, while the English were friendly with the Iroquois—the Five Nations who inhabited Central New York.

"Queen Anne's War" was in Europe the War of the Spanish Succession. beginning in 1702, ending with the Treaty of Utrecht, in 1713. This was the last of Louis the Fourteenth's wars, as he died in 1715. In this war the colonies were involved; the frontiers of New England were kept in continual alarm. The town of Deerfield, in

GARRISON HOUSE, IN DEERFIELD, MASS.

Massachusetts, was attacked and destroyed by a party of French and Indians, and for several years the frontiers of Canada and New England were the continued scene of massacre and devastation. This was a war of religions, for both on the Continent and in America, Protestant English were arrayed against Roman Catholic French.

"King George's War," called after George the Second, is the same as the war about the Austrian Succession; the Protestant countries of Europe, England and Holland, defending the claim of Maria Theresa against Frederick the Great, and also France and Spain, who took up the cause of her opponent, the Elector of Bavaria. War was declared between France and England in 1744; Louis the Fifteenth had succeeded his grandfather on the French throne; and George the Third was reigning in England. Again the colonies shared in the warfare. In 1748 a treaty was concluded at Aix-la-Chapelle, by which all nations were pacified, and peace prevailed in Europe; but in America the encroachments of France on the English led to resistance, and the events of which Lake George and Lake Champlain were the scene, preceded the outbreak of the Seven Years' War in Europe.

PITCHER-PLANT.

The Horners had a whole day going to and coming from the lake named after Madame Scarron. They found the way beautiful with flowers, some of them new to all. Hubert wished for Professor Bruce, who would have told them all about the botany.

Beautiful blue flags grew in a sort of bog, where there was kalmia different from the common sheep's laurel, or the splendid kalmia latifolia, not yet in blossom. They found, too, the curious side-saddle-flower (*Saracenia*) with its pitcher-shaped leaves.

In 1749, when Indians, French and English were enjoying a short peace, but all sharpening their weapons for renewed contest,

Peter Kalm, a Swedish botanist, travelled over this region. He made discoveries of many plants not known in Europe, and gave his name to the kalmia.

The long sunny day on which they took this expedition was the last day of their stay at Lake George. On the next they went to Fort Edward, where the party separated, Hubert and Tom escorting Mrs. Horner and Bessie to Utopia, by the way of Rutland and Burlington, whence the way was the same as that by which Hubert had joined them.

Miss Lejeune and Mr. Horner returned to New York, where each had affairs to look after. A fortnight had slipped by among the associations and legends of early warfare on the lakes, and it was now the middle of June.

"Well, aunt Dut," said Bessie, as they stood on the platform, "I am sorry to part from you. I wish you were coming with us to Utopia."

"So do I," said Hubert. "I am sure you would enjoy it, Miss Augusta. You would have immense fun with Professor Bruce. He is a great talker, and there is nothing he does not know."

"Perhaps I will come later," said Miss Lejeune; "but having once surrendered myself to a summer of visits, there is no end to engagements. It really requires book-keeping by double entry to keep the run of them. As soon as my trunks are ready, I am off for Beverly, then Nahant, and so on. I am only afraid," she added, in a low tone to Bessie, "that your mother will be fearfully bored at Utopia."

"I do not believe she will stay long," replied Bessie. "You know papa also thought it would be too dull, but she was possessed with the idea she would enjoy some real country. You know Philip's vacation begins soon, and I think he will invent something for her."

"How about yourself, Bessie?" asked Miss Lejeune; "it is rather tame for you, settling down here in Vermont."

"Tame with my old Hubert here to squabble with and instruct," exclaimed Bessie, "and Tom besides: I assure you, we are going to have a wildly exciting summer, are we not, Tom?"

Tom and his father were walking up and down the platform, while Mrs. Horner was resting in a rocking-chair in the ladies' waiting-room. They joined the conversation.

"It will be wildly exciting if my father sends us the Stuyvesant boys," said Tom; "we have just been talking about that."

"I shall go and see Stuyvesant directly," said Mr. Horner, "and see what he thinks of the plan. Meanwhile you must lay it before the Bruces. If it is decided the boys are to come, I can bring them with me next week or so. whenever I find time to come up.

"You see," he continued, speaking to Miss Lejeune. "this troublesome affair of Brown's I was telling you about. will keep me pretty close to New York all summer; but it will not be difficult to run up to Utopia occasionally to see how the family agree."

"Of all of us," cried Bessie. "you. papa, have arranged the vilest programme for yourself!"

"My dear, I feel quite light-hearted at the idea of a hard-working summer. I want to prove to my own satisfaction that several years' travelling has not unfitted me for it."

The scheme presented to Mr. Stuyvesant pleased him greatly, and was carried out. as the Bruces did not object to receiving the twins.

Mrs. Horner and Bessie, as the boys expected. were delighted with the drive over the mountain from East Utopia. The road through the woods was carpeted with mosses, ferns, and the bright red partridge berry.

"It looked very different, you had better believe, when I was here before," said Tom, remembering with a shiver the snow-covered landscape. It was now the perfection of early midsummer.

PARTRIDGE-BERRY.

The woods were full of kalmia latifolia, mountain laurel, in dense thickets sometimes twenty feet high. There was one place where it grew upon a slope surrounding a little pond like an amphitheatre, and here the masses of its bright pink blossoms prevailed over the green of the foliage.

"It is like a pink snow storm!" cried Hubert.

They drove slowly up the hill to the homestead towards the end of the afternoon. Mr. and Mrs. Bruce were both awaiting them on the doorstep, and Alice ran across from her house as soon as she saw the wagon in the distance, for which she was on the watch.

"Look, Mrs. Horner! is not the view lovely?" demanded Hubert.

The broad river below swept away for several miles; across it were the hills of New Hampshire, now brilliant with the perfect greens of June. Opposite, the sun was already giving golden tones to the scene as he approached the west.

A BIT OF THE LAKE.

# CHAPTER XVIII.



MR. HORNER went back to New York, the Stuyvesant boys came, and little Mrs. Bruce had a house full, and her hands full of responsibilities, for which she was quite equal. Reinforced by two friendly young ladies in the kitchen, "who did not mind helpin' Mrs. Bruce for a spell, seein' she had so many to do for," the housekeeping ran smoothly enough.

Bessie and her mother occupied the "best spare," a room containing the most stately furniture of the house; a huge mahogany four-post bedstead, with a delightful "quilt," occupied one side of the room between the windows. The first night when tired Bessie threw herself upon this bed, she found herself sinking down, down, to unknown depths. She shrieked for help to her mother and Mrs. Bruce, who having come up-stairs late, were chatting in the doorway. They came and rescued her. The down was eider-down. Mrs. Bruce sat down in the rocking chair and laughed a quiet little laugh she had.

"That's Lavinia Mary's doing," she said. "She must have brought the down-bed from the garret on purpose to make you comfortable. In January it might have been hospitably imagined, but to-night!"

Bessie was afraid of making trouble, but she was so sure that her mother would be smothered during the night if she tried sleeping in a bed of cider-down, that she allowed Mrs. Bruce to pull it off, and lent her help in re-making the bed, of which the basis was an excellent hair-mattress.

The kingdom of the boys was up stairs. Two large rooms occupied the whole front of the house, behind which, in an L, down a few steps, and over the "Hall," was the garret where Molly Stark's bonnet lived.

At first the Stuyvesants were very meek and well behaved, and as Tom and Hubert did not wish to encourage over familiarity, the door of communication between the rooms was kept closed. Later on — but it is unwise to anticipate.

It was a very cheerful party; and the time it shone to best advantage was at breakfast-time. Mrs. Bruce believed in feeding young and growing persons. The things she had for breakfast were likely to tempt the most timid appetite, and delight the most robust.

The table was adorned with a bunch of wild roses. Mr. Bruce sat at his end of it, and administered broiled chicken, and ham and eggs. Mrs. Bruce, opposite him, poured out steaming coffee with boiled milk and real cream in it; and Lavinia Mary came in at intervals of five minutes, with plates of steaming griddles which she applied all round the table with appropriate remarks. "Now, Mrs. Horner, you'll have another. What! given out al-

WILD ROSES.

ready? Well, I declare! I told Belinda I thought you'd take once more. Mr. Hubert will, I know. Land's sakes, he's just begun. Well, there's plenty more batter; it ris well this time. Now, Mr. Augustine!"

The boys, Ernest and Augustine Stuyvesant, were pale, thin boys, looking as if they had had too much between meals in the way of candy and fruit. Even at Utopia, their leading idea of filling up the time was to go over to the store and spend their plentiful pocket money on certain large balls of sweetness,

UNDER THE TREES.

one of which entirely filled the mouth and precluded speech until it had disappeared. Mrs. Bruce hoped to counteract this practice by feeding them heartily at regular hours, and giving them plenty of more rational employment in the intervals of regular meals.

"What are you going to do to-day?" asked the professor, for lessons had not yet begun. It was agreed on all hands that there should be an interval of real vacation, which was to close on this seventeenth of June with some occasion worthy to celebrate together the anniversary of the Battle or Bunker Hill.

In plans of amusement, Hubert took the place of master of ceremonies, on account of his prior knowledge of the place. This seemed very funny to Tom, who was well accustomed to be the leader, especially with Hubert, but he willingly accepted, though for this occasion only, the part of second fiddler.

Therefore he remained silent, putting his hands in his pockets and tipping back his chair, a custom which Mrs. Horner disapproved of, but which gentle Mrs. Bruce allowed, while Hubert replied:

POND LILIES.

" Alice says, sir, that there are pond lilies out in the pond beyond the upper farm, and we thought we might go up and picnic there."

" Pond lilies so early! I can hardly believe it!" replied the professor.

" She saw two of Burdick's boys with some yesterday, and they told her where they got them."

The professor roamed off into the library, and finding the right page in his *Gray's Manual*, glanced at the pencil annotations in the margin, giving the dates when he had found lilies in previous years.

"Well, yes, — 'June 17, 1865;' — yes, there may be some; at any rate, it is a delightful place to go to."

"We thought, sir, we might go up the big river in the two boats, and then push the little boat through the creek, so as to have it in the pond to get the lilies."

"It's flat and swampy there; you cannot get the boat through, I'm afraid," objected the professor.

"We can try," said Hubert with a smile.

"We can try" was a form of expression beloved of Professor Bruce in connection with mental problems.

"May I come in?" asked Alice, pushing wider open the front door, which was already ajar, and close to the dining-room.

Alice was still terribly afraid of Bessie, stood in awe of Tom, had her doubts about Ernest and Augustine, and even found her relations with Hubert changed, now that he was no longer dependent on her for society. She liked the fun of such a crowd, as she called it, but looked back with some regret on the delightful quarrelling days when she and Hubert had the whole of Utopia to themselves.

"What's this, Alice, about pond lilies?" asked the professor.

"I have brought this one to show you, sir; it is not a very good one, but the Burdicks wouldn't let me have any other."

"It is three days old," he replied; "that shows they are well forward; if that is so, we may find cardinals too."

"That ham, marm," said Lavinia Mary, "is just in the condition for sandwiches."

Mrs. Bruce, thus reminded of the material part of a picnic, now asked who was going.

"I do not like these marine excursions," said Mrs. Horner, who had heard the suggestion of boats, "and think I may be counted out."

"My dear madam," said the Professor gallantly, "I propose to leave the young people to solve the boat problem. I will put

Lucy in the carryall, and take you and my wife, and any one else, indeed, who cares for dry feet."

"Then do start soon," cried Hubert, "for we want to get back before dark."

Lucy was not a very fast horse.

"The baskets can go with us, then," said Mrs. Bruce, and she withdrew with her adviser-in-chief to prepare the substantial.

The young people darted off, careless of preparations, to the shore of the river. Only Bessie paused to offer her services, but Lavinia Mary called out, "Now you go with them, Miss Bessie, and we'll see all is right."

CARDINALS.

"Dear mama, I'm so glad you are going," cried Bessie; "do you mind taking this book? I may get a chance to read to Hubert."

"O Bessie!" cried her mother, "don't try to improve his mind to-day!"

"But it is interesting, mama!" and she was off. The book was Parkman's Pontiac.

Bessie could not be missed from the rowing party, for she pulled the best oar, except Tom. She therefore manned one boat, he the other. She took Hubert, Tom took Alice, and the twins were equally divided between the two boats.

They proceeded but slowly up the stream, but the current close to the shore was not strong, and the distance not more than quarter of a mile. The tug of war was at the entrance of a sluggish little creek through a swamp thickly grown with marsh grass. The smaller boat was left below, where a good landing could be made. Alice and the twins were sent round by a dry path to the pond, while Hubert and Tom pulled off their shoes and stockings, rolled up their trousers and became outside passengers. Bessie stayed in the boat to pole with an oar and to guide the flat-bottomed craft. She pushed, the boys tugged. They stuck in the mud, but got off again. The channel became narrower and narrower. Bessie had to alight on a rock, while they lifted the boat over the submerged part of it; getting back into the boat required a long step, but Bessie was equal to it. Finally they came out where they longed to come,— a deep, cool arm of the pond, where great trees came down to the shore. Here all was changed. They shoved the boat to land, shouted to the other children, and threw themselves down, panting and exhausted.

"Oh, I'm that hot!" cried Bessie.

Hubert dipped up some water in a cup he carried in his pocket.

"It is not very cool, but it is better than nothing," he said.

The picnic place was just round the corner in the same woods. For a wonder, Lucy had arrived before the boating party.

The two boys brought the boat round to the spot where the

rest were assembled, and after a brief rest, Tom pushed across to the part of the pond where the lilies were, taking the two girls to pull them up.

They found them not very plenty as yet, but with promise of a large crop later on. Alice showed Bessie how to put her hand deep down and pull on the stem steadily in a perpendicular direction, so as not to break it off short. For Bessie had never gathered pond lilies before.

As they were eating their good lunch under the trees, the professor told them that the true way to gather lilies is to come before sunrise and to see them as the first light touches and opens the buds. They resolved to do this, and with his permission, they left the smaller boat there for future excursions, perfectly safe in that unfrequented region. Coming home, the twins were packed into the wagon, the other four drifting merrily down the river in the other boat.

PULLING UP LILIES.

# CHAPTER XIX.

## WORK IN EARNEST.

WORK began in earnest on the next Monday, with reservations in favor of the coming Fourth. The library was converted into a real schoolroom. Two desks, joined together, hacked and ink-stained with good service of years, were brought out from retirement for Ernest and Augustine Stuyvesant. Hubert still kept his table in one corner, by a window overlooking the Connecticut, while Tom was allowed one end of Mr. Bruce's own writing-table, in the middle of the room. But Tom was only an honorary member of the class. He had been working hard all winter, and was at liberty to please himself now in the matter of study. Nevertheless, as the theory of the Horners was in favor of doing something useful in the course of every day, Tom was reading German by himself with a dictionary, and was generally to be found at his end of the study-table while the others were at work.

Professor Bruce presided, "grinding" the little boys at Latin, reading, writing, arithmetic, etc., and suppressing their occasional tendency to kick each other's shins. Maps and slates pervaded the library. Bessie did not mix herself with this studious retreat, but established herself and books in a corner of her own room, near a window with a deep low window-seat, commanding the same wide view of the river and distance that Hubert's did below. She had free access to the books in Professor Bruce's library, and had prepared for herself a course of American History; besides which Bessie was always getting up a new language. At present, it was Italian, with which she was less familiar than the other modern ones.

PROFESSOR BRUCE.

Meanwhile, Mrs. Horner accompanied Mrs. Bruce daily around the garden, advised or agreed about the housekeeping, helped Lavinia Mary make the beds, cut and disposed of flowers from the gar-den, and gave that light final touch to the dust-ing and arrangement of the parlors which makes the difference in charm between a room so cared for and the one me-chanically set to rights.

As Bessie sat day after day at her books, and heard her mother's gentle voice conferring with Lavinia Mary, it often happened that she sighed a little sigh, and said to herself, "Poor mamma, it is awfully dull for her here!"

HUBERT'S CORNER.

"Take these towels, Lavinia," she heard her mother saying one Monday morning, adding cheerfully, "you will have a nice day to wash."

"Yes'm. The great things are all out now on the lines. I told Belinda I did not know but the wind might be a little too high, but it has gone down considerable since sunrise."

"It is much nicer to have the things all washed every week," remarked Mrs. Horner, as she smoothed down her side of the bed, and paused for a simultaneous turnover, with her fellow bed-maker, of the edge of the clean white sheet.

"I expect so," said Lavinia Mary, without in the least knowing what was meant.

"In Germany, you know, they only wash once in six months," continued Mrs. Horner.

"Land's sakes!" cried Lavinia Mary. "Do the things keep clean so long in them climates?"

"Oh, dear, no! but they have quantities and quantities of sheets, pillow-cases, and all wash-things. They change as often as we do, throwing all the soiled linen into a dark closet; and when the time for the grand wash comes, these are taken out, sorted and counted, and then they wash and wash till all is clean again."

"Heathen customs," remarked Lavinia Mary as she left the room and went back to her weekly tub.

It was that same morning that as Bessie came out of the library, which she had entered for a moment to look at a book of reference, leaving the students busily and quietly employed, she came upon Alice Martin, who was not usually to be seen at the house so early. She brought a tastefully grouped bunch of buttercups and dandelions which she shyly presented to Bessie, and then said, "Is Tom in the library?"

"Tom?" demanded Bessie without another word, but in a manner which implied, "What in the world can be your business with Tom!"

"I,—that is, he,—I mean, we are going to begin German together," explained Alice, embarrassed at Bessie's sternness.

Luckily for her, Tom, hearing the voices, came to the door, and assuming a severe manner to cover his own slight sheepishness, he said, "Oh, you have come, Alice! you are late. I supposed you had changed your mind. The grammar is all ready for you. Come in!"

"So you have turned pedagogue, Tom! It must be in the air!" cried Bessie. The door was quickly shut, almost in her face, and she went up-stairs, laughing.

"Tom and Alice!" she said to herself, "that is a new combination. I must write to aunt Dut about it. That Tom should be teaching German! It is a capital thing to fill up his time."

As it happened, the mail that day brought other combinations.

Mary Horner, the oldest of the family, had been married about a year, during which time she had been travelling or resting in the south of Europe, with her husband, Mr. Clarence Hervey. Letters came every week from the young couple, describing the pleasures of Pau and the Pyrénées, with favorable accounts of Mary's health, which had never been so robust as that of the rest of the family. The budget which now arrived was full of but one theme and entreaty, that the mamma should come out and join her daughter, and her very great favorite, the new son-in-law. The Herveys had heard the scheme of a Vermont summer without greatly approving of it, for their mother at least.

"For the young ones," wrote Mr. Hervey, "it is all very well; but, dear Mrs. Horner, you are buried alive in the wilds of your native land. You have not even your own closets to keep in order, any more than you did while travelling in Europe. Come and keep us in order. We need you more than the rest of your family does. Bessie can matronize the young crowd at Utopia, and Mrs. Bruce can matronize her. You must come to us. We will spend the summer wherever you like best; but we think you will like our little Chateau Henri Quatre. It is just far enough from Pau to be quiet, and near enough to be amusing, and the view of the mountains is superb."

Mrs. Horner was a good deal upset by these letters, among which was a private one from her husband, which seemed to much urge the same thing. His plan, to make everything simple, was that Philip should cross with his mother, in that same Bordeaux steamer they were so fond of.

Philip, the second Horner, and eldest son, had finished his first year at Harvard. Class day was just over, and he was lingering in the neighborhood of Cambridge with a college friend. No sooner did he hear the plan than he rejoiced greatly. Meeting, oddly enough, Miss Lejeune at the Country Club, one day, he had a chance of briefly talking the matter over with her. The result of this was a sheaf of letters from these two, which hardly left Mrs.

THE FRENCH CHATEAU.

Horner an opportunity to protest. "But, my dear," she said to Bessie, "how can I cross that dreadful Atlantic again, and without your father? and then, he is so forlorn by himself in New York." She fell to crying, but Bessie held firm.

"Papa will do well enough, mamma. I think he is really younger for having this business on his shoulders. He can come here, or I can go to him, by and by. He can go to Newport while aunt Augusta is there. What trunk shall you take, mamma?"

"I thought the black one, Bessie, would be enough with the little state-room valise."

Bessie smiled to herself. The fact that her mother had already suffered her mind to dwell on the matter of baggage showed that she was not invincibly opposed to the scheme.

"The fact is," said Tom, talking it over with Hubert, "that our family go to Europe as easily as turtles slip off a log. Just you notice that one."

He neatly aimed a stone at a happy turtle who was sunning himself a rod or two off. The boys were strolling along the river-side, just below the house. The stone struck the log; the turtle vanished.

Without more ado the plan was settled. Philip went to New York; Tom took his mother there. They met Mr. Horner and passed a couple of days at the Fifth Avenue Hotel together before the two travellers sailed.

Bessie felt a little gloomy as she saw her mother drive from the door, with trunks and shawl-straps, and the little state-room valise which she had herself so many times packed and unpacked. She had misgivings about her mother. alone and sick in her state-room, but the very next one had been secured for Philip, who was never sick himself, and who was as good a nurse as one of the girls. But Bessie wished she were to be with them; as she turned from the door, the sunlight seemed dark within the house. She felt that her own fate was rather dreary, "poked off with a lot of boys up in the country, while the rest of the family were enjoying themselves." In fact, left to herself,—for the house was empty,—Bessie retired to her room,— now all hers since her mother had deserted it,— and indulged herself in the rare luxury of one of what in her childhood had been called "Bessie's tantrums," an access of crying. accompanied by the darkest view of her situation in life.

It lasted perhaps ten minutes, during which her nature worked off the excitement of the last week. Then she became reasonable, and thought of a great many things which made her position not only desirable, but delightful. Washing her face to remove the tears, she set herself to the active hard work of changing all the furniture in the room from one place to another, and putting finally away the remains of her mother's packing.

By the time the early dinner hour had arrived, she was not only cheerful, but in ridiculously good spirits, and Tom being absent, she carried off the blank caused by the two vacant places in a manner which surprised Mr. Bruce, and every one but Hubert, who had seen her just like this before, in similar circumstances.

DANDELIONS AND BUTTERCUPS.

# CHAPTER XX.

## TWO HEROES.

IT is evident that the stirring events of the early half of the eighteenth century were raising a crop of heroes ready to stand forth fully equipped in the service of freedom when the time came to resist the oppression of the mother-country. The boys who were born at that period grew up familiar with the smell of powder and smoke, and accustomed to the use of arms. To resist, to defend, were a part of their natural lives, and to do and dare great things. Thus the names of young men who took brave parts in the contests on the Lakes, reappear again as patriots in the cause of liberty.

The French War was a grand field for the military training of men, officers and soldiers for the scenes to be enacted a few years later. The young men of the country who displayed military genius in that war were all the time rising from the ranks of the common soldier to positions of command and responsibility. Israel Putnam was among the young men who distinguished himself at Fort Edward, which he once saved by the example of his own immense exertions from being utterly destroyed by fire.

In the winter of 1756 the barracks took fire. The magazine containing three hundred barrels of gunpowder was only twelve feet distant. Putnam took his station on the roof of the barracks, and poured on water, handed him by a line of soldiers, until the fabric began to totter. He succeeded in subduing the flames only when the outside planks of the magazine had been consumed, so that but a thin partition protected the powder.

This Putnam is the hero of the well-known adventure with the wolf, which happened in Pomfret, Con., when he was a young farmer there, in 1743. Every boy knows how he descended into the wolf's den, a rope round his body, and a blazing torch in his hand, and

ISRAEL PUTNAM.

descried at the farthest end of the cave the glaring eyeballs of his terrified foe. With a dexterous shot he killed the wolf just as she was preparing to spring; and the people above, with no small exultation, dragged them out together.

Putnam's life was full of similar bold deeds and hair-breadth escapes. In the French War he was often brought into the closest quarters, where escape seemed impossible, but by his quick perceptions and amazing energy could wrest a victory from what seemed defeat.

The Indians thought Putnam bore a charmed life, and no wonder, for he was always coming out alive and unharmed from the most dangerous encounters. From the day that he entered the den at Pomfret till he rode down the steep stone steps at Greenwich, Con., to escape his pursuers,—when he was sixty years old and weighed two hundred pounds,— he was going through a series of wonderful adventures and escapes. He gained many a wound and scar, but preserved through all his life, and died at home in a good old age.

Another young hero, ripening for the Revolution, was Ethan Allen, also famous at Ticonderoga. The school in which his bravery was developed was the difficulty which arose in Vermont about the possessions of his lands.

No permanent settlement was effected in Vermont, on the west

MRS. BRUCE IN HER CAPE BONNET.

side of the Green Mountains, till after the conquest of Canada by
the English. In their expeditions against the French, English colonists had made themselves acquainted with the fertility and value
of the lands lying between the Connecticut River and Lake Champlain, and the conquest of

Canada having now removed
the danger of settling there,
swarms of adventurers began
to arrive. From the year
1760, the population of Vermont began to increase with
some rapidity. During the
war a road had been opened
from Charleston, N. H., to
Crown Point, which helped
to open the land of Vermont
to the attention of settlers.

Governor Wentworth, of
New Hampshire, laid out
townships on both sides of
the Connecticut River, and
by granting lands, with fees and emoluments, and by reserving
five hundred acres in each township for himself, was accumulating
a fortune. The government of New York, on the other side of
these lands, determined to check this, in order to possess themselves of the advantage. This was the beginning of great difficulties, as the original grants made in the time of Charles the Second were absurd and conflicting.

Among the settlers in this disputed territory was the family of
Ethan Allen, who became first conspicuous in resisting the decrees
of New York law. Allen was made colonel of an armed force
organized to protect the New Hampshire granters and remove the
New York settlers.

At the head of his Green Mountain boys, he resisted all the proceedings of the New York authorities. Whenever a sheriff appeared upon the grants for the purpose of arresting rioters or ejecting settlers, he was sure to be met by a party larger than his own, ready and able to frustrate his object. Repeated aggressions took place, until the indignation of the settlers throughout the New Hampshire grants was raised to the highest pitch; open hostilities were prevented only by the commencement of the American War, at Lexington (nineteenth of April, 1775), an event which produced a shock felt throughout the colonies. Local and provincial contests were at once swallowed up by the importance of the struggle thus began between Great Britian and her colonies.

Here was another hero ready for the emergency. As soon as war with the mother-country had become inevitable, the occupation of Ticonderoga was determined on, and the task confided to Allen, who repaired thither at once, at the head of his well-tried Green Mountain boys.

Ethan Allen was born in Connecticut, in 1737. It was in 1766 that he moved to Vermont, and became outlawed by New York for his bold and defiant action. In 1775 he took Fort Ticonderoga. Later in the year, attacking Montreal with one hundred and ten men, he was captured, with his whole command. He was carried to England and kept a prisoner in Pendennis Castle for a short time, but was exchanged in 1778. His life was always eventful, sharing the later troubles of his adopted State. He died at Burlington in 1789.

At Montpelier, the capital of the State, is a fine statue, in Vermont marble, of Vermont's hero, made by Larkin Mead. The State House is a handsome building of light-colored granite, with a portico supported by Doric columns, and under it the statue stands with a fine imposing effect.

"I might have stopped at Montpelier," said Hubert, "when I went to Burlington to meet you, but I never thought of such a

PUTNAM RIDING DOWN THE STEPS.

thing. If they had shown me Ethan Allen, I should not have known whom they meant."

"I'll tell you what, Hubert," said Bessie, "you and I will quietly go there some day, and have an 'excursion of historic in-

ISRAEL PUTNAM'S BIRTHPLACE.

terest.' There are friends of the family who will be pleasant to us, without any doubt."

Hubert and Bessie did accomplish this little trip later on in the summer, and it may as well be here described.

Montpelier is a pretty town, with broad streets well laid out, and surrounded by hills highly cultivated. There are several handsome churches, each denomination vying with the rest, it would seem, to erect the finest.

The old State House was burned in 1857, and the new one has since taken its place. It stands on a slight elevation approached from a green common, by granite steps in terraces.   Under the portico are kept two cannon taken from the Hessians at the bat- tle of Bennington (1777), after a desperate struggle.   The British got them back at the surrender of Detroit, in the War of 1812, but they were retaken by the Americans during the Canada Cam-

ONE HUNDRED YEARS AGO.

paign.   They were sent to Washington, and Congress pre- sented them to the State of Vermont.

" Probably Molly Stark wore her bon- net when she was congratulating t h e General for taking these cannons," re- marked Hubert.

" What ? " asked Bessie.

" Oh, I forgot! it was Alice," said Hu- bert, and then told her about the gar- ret and the bonnets, which had never been again thought of, in the open air summer life they were lead- ing.

" That was the first I knew about the battle of Bennington," said Hubert.

Carefully kept behind glass, in the State House at Montpelier, are preserved all the battle flags and pennons of the Vermont regiments in the War of Secession. They are tattered and weather-stained, with the names of the battles in which they were borne inscribed upon them in gold letters.

The State House contains portraits of different Governors of Vermont.

Bessie and Hubert dined and spent the night at a large hotel called the Pavilion, the side windows of which overlook the grounds of the State House.

Some old friend of the family very kindly showed them the lions, and they returned to Utopia highly pleased with their visit to the Metropolis.

"I feel exactly," said Bessie, "as if I had been to Paris, or London. There is so much going on in the streets, which have real sidewalks, shops with lace and ribbons, and all like a large town. It is long since I have seen any sort of a street!"

This was after Bessie had been at Utopia more than a month, where there was but one store, and that not on the scale of the Bon Marché, or Arnold and Constable's. One counter occupied the side of a large room, on the end of which was erected the set of pigeon-holes which proclaimed the post-office. Shelves behind the counter contained red and yellow flannel, and a few pieces of dark calico, and unbleached cotton cloth. Salt fish contended for the prevailing odor with molasses and tobacco, for the wall opposite the counter was left to accommodate a row of chairs, tipped up against it, where the worthies of the neighborhood installed themselves in their leisure moments, and might be found any day awaiting the arrival of the mail, chewing tobacco, reading the newspaper, and talking a little, but not much. Few and short were the sentences which fell habitually from their lips; the pleasure of these occasions was apparently a kind of dumb companionship.

"The store is such as it was when I used to go there, a little mite of a thing, in my cape bonnet, forty years ago," said

Mrs. Bruce. "It has fallen off, however, since the war, like everything else in Utopia."

"I am inclined to think," said the professor, "that it has looked pretty much the same these hundred years."

READING THE NEWS.

# CHAPTER XXI.

## MOVING TABLEAUX.

A WEEK now remained before the Fourth of July, and great preparations began in honor of the occasion. These preparations were a secret from the grown people, and what was more, they were a secret from Bessie. It made her feel very old to find herself thus put on the side of dignity,—among the spectators instead of being a prominent performer in whatever was going forward.

"We had just as lief have you, Bessie," explained Hubert, "in fact, we want to consult you all the time ; but, you see, if you are with us there will not be anybody to look on, except the professor and Mrs. Bruce, and they may not laugh in the right place !"

They drew the line at Bessie, for Tom was required as chief counsellor ; but the scheme was Hubert's and Alice's. The twins worked with a will.

As soon as lessons were over, all the party disappeared in the direction of the large barn over at the Martin's. They came back breathless, heated and late, and returned after a hasty meal to their labors. In the evening the conspirators all sat grouped together about Tom, on the doorstep, and discussed their plans. Bursts of laughter came from the boys, followed by "Sh! sh!" from Tom. "You must not let them hear beforehand."

In these days, Bessie felt melancholy. She leaned on the bar of the side-piazza and looked at the moon over the Connecticut valley. She seemed to herself suddenly to be grown up, without having noticed it coming on; she thought of her mother and Philip, of their steamer plunging along through the waves, and of Mary and Clarence Hervey awaiting them at Bordeaux; then with a sigh, she would turn away to the library, and rouse the professor to a vigorous discussion of some literary or historic point.

Meantime, Alice as head-manager of that part of the business, sought the barn every day, and with a broom in her hand, and her head tied up in a blue spotted handkerchief, directed the work of renovation. The rubbish which the children had no authority to destroy, was gathered together in one corner, and concealed behind some small young spruce-trees which the boys cut down and dragged in from the woods; fortunately there were plenty to be had not very far off.

"It will be very useful," said Tom, "to resemble a forest," as the business began of disposing of the trees after he had decreed that enough had been brought.

He was sitting on top of a barrel giving out his orders.

"Don't throw them down like that, Ernest!" he called out. "Cannot you make it look like a primeval forest?"

Hubert scrambled up to the top of the pile of barrels and boxes, and succeeded in sticking the stem of a little tree into a knot-hole in one of them.

"Good," said Tom, "now work up to that;" and taking compassion on the little boys who were tugging at the pile of trees, he fell to himself with such vigor that a very respectable forest soon concealed the rubbish.

Festoons of ground pine were pulled up in the woods to decorate the long sides of the great chamber. The children were anxious about the darkness of the place, as there were but two windows, one at each end, and these were small; but when Alice, with her dusting-brush and much soap and water, had removed the cobwebs and scrubbed the panes, the quantity of light was greatly increased.

As the plan progressed and improved in importance, it was decided to invite all the people of Utopia with whom the Bruces were on visiting terms; this included about everybody, and the children were surprised to find that they had sent out seventeen invitations. These were given by word of mouth, through Alice, and they were all accepted. It now became necessary to borrow settees from the vestry of the meeting-house; their first plan had been to provide only old boxes and barrel-tops for the audience.

The day came, and two o'clock P. M. came, the hour fixed for the entertainment. This was chosen because all Utopia dined at noon, or half-past twelve at latest. No tickets were sold or issued, as the occasion was wholly complimentary, so there was no need of any ticket.

Mr. and Mrs. Bruce came early, and received the guests. The steep flight of narrow stairs was a little awkward, but the door at the top was fastened open. Punctual to the hour, they began to arrive, in best bonnets and Sunday coats.

"Well, I declare!" was the general sentiment from one and all as they entered the room. The farthest end, which contained the primeval forest in one corner, was left clear for the performances. A sort of trophy had been arranged high up over the windows, of American flags, and a stuffed eagle, which, rather the worse for wear, had long ornamented the top of a bookcase in the professor's library.   Two screens, which were in reality clothes-horses of the large old-fashioned type, stood on either side, to make retiring places for the performers.   These were hung with patch-quilts, one of which very appropriately contained for its centre square a portrait of George Washington printed on calico, and the other that of Martha his wife.   They had been borrowed by Alice from an old lady of the town, for Alice knew well the ins and outs of Utopia, and every piece of furniture possessed by every inhabitant.

The sides of the chamber were festooned with green, and bunches of laurel, which still lingered in blossom, were stuck up at intervals.   The settees occupied the nearer end of the room, rocking-chairs being placed for guests of advanced age and distinction.   Bessie modestly seated herself at the back of the hall, to leave the best places for the guests.   Just as all seemed ready

PULLING UP GROUND-PINE.

to begin, Tom, looking hot and flurried, came to her and said:

INDIANS ATTACKING A NEW ENGLAND STAGE-COACH.

"Look here, Bessie, I wish you would come behind the scenes and help. We don't know how to put on the things very well."

It was a moment of triumph for Bessie, revealing that they could not get on without her, after all. Wasting no time in exultation, she quietly followed him. Behind each screen was a pile of costumes, or rather the materials for them. A couple of cocked hats, two swords, with belts, a pair of top-boots, lay on the floor on one side of the stage. Crossing to the other without any regard to the audience, although there was no curtain, Bessie found the twins, trembling, in the costumes of wild Indians; that is, two very good feather dusters had been sacrificed for their head-dresses, bright scarfs were bound about their waists, and their feet were bound in something like leggings. Alice was engaged at that late moment in putting a spot of the water-color called "Indian Red," upon each of their four cheeks.

"It does not stick very well," said Alice, "but that's no matter. Do not they look splendid, Bessie? I am thankful you have come!"

"They are to be Indians throughout,' explained Tom, "and come on for either side, just as it happens."

The programme consisted of a number of moving tableaux, without speaking, representing stirring scenes in the French and Indian wars. The first series represented the surrender of Fort William Henry. Tom retired and put on the cocked hat, sword and cloak, to appear as Colonel Munro; when he was ready, Hubert advanced, in a uniform shown to be French by its tri-colored sash, as General Montcalm. The interview between these two worthies was a little embarrassed, consisting chiefly of stiff bows up and down on both sides. Alice entered as the daughter of Colonel Munro and wept upon the shoulder of her father.

This was the first scene; the second was more exciting when the departure from the fortress began, Hubert having changed rapidly to Duncan, an officer on the American side. The Indians rushed in with tomahawks. They had been instructed to keep moving round the screen from the stage and coming out again as more Indians. This must have confused the audience, but confusion was a part of the occasion. There was much stamping, and flashing of

STUART'S PORTRAIT OF WASHINGTON.

swords and tomahawks. It ended in a tableau of everybody lying wounded on the ground except the Indians, one of whom supported the swooning form of Alice, while the other vindictively waved a murderous weapon,— a rusty hatchet. Then the stage was cleared. The Utopians sat pleased, but silent, and such silence is always depressing to dramatic performers. But Bessie came forward, and resuming her seat among the audience, began to clap her hands and applaud vigorously. Professor Bruce followed her example. The spirits of the company revived, and they went on. It would be difficult to describe all the scenes which followed; indeed it is to be feared the audience failed to keep the run of them. There was a great deal of bravery, courage and bloodshed. Major Putnam descended from the top of the forest, riding a savage saw-horse, with an old broom for a head. This was a really daring feat, in which Tom might have broken his neck or a leg. for in spite of due previous precautions, the whole forest, and indeed the heap of boxes of which it was made, came down with him.

Scene after scene followed each other in rapid succession. The Americans dared, the English resisted, the Indians scalped, the maiden swooned continuously. The air of the old barn-chamber became thick with dust, and the floor shook with the violence of the combatants.

"I guess that's enough, boys," said Tom finally, and they all dropped their arms and advanced in a row towards imaginary footlights.

"Ladies and gentlemen, I have the honor to tell you that the performance is concluded," said Tom. The audience retired, asserting that it was a beautiful show.

# CHAPTER XXII.

### THE REVOLUTION BEGUN.

"I TELL you, Tom, those boys are just as stupid and ignorant as can be," said Hubert.

"You wanted them up here," retorted Tom.

"Oh," said Hubert, "they do very well for Indians, but, you know, I believe they had not the faintest idea what we were celebrating yesterday. I heard one of them asking Mrs. Bruce if Independence Day came more than once a year!"

Tom threw himself back in the bushes and laughed joyfully.

"I'm glad it does not," said he, "for my back is stiff with that ride of Major Putnam's."

The two older boys had strolled off for a walk by themselves the afternoon following the great performance in honor of the national holiday. They had reached a high opening in the woods overlooking the broad valley of the Connecticut, and Tom was reposing hidden in a nest of moss and bushes, while Hubert lay flat on the ground near him.

"They read, when they are reading aloud, like parrots," continued Hubert, "without taking the sense of the sentences they repeat. They have been reading in "Gilman's American People" about the Revolution ever since they came."

"I do not call them really dull boys," said Tom; "simply, they are not used to books. I suppose Mrs. Stuyvesant never reads any thing but the Duchess's novels. In fact, I think one of the twins is very intelligent, only I am never quite sure which one it is. I should have been that kind of a boy, only that Bessie and the rest are continually driving in information."

The Stuyvesant boys, it was true, diligently read without receiving ideas from their books. Professor Bruce, perceiving this,—not for the first time in his long experience of teaching all sorts of boys,—saw that it was necessary to rouse their minds by talking with them much on the subjects they were busy on. In this way he hoped to awaken enough curiosity to give them power to fasten some meaning upon printed words.

The history of our country down to the Revolution is the history of thirteen colonies. Besides the Massachusetts colony, and New Hampshire, which included a part of Vermont until some years later, there were eleven others making the list:

New Hampshire, Massachusetts, Rhode Island, Connecticut, New York, New Jersey, Pennsylvania, Delaware, Maryland, Virginia, North Carolina, South Carolina and Georgia.

TALKING IT OVER.

These were not all established at the same time, nor all by Englishmen, but however differently founded or governed, they were all alike in some things. They all made their own laws, to a certain extent, while they all had become, at last, subject to Great Britain ; and they all thought themselves ill-treated by the British Government. This common discontent made them finally separate themselves from England, and unite with one another, but it was a long time before this union was complete.

The colonies would have been satisfied to go on as colonies if Great Britain had either not taxed them, or had let them send representatives to Parliament in return for being taxed. The wisest English statesmen would have consented to either of these measures ; but King George the Third and his advisers would not agree to either; and so they not only lost the power of taxing the American colonies, but in the end lost the colonies themselves.

The excitement about the "Stamp Act" was the real beginning of the war. This famous act only required that all deeds, and such legal documents, should be written or printed on paper with a stamp on it, only to be bought of tax-collectors, the money received for it going to the Government. This is a common way of raising money for government purposes in small sums, but the colonists were in the mood to object to any tax. In one colony after another opposition was made to such an extent that nobody dared to act as stamp officer, and the law was never enforced.

The Stamp Act was repealed just a year after its passage. There was great rejoicing throughout the colonies. In Boston, bells were rung, flags displayed, and houses illuminated. British troops were stationed in Boston and New York to keep people quiet, but the effect was just the other way. The boys used to insult the soldiers, and they in return taunted the people. Such events as the Boston Massacre, the throwing the tea into the harbor to prevent any tax being paid upon it, and similar instances of resistance, only made King George and his ministers increase the strictness of the laws, hoping to frighten the colonies. The severest of these measures was the Boston Port Bill, closing the port of Boston, cutting off all water communication between it and neighboring towns, except by the way of Marblehead, where everything must be entered at the custom house, and brought to Boston in the care of an officer.

The Boston Port Bill helped to make the scattered colonies a nation, for it united them in a common cause of resistance.

There were now two million Americans, perhaps three millions, of whom a fifth were fighting men trained in Indian warfare. In Braddock's expedition, some of them had seen the red coats run for their lives before the French and Indians, while the Virginia riflemen stood their ground. Such men as General Putnam, who had been tied to a tree by Indians, and had seen the fire

GENERAL GAGE.

blaze up around him, without flinching, was not likely to flinch before English muskets. Such was the way the patriots regarded the chances of success, although there were many colonists who thought it not only wrong, but dangerous, to resist the British Government.

In the midst of this excitement, General Gage, the royal Governor of Massachusetts, called the legislature together, and then, changing his mind, dissolved it before it met, by a proclamation dated September 28, 1774. Upon this all the members elected to the legislature came together by agreement, without asking his leave, and formed themselves into a Provincial Congress. They at once began to get the militia into good order. A quarter of the militiamen were called "minutemen," and were bound to assemble at the very shortest notice. Then the Provincial Congress set about the collecting of arms and ammunition, and had them stored at Concord and Worcester. Meanwhile British troops kept arriving in Boston, and General Gage kept sending out spies to find out where these military stores were, and the patriots had their own spies to watch his movements in case he should send out to capture these stores.

MINUTE-MAN.

It was one of these watchers on the Charlestown side of Charles River, who learned one night, by seeing the signal of a lantern gleaming in the steeple of the North Church in Boston, across the water, that a large force of British troops was preparing to leave Boston. Instantly all was in motion, and messengers went riding in all directions to spread the alarm that the stores were in danger. It was then that Paul Revere mounted his horse and galloped out through Medford to a house where the patriotic leaders, John Hancock and Samuel Adams, were, awaking the principal farmers as he passed from house to house.

So as the eight hundred British soldiers, having crossed the water in boats, marched silently along the marshes, they knew by the sudden ringing of all the bells in the towns around, that their plan had been found out. Paul Revere, and the other scouts, had done their work well. The commanding officer of the British then sent back for more troops, and Major Pitcairn went forward with two or three hundred infantry, having orders to secure the two bridges at Concord. But when on his way Pitcairn passed through Lexington, at four in the morning, April 19, 1775, he found sixty or seventy militia collected on the Green to resist him. The British soldiers fired upon them. The Americans fired in return, but did little damage. Eight of the Americans were killed and ten wounded, while the British marched on towards Concord.

Although the British troops succeeded in destroying all the military stores they could find in Concord, they did not return to Boston so easily as they came. It was sixteen miles, and the whole country round was now roused by the guns and bells. Men came hurrying from all directions; it seemed to the British as if they dropped from the clouds, and with every mile the number of their opponents increased. Before they reached Lexington they fairly ran, and they would have had to surrender, but for the protection of Lord Percy, who had marched out to meet them with re-enforcements.

The British now retreated more slowly, but they were glad, at sunset, to find themselves under cover of the guns of their men-of-war, having suffered, in killed, wounded and missing, nearly three times as much as their opponents.

This day was the real beginning of the Revolution. It was

THE NORTH BRIDGE AT CONCORD.

soon after, on the tenth of May, 1775, that Ethan Allen captured Fort Ticonderoga. An army of fifteen thousand men was collected. Among the list of generals were to be found the names of Putnam and Stark, whose bravery was well known already.

The Battle of Bunker Hill, June 17, 1775, came next; the Americans were then obliged to retreat, but the inexperienced soldiers showed that they could resist regular fire, and although they claimed no victory, the colonists felt greatly encouraged. The ranks of the Continental Army were filled up, and the troops were full of enthusiasm.

The army was now adopted as a national army, and George Washington was chosen General-in-chief, for there was no man in America who could claim to equal him in military reputation.

Under the great elm in Cambridge, still known as the Washington Elm, he took command of the Continental Army.

When the British government heard of the Battle of Bunker Hill, it was resolved to subdue the American colonies, no matter at what cost. Some fifty thousand men were employed against not more than twelve thousand. But the Americans felt they had gone too far to retreat, and resolved to persevere.

THE OLD ELM AT CAMBRIDGE.

# CHAPTER XXIII.

## THE DECLARATION OF INDEPENDENCE.

THE Massachusetts Legislature had issued a circular inviting all the colonies to send delegates to a Congress at New York. This Congress met, drew up a declaration of rights, a memorial to Parliament, and a petition to the King, in which they claimed the right of being taxed only by their own representatives. The colonial assemblies approved the proceedings of the Congress, and thus for the first time in their history, a bond of union was formed among the American colonies.

This Continental Congress was composed of the best thinkers, the most patriotic and the bravest men of the colonies, and it was upon these that the responsibility of the situation rested, more than on the farmers who fought at Lexington and Bunker Hill. Even after one or two fights, the Americans might have drawn back, and made peace again ; but after Congress had declared that "these United Colonies are, and of right ought to be, FREE AND INDE-PENDENT STATES," they were obliged to support the assertion, and take the consequences. The Congress had the difficult work of raising soldiers, choosing efficient officers, and worst of all, collecting money to pay the expenses of a war. Some of these men, even Washington himself, were at first not prepared for an absolute separation from the mother-country; but they became convinced that nothing else would do. Doctor Franklin, who was one of the wisest of the patriots, was always cheerful and hopeful, and when the time came, the delegates from all the colonies voted to declare independ-·ence, except New York, and New York didn't vote against it.

Thomas Jefferson wrote the Declaration of Independence. It was discussed in Congress and severely attacked, but it was finally adopted without much alteration, on the Fourth of July, 1776, and signed some weeks later. There were rejoicings everywhere, and on the tenth of July the document was read at the head of each brigade of the Continental Army posted at and in the vicinity of

HOUSE WHERE THE DECLARATION OF INDEPENDENCE WAS DRAWN UP.

New York. "It was received everywhere with the utmost demonstrations of joy."

"So, boys," said Mr. Bruce as Ernest finished reading the last sentence, stumbling a good deal over the word *demonstrations*, "now you see why we celebrate the Fourth of July every year."

"And why," said Tom, looking up from his German, "all good little American boys fire crackers all day long."

"And why," said Bessie who happened to be in the library, "cannons resound, and bells ring, all over the United States, and fireworks are sent off in the evening."

" Like the destruction of the Bastile," said Augustine, with a gleam of intelligence.

Alice stared, and did not cease when Tom and Bessie readily agreed, saying both together, "yes, exactly."

Ernest and Augustine, little absentees as they were, had never seen a popular celebration of any sort in their own country, but

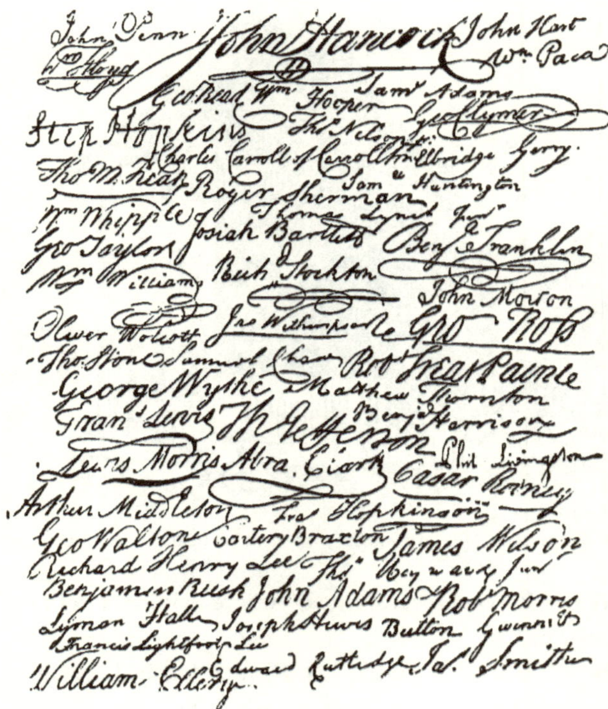

AUTOGRAPHS OF SIGNERS OF THE DECLARATION OF INDEPENDENCE.

they were perfectly familiar with similar demonstrations in France, where the fourteenth of July is recognized much in the same manner.

The Bastile was a prison in Paris, where for centuries state pris-

MEADOW INTERVALE.

oners were immured, and tortured with great cruelty. It continued to be used for much the same purposes down to the fourteenth of July, 1789, when the people rose in their fury and utterly destroyed it. This is one of the acts of the French Revolution, to be balanced against its numerous crimes. The day is celebrated in France as we celebrate the Fourth of July, because of its importance in the annals of liberty.

"We ought to have read the Declaration on the Fourth," said Bessie, "and Tom, you ought to be able to repeat it."

"WHEN, IN THE COURSE OF HUMAN EVENTS," began Tom, in an oratorical manner, then changing to his usual voice, he continued, "that is as far as I know."

"I have it here, in a dozen books," said the professor, as he looked along the shelves.

Bessie said to him in a low tone, "Do not find it for a few minutes, — not till I come back."

"Here it is," cried Hubert, "in the end of Mr. Gilman's history."

Just then Bessie reappeared, having hastily draped herself in an American flag which she had found, still lying in a heap in the best parlor, with the rest of the decorations used on the recent occasion. Her white handkerchief was tied over her head after the manner of a Liberty cap. Thus converted, for the moment, into the Goddess of Freedom, she stepped lightly upon a chair, thence to the middle of the large study-table, and taking the book from the astonished professor, who, a little nervously, moved the inkstand away from her feet, she declaimed, in as theatrical manner, the famous document upon which rests the liberty of America.

Tom set the example of applause at the appropriate pauses. This was an idea readily received by the twins, who found that banging their desk-lids was so effective that they introduced this form of approval oftener than was absolutely necessary.

When it was over, and something like quiet was restored, Tom turned to Hubert, and shaking hands with him, said in an exaggerated manner:

"Sir!—you have behaved like a gentleman. You have suppressed your feelings as an Englishman, and applauded those sentiments of patriotism and freedom which fill every American breast. And now," he continued, "let us go and have a swim, for it is warm,—with your leave, sir," he added, turning to the professor.

"The school is dismissed for the day," said the professor, with alacrity, using a formula which had been familiar to him through many a long year.

The days, as is their custom in the beginning of July, had become very warm, and the boys took advantage of this for delightful aquatic excursions, of which there was every variety. There was the cold brook on the mountain road, where water fell babbling and bubbling over great stones, where they could sit on submerged sofas of rock and let the ice-cold stream fall over their shoulders. There was the dark pool below the mill at the foot of Stevens' Fall, good for diving, where those who were bold and skilful enough could get long headers in the wine-gold depths.

There was the west end of the lily pond where they had the picnic; under the trees the shore sloped down rapidly, so that two strokes away the water was many feet deep,—cool, still, delicious for floating, or treading water.

But to-day the boys were going to a place in the meadow intervale, where the Connecticut made a bend, among tall American elms; the hay had just been cut there, and was now to be brought home to Farmer Martin's great barns. The plan was to take their bath under the elms, in a spot with a pebbly bottom, and perhaps "loaf round" through the afternoon, and come home on top of the hay.

Tom was a fairly good swimmer, and Hubert an excellent one. At Gibraltar he had been taught many an aquatic feat by an old soldier in garrison there. The twins were helpless, as yet, in deep water. It was for their benefit that the shallow place had been chosen for that day's bath. Bullied, scolded, encouraged and instructed by the older boys, they were beginning to make some progress. Ernest could already float, and Augustine make several strokes, if somebody would stand by to catch him by the chin. When Tom and Hubert were amiable, they performed these offices: when the reverse, they went off to their favorite diving pool, when

WASHINGTON CROSSING THE DELAWARE.

the twins had to give up their bath altogether, or take their bathing-clothes and accompany the girls.

For Bessie was an admirable swimmer, and never missed any day a dip in the river, if she could help it. Her usual resort was under the pines by the lily pond, and she and Alice either went there by boat, walked, or drove.

"Let us take up some lunch, Alice," she said on this occasion, "and not come home until it is cool."

"Why do not you?" said Tom, "and perhaps we will come along in time to bring you back."

"All right," said Alice, "then we will walk up, and you can come for us in the boat if you like."

"Very well," replied Tom, "only mind, we do not promise!"

Then there was a rush for towels, bathing-dresses and luncheon.

"Land's sakes!" exclaimed Lavinia Mary. "It is on the line, Miss Bessie. So you won't none of you be here to dinner! Well, it's a mercy, for there is nothing but boiled dish; for Jacob, he did not kill, after all, yesterday."

This strange remark had reference to lamb, which would have been roasted to-day, but that it was still gambolling in the fields, or more likely sheltering its broad proportions from the sun under a stone wall.

"Land's sakes!" cried Tom, "is it boiled dish! I have a great mind to come home to dinner!"

"Tom," said Bessie, "you must not say 'land's sakes!' Mother dislikes it very much, and if you get the habit, you will never give it up, — like *Ach du!* in Germany."

"Well, give me my towel, Liberty, and do not boss, it becomes you ill!"

Bessie had not yet taken off her Liberty cap, and the Stars and Stripes were still wound about her, impeding her progress. So she did not pursue her brother, but let him go off, and went to make her own preparations. Alice was seen flying home across the fields to inform her mother of the programme. The boys scrambled down the steep hill to the boat-landing, and were soon pulling across the river in the hot sun, in the direction of the meadow-intervale.

"Well," said Lavinia Mary, "I do not say but it's a comfort to see the last of them. I guess I'll shut the blinds and give one drive to them flies. It is about time to put on the cabbage, unless Belinda, she may have seen to it."

The professor settled himself to his books, and Mrs. Bruce coming down from her room, looked in upon him and said:

"Was not there rather more noise than usual, my dear, about the lessons?"

"Yes, dear, it was the Declaration of Independence," said the good professor.

BELOW THE MILL.

# CHAPTER XXIV.

## THE WAR.

AT first, the American troops were defeated. They lost several battles, and Washington, with his main army, had to leave New York to the British troops, and retreat, much to the encouragement of the British.

Washington felt that the courage of his army must be kept up by some great success. There was a body of about a thousand British troops at Trenton. These soldiers, although they belonged to the British army, were Germans, hired and paid for by the British Government, to which they were furnished by their respective sovereigns, one of whom was the Prince of Hesse-Cassel, and therefore they went, in this country, under the name of Hessians.

On Christmas Day (1776), which is a great holiday with all Germans, Washington crossed the Delaware from his camp, and took them by surprise. The German commander was killed, and all his soldiers were taken prisoners.

In spite of this and other successes, Washington's army spent a gloomy and suffering winter at Valley Forge where they were encamped. The soldiers slept without blankets, went without shoes, and food was scarce. For there was scarcely any money to furnish supplies, and still less to pay the troops.

Lafayette and other brave men who had come from Europe to fight on the American side, for the sake of the cause of liberty, suffered alike with Washington and his army. Meanwhile the British were living comfortably in Philadelphia, and their officers enjoyed every luxury.

WASHINGTON AT VALLEY FORGE.

Early in 1777, General Burgoyne, with a part of the British army, came up Lake Champlain from Canada, took Ticonderoga, and sent a detachment to destroy military stores at Bennington. This was the time when General Stark carried the day. A still greater event followed. Burgoyne, with his whole army, encamped at Saratoga, and after two battles at Stillwater were hemmed in by General Gates and his troops, and forced to surrender October 17, 1777.

This was a great advantage to the Americans. It made the French Government think there was a chance of success for the colonies, and Doctor Franklin, who was in Paris, obtained a treaty and promises of aid from France.

Yet the war dragged on slowly for three years more, with varying success. Sometimes the Americans won the day, sometimes they were beaten. There was fighting at sea as well as on land, with the same results.

The struggle closed with one great victory, in which the French troops sent to aid the colonists played an important part. It was at Yorktown, Va., where the British General Cornwallis had made his headquarters. General Washington was there with American troops, and Count Rochambeau with French soldiers, while York River was blockaded by French ships. After a siege of ten days, Lord Cornwallis, who had planned to retreat across York River, one night, was prevented by a storm, and he surrendered to Washington.

This was October 19, 1781. There was great rejoicing everywhere, and well might the Americans rejoice, for it was acknowledged by both sides that the surrender of Cornwallis decided the result of the war.

It had lasted nearly seven years, had cost Great Britain a great deal of money, and the lives of many brave men, besides which the colonies were lost. There was more fighting, here and there, after the surrender of Cornwallis, and the British kept the city of New York, and also Charleston and Savannah, for nearly two years more. At last, on September 3, 1783, a treaty was made at Paris, between English and American Commissioners, by which

LORD CORNWALLIS.

all that the Declaration of Independence had claimed was conceded, and the United States of America took its place as a nation.

There was one great act of treason committed during the war, by one of the most distinguished of the American officers, General Benedict Arnold. He had taken part from the beginning; was at the side of Ethan Allen at the time he marched into the fort at Ticonderoga; and had distinguished himself in other ways. But he was carrying on all along a secret correspondence with the British commander-in-chief; and letters from him were found concealed upon the person of Major André, a British officer who was carrying them to his general. These papers contained full information in regard to the defences of West Point, and a plan for its surrender.

Major André was detected on the twenty-third of September, 1780. He was tried by court-martial and hanged as a spy. Much sympathy was felt for him, as he was but obeying the orders of his superior in transmitting the papers of Arnold; but it was remembered that a brave young American officer, Captain Nathan Hale, had been hanged as a spy by the British, four years before. Arnold himself escaped to the British lines, and joined the British army. He fought against his own countrymen and was made a brigadier-general by the English. The thought of André, sacrificed to his disloyal intentions, must have been ever after a dark thread in whatever bright schemes he might weave for his ambition.

MAJOR ANDRÉ.

In all the course of reading and talk which Professor Bruce encouraged on the subject of the Revolutionary War, Hubert was staunch in maintaining the bravery of his countrymen. At this distance of time from the conflict, all Americans are not always ready to concede this. The account of Burgoyne's surrender at Saratoga cannot fail to enlist the sympathies of those who read it.

He was completely surrounded. The main body of the American army, under General Gates, was close at hand; every part of his camp was exposed to fire. There was not a place of safety for the sick and wounded; no one dared to go to the river for water.

Desertions of Indians and Canadians, and losses in killed and wounded, had reduced Burgoyne's army one half, and a large proportion of those who remained were not Englishmen.

When General Burgoyne was holding a council of officers, in a large tent, it was several times perforated by musket balls from the Americans. Grape-shot struck near the tent, and an eighteen-pound cannon ball swept across the table where the generals were sitting.

Their deliberations were short, as might be expected under these circumstances, and it was unanimously resolved to open a treaty with the American general for an honorable surrender. It was bitter, but there was no alternative.

A flag was sent to General Gates, who ordered a cessation of hostilities till sunset. After long negotiations, everything was agreed upon.

Just before signing the articles, Burgoyne heard news of English successes on the Hudson, and this ray of hope disposed him to withhold his signature from the "convention," as the agreement of surrender was called. General Gates, who also heard the news, drew up his army in order of battle, and sent a peremptory message to Burgoyne that if he did not sign the articles immediately, fire would be opened upon him. With reluctance, Burgoyne subscribed his name.

The British army left their camp upon the hills, and marched sorrowfully down upon the Green, where the different companies were drawn up in parallel lines, and grounded their arms, and emptied their cartridge boxes. General Gates, with generous delicacy, ordered all his army into their camp, out of sight of their conquered enemy.

General Burgoyne now rode forward to be introduced to General Gates. He met him with his staff at the head of his camp. Burgoyne was in a rich uniform of scarlet and gold. Gates in a plain blue frock-coat.

THE CONTINENTAL ARMY.

When within about a sword's length, they reined up and halted. The names of the two generals were mentioned to each other, as in any ordinary introduction, and General Burgoyne, raising his hat, said:

"The fortune of war, General Gates, has made me your prisoner."

The victor promptly replied:

"I shall always be ready to bear testimony that it has not been through any fault of Your Excellency."

The other officers were introduced in turn, and the whole company repaired to Gates's headquarters, where a sumptuous dinner was served.

After dinner, the American army was drawn up in parallel lines on each side of the road, extending nearly a mile. Between these troops the British army, preceded by two mounted officers, bearing the American flag, had to march to the lively tune of Yankee Doodle. As they passed, the two commanding generals came out together from Gates's tent, and gazed upon the procession.

Burgoyne had a large and commanding person, and was in all the splendor of scarlet and gold. Gates was less dignified in appearance, and plainly dressed, but he was flushed with a great victory, while his opponent was foiled and disappointed.

Without exchanging a word, Burgoyne stepped back, drew his sword, and in the presence of the two armies, presented it to General Gates. He received it with a courteous inclination of the head, and instantly returned it to the vanquished general. They then retired to the marquee, while the British army filed off on the march for Boston.

"Oh, dear me!" said Hubert, with a long-drawn sigh, "it reminds me of that picture by Velasquez, in the Madrid gallery, where Spinola is receiving the key to Breda."

"Or Boabdil," added Bessie, "giving up his keys to the Christian conquerors at Grenada. All such occasions are picturesque."

"The Alhambra," remarked Tom, "is a more picturesque setting for such a scene than the heights of Saratoga."

"I do not know," said Professor Bruce, reflecting, "it was October, you see. The woods were all brilliant with scarlet and gold, to make up for Gates's plain uniform. The scenery all about Saratoga is very fine, especially in autumn."

"Is it?" said Bessie. "I thought Saratoga was a sand plain, full of springs and fashionable people."

"Ah, but the battle field is at some distance from the Springs, and the whole region is very pretty," replied the professor.

NEAR SARATOGA

## CHAPTER XXV.

### PAINTING LESSONS.

ABOUT this time Bessie and Alice found themselves most unexpectedly left much alone. The boys were building a House in the woods, on the steep bank at the upper end of the pond, and although the girls were permitted, and even invited, to give their opinion, in choosing the site of the House, their presence was neither desirable nor helpful through the hard-working process of building. Soon after the project was started, too, they all agreed that it would be well to have the finished house a surprise for all except the workmen.

Every day the boys disappeared as soon as lessons were over, and this brought about a little change in the household arrangements, which greatly pleased Bessie, who detested a hearty dinner in the middle of the day.

Lavinia Mary, Belinda, and even Mrs. Bruce herself, would have been outraged by the idea of a late dinner. "Them Frenchified notions" did not suit the atmosphere of Utopia; but it suited their practical minds still less to prepare "a square meal of victuals," when there was nobody but women-folks to eat it.

So the boys took with them daily a substantial lunch; and the professor, his wife, and Bessie had a light noon meal, which the latter secretly considered her second breakfast. When all the family had assembled, about sunset, there was a copious meal of hot beefsteak, or a broiled chicken, with plenty of cream, and all kinds of good things.

"Alice!" called Bessie from her window one day. Lessons were just over ; the boys were preparing to start off for the woods, in flannel shirts, armed with axes, hammers, and carpenter's tools. "What are you going to do now?"

"I'm going home," said Alice disconsolately.

"I know ; but I mean, what do you do every day now, when you go home?"

"Mother wants me to sew," replied Alice. "I was hemming towels yesterday, but they might just as well be done on the machine."

"Suppose you stay over here till your dinner time," said Bessie. "I have got an idea. Come up in my room, and I'll explain."

When Alice appeared in the doorway, Bessie drew in her head from the window, and went on:

"You see I am left by myself, now the boys are off all the time, and I thought you might like to come and work at something with me."

Alice's face looked very bright. Bessie had not as yet taken much notice of her, and the younger girl felt that any attention was flattering and pleasant from so important and grown-up a person as Tom's sister.

"What kind of work do you mean, Bessie?"

"You'll laugh," said Bessie, "but I was thinking of giving you painting lessons."

"Painting lessons!" repeated Alice, "but you " — don't paint yourself, she was about to add, when it occurred to her that it might be rude.

"Don't paint myself," said Bessie, quietly finishing the sentence just as Alice had thought it. "That is true, but that does not make any difference. I mean, I have been taught water-colors, only I have no vocation for it myself. I have paints and things, and I could tell you how to do it."

"O, Bessie! what put such a nice idea into your head?"

"I'll tell you, Alice, it was seeing how gracefully you put flowers

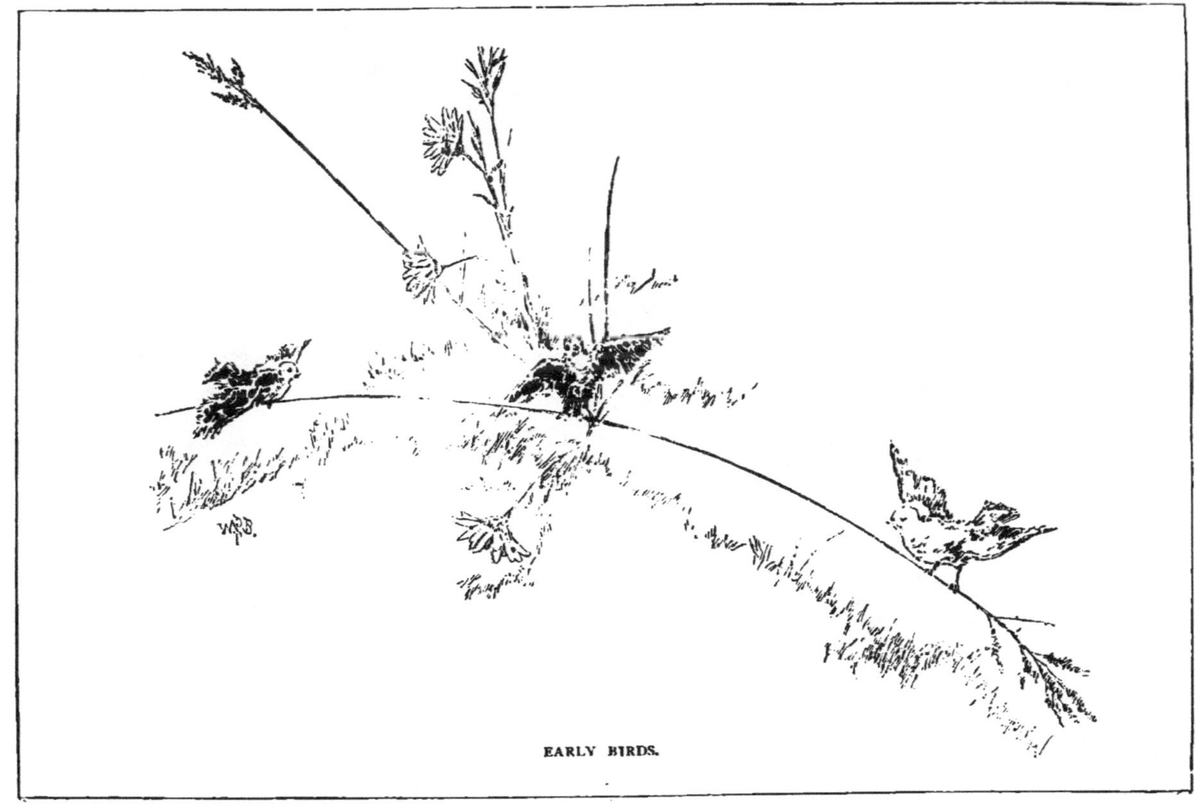

EARLY BIRDS.

together. I have a theory that people that arrange flowers well, are natural artists."

Alice colored all over. "I did not think you were watching me," she said; "oh, thank you, thank you, ever so much!"

"Well, let's begin," said Bessie abruptly, in order to cut off too much gratitude.

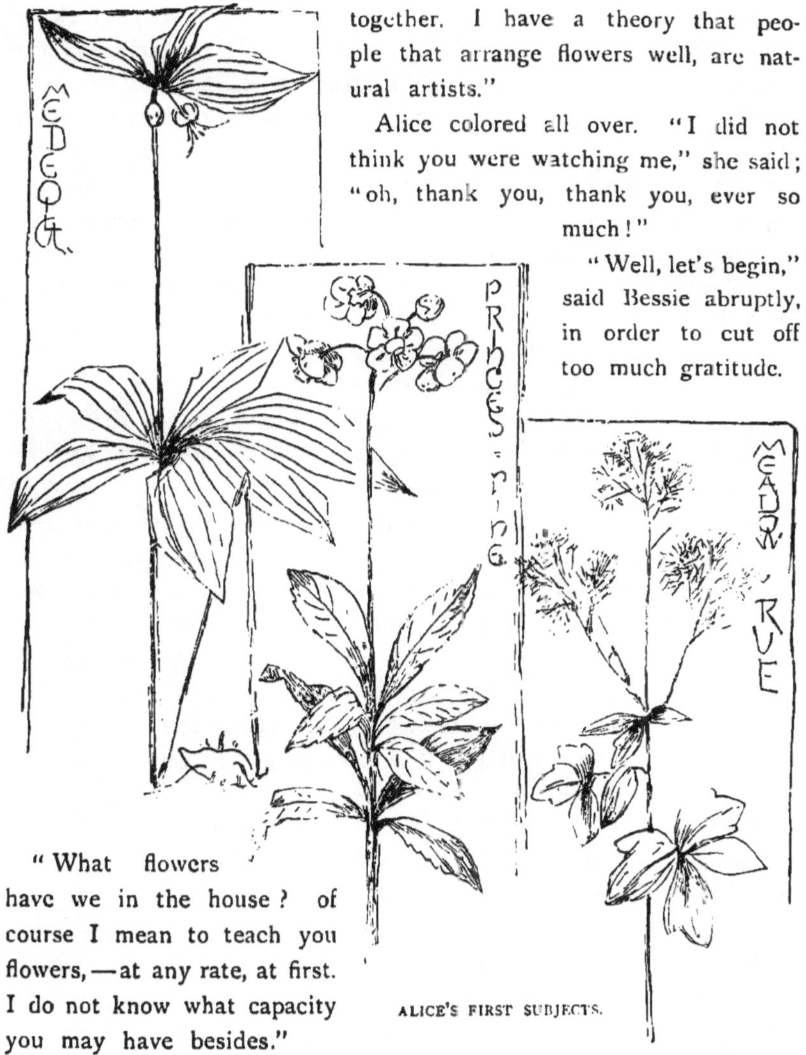


ALICE'S FIRST SUBJECTS.

"What flowers have we in the house? of course I mean to teach you flowers,—at any rate, at first. I do not know what capacity you may have besides."

"I will run down and fetch them," said Alice, and in a moment she returned from the sitting-room with a jug full of pretty wild flowers they had brought in from the woods.

Bessie was fitting out a table for her, when she came back in her dressing-room, a sort of large closet off her chamber where there was but one window with a steady north light.

"Let us take this Prince's pine, to begin with," said she. "This medeola · will do very well too," and fastening one of them up with a pin upon the white shutter, so that the light fell sideways upon it, she showed Alice how to draw the outline lightly with a pencil, copying the forms carefully.

"There, while you are drawing it, I will hunt up the paints," said Bessie.

"What, paint already! paint to-day!"

"Certainly," replied Bessie, "why not?"

The delighted Alice set to work, and in the course of the lesson, which was to last two hours, had produced not unsatisfactory likenesses of two or three flowers.

The reasons why Bessie took this task upon herself were mixed. She had a great feeling of loneliness, off in the country, of which neither Tom nor Hubert took any account. Finding it was gaining upon her, she set about to invent some way of giving pleasure to somebody, after a receipt of Miss Lejeune's for dull spirits.

She hit upon Alice through a sort of fellow feeling for the girl, who had led a lonely life almost always. These were her highest motives; Tom accounted for the proceeding otherwise, in a way which contained some truth.

" Bessie loves to boss!" he remarked to Hubert, after the arrangement had been announced. "She cannot get along without expounding something to somebody."

The very next day Bessie had a new recruit, little expected. Alice had been settled scarcely more than an hour at her work, after the boys' departure, when they heard footsteps coming towards the house. Bessie, as usual, put her head out of the window to reconnoitre.

"What! Augustine, have you come back?"

"Yes; my head aches," he replied pitifully. "I could not do anything, so they sent me home."

"Well, come up here, and I will look at your tongue," said Doctor Bessie jocosely.

"That will spoil everything!" cried Alice, "how provoking!"

"You see," explained Augustine, "they are carrying planks up from the boat to the house, and I kept resting, and went to lie down by the water to cool off, and Ernest and Hubert scolded me; but when I stood up I was so dizzy Tom told me to come home."

"You poor thing," said Bessie, "it is the heat. Go up and change your flannel shirt for something cool, and then you can come back here."

"The lazy lump!" cried Alice, stopping from her work; "all the boys say he is not half so plucky as Ernest."

AUGUSTINE COOLING OFF.

"Those boys are remarkably different," replied Bessie. "I dare say he is not strong enough for such violent exercise. I only hope they won't all overwork themselves. I must speak to Tom about it."

"He has spoiled our fun," grumbled Alice.

"Oh, no," said Bessie a little sharply; "do not consider yourself the only person of importance in the world."

Augustine returned, having washed his face, looking fresh and cool, and began to take a deep interest in Alice's work, who, silenced by Bessie's remark, made no objection, but it was evident she could not be watched and go on to any advantage.

"Augustine, you used to paint," said Bessie.

"Yes," he answered; "and I have a box of paints here."

"Get it," said Bessie, "and I will set you up in this corner of my table."

She made no effort to give him instructions, but furnished him with a large block of paper, not first-class, but good enough.

The boy was well satisfied, and worked diligently until luncheon time, when he exhibited his great work. It proved to be "The Surrender at Saratoga," and represented, in a crude way, the two armies drawn up, while Burgoyne was delivering his sword to the victorious Gates. A blotch of indigo represented the sky, which had run down into the autumn tints of the foliage somewhat painfully, and these in their turn interfered with the splendor of General Burgoyne's scarlet coat; but there was plenty of action in the scene, sharply delineated with a very black pencil before the colors were put on.

This masterpiece received due praise from Mr. and Mrs. Bruce when it was exhibited to them at lunch. The good professor was pleased to find that any impression was left on the boy's mind by his reading, and Bessie was pleased with herself for being patient with him.

But when the other boys came home, hot, tired and hungry, they treated the performance with contempt, and Ernest especially accused his brother of all the sins of slothfulness.

"Anybody that chose to tie an apron round his neck," he said, "and sit up at a table, to paint like a baby, could do as well as that."

Augustine was crestfallen.

"But my head ached," he whined, falling back upon a suffering tone, unused throughout the whole day.

"Fiddlesticks!" shouted Ernest.

To change the conversation, Bessie called upon the others to tell about the House, and they were soon describing their labors with animation. There was a saw-mill on a stream not very far from their chosen spot, where they had bought boards, and brought them down in a flat-bottomed craft belonging to the mill.

"I tell you, it is hard work," said Hubert, "and here is a splinter I cannot get out."

Mrs. Bruce, with spectacles on her nose, and a fine needle, extracted the uncomfortable splinter. The boys were too tired for anything but bed, and the evening broke up early.

"Tom," said Bessie, "Augustine looked really very pale when he came home. I think it is too much for him to work so hard."

"I know it," said Tom, "I sent him home. I ought to have praised his picture. But you will make him too soft."

VIGNETTE.

# CHAPTER XXVI

DOCTOR GOODKIN, being consulted about Augustine, readily pronounced sentence upon his working in the hot part of the day. The other boys were afraid of a similar verdict in their own cases, and carefully kept out of his way.

Thus there came about a marked difference in the habits of the twins. Ernest kept at work with the others, and became brown, stout and strong, while his brother remained pale and slender, though his health visibly improved. The girls found him a valuable cavalier and companion on their afternoon excursions after flowers.

Alice's interest in flowers increased rapidly in consequence of Bessie's praise of her taste in arranging them, and her growing skill in drawing. The beautiful nodding yellow lilies, which filled the meadows at that time, were too much for her brush and pencil, but she grouped together masses of the real flowers on tall stems, to decorate the parlor.

White-weed was everywhere, — blanching the green of the fields, and imbittering the browsing of cows. Alice had to be taught to love this; it was too common, she thought, and could scarcely believe that it is raised in greenhouses in winter, and sold in cities at ten cents a head.

"Alice, you can make about two dollars with that bunch, if you can keep it fresh till next January," said Tom.

Thus hot July went by, a succession of long sunny days. While the interest in the boys' house increased, they allowed themselves no holidays on account of it; on the contrary, the two hours of reading and study in the morning were a healthful balance to the steady hard work outdoors of the rest of the day.

After the signing of the treaty at Paris, on the third of September, 1783, the return of peace was celebrated throughout America with bonfires, rockets, and speeches, and with thanksgiving, on the nineteenth of the next April, the eighth anniversary of the fight at Lexington. The last remnant of the British army in the east had sailed down the Narrows on the twenty-fifth of November, a day called in consequence Evacuation Day, and celebrated with fireworks and military processions.

His great work of deliverance over, Washington resigned his commission and made ready to go back to his estate on the banks of the Potomac, to the habits of a private gentleman.

ALICE'S LILIES.

About noon on Tuesday, the fourth of December, Washington bade adieu to his officers. The chiefs of the army were assembled, and he joined them, deeply moved as he beheld drawn up before him the men who for eight long years had shared with him the perils and hardships of the war. He said :

"With a heart full of love and gratitude, I now take leave of you, and most devoutly wish your latter days may be as prosperous and happy as your former ones have been glorious and honorable."

The officers then approached one by one and took leave of him, and then they walked, through a line of infantry drawn up all the way, to the water, where a barge awaited the hero to carry him across the Hudson. The streets, balconies and windows were crowded with gazers; the church bells were all ringing. Arrived at the ferry, he entered the barge in silence, stood up, took off his hat, and waved farewell. Then as the boat moved slowly out into the stream, amid the shouts of the citizens, his companions in arms stood bareheaded on the shore till the form of their illustrious commander was lost to view.

After this, he publicly resigned his commission at an audience of Congress, when the Hall was crowded, in a short and solemn address.

The outburst of love and gratitude soon subsided. The Revolution, it was true, was accomplished, and it might be thought that the path of the young country was now made plain before it, and easy to follow. But the war had brought many evils, which were now pressing heavily upon the people, so that they forgot those which had been removed.

The different States had been for a few years united by a common danger; but now that danger was gone, old quarrels broke forth again, and the union so lately formed seemed likely to be dissolved.

The condition of the country was indeed critical. The people had just emerged from a long and exhausting war. After their struggles, their suffering, their narrow escape, they were irritable and wavering. Everything about them was new. Old parties, old leaders, old forms of government had gone down in the storm of

WASHINGTON ON THE BATTLE-FIELD.

revolution, and no new ones had as yet arisen to take their places. They had yet to frame some foreign policy fit for the high place they were soon to take among the nations, and a home policy which would unite the conflicting interests of thirteen jealous republics. They had to pay off an enormous debt, to restore a depreciated currency, and to replace it by a national one; to establish public credit, and create a national commerce. Towards furthering all these things, Congress could do next to nothing but advise, recommend, and suggest.

In these early days it had no fundamental power. It was held in but little esteem by the people, and its recommendations were often treated with open contempt. Each of the thirteen States reserved to itself all the rights of control, and treated the Continental Government as if they were dealing with a foreign power. It was difficult even to assemble the delegates. The House was frequently forced to adjourn day after day for want of a quorum; for as the journey to the capital,—then New York,—was for many of the members long and expensive, and as they were by no means sure of being paid for their trouble, many preferred to stay at home.

Only the strong patriotism of such men as Alexander Hamilton, Benjamin Franklin and others, could have brought order out of such a condition of things. It was the custom then to influence the people by papers, written on all public questions. Squibs, broadsides and handbills were issued by every one who had a fancy to express an opinion. Hamilton's papers had great influence in a right direction.

A convention of delegates was called to meet in Philadelphia, to make, if possible, the government stronger, without doing harm to the liberties of the people. This convention lasted many weeks, and so did the discussion; but at last the present Constitution of the United States was adopted on September 17, 1787. Only ten of the thirteen States accepted it at first, but these were more than enough for a majority, and it went into effect in 1788. New York, North Carolina, and Rhode Island were the three who refused at first to accept the conditions of the Constitution, but they had all come into it by 1790.

The nation has been governed by this Constitution ever since, with a few amendments which have been since made by act of Congress.

During all this time, Vermont, which was not one of the original thirteen States, remained "out in the cold." New York and New Hampshire as we have seen, and also Massachusetts, laid claim each to a part of her territory; while Ethan Allen and other patriotic Vermonters demanded a separate and individual State government for themselves  This occasioned much trouble to the old Continental Congress.  As Vermont would not agree to the demands of the neighboring States, it was refused admission to

CONTINENTAL CURRENCY.

the Union. The British generals in America, in 1780, before the signing of peace, entertained hopes of turning these disputes to the account of their cause, by detaching the district from the American cause and making it a British province.  But this suited Ethan Allen as little as being swallowed up in New York or New Hampshire.  He informed Congress, however, of the overtures the British were making to him, saying in addition:

"I am as absolutely determined to defend the independence of Vermont as Congress is that of the United States, and rather than fail, I will retire with the hardy Green Mountain boys into the desolate caverns of the mountains, and wage war with human nature at large."

During this time, the condition of Vermont was better in some

STATUE OF BENJAMIN FRANKLIN AT PHILADELPHIA.

respects than that of the Confederated States. She had managed to pay her own troops during the war, and as she had no connection with Congress, no part of the burden of the public debt of the United States rested on her. The people, observing that their own condition was improving, while that of their neighbors was constantly growing worse, ceased to regard their admission to the Union as an event to be desired, especially when by the removal of British troops, on the treaty of peace, she was relieved from danger of foreign attack.

But after the adoption of the Federal Constitution, all parties became anxious to admit the independence of Vermont. The difficulties with New York were adjusted, and a controversy was ended which had been carried on with great spirit for more than twenty years, calling into exercise the native courage and talents of the Vermont leaders. The State of Vermont was admitted into the Union on the fourth day of March, 1791.

Vermont was unlike any other State, in having no provincial government of her own, previous to the Revolution, while the original thirteen were all provinces under the Crown of England. Vermont had never been separately recognized by the Crown, nor, although placed under New York, had she recognized the authority of that province, or of any other external power. Her citizens had formed themselves, in fact, into a little independent republic, like the sturdy mountaineers of Switzerland, and by the boldness, wisdom and prudence of her statesmen, she had succeeded in regulating her internal affairs to the great advantage of her people. So that Vermont may be called the most independent of all the independent States of America.

Governor Chittenden, the first Governor of Vermont, was well fitted to be the leader of such independent, dauntless, uncultivated settlers. He was born in Guilford, Conn., in 1729. Early in the spring of 1774, he removed with his family to the New Hampshire grants, and from that time shared the fortunes of the growing State. He was elected Governor in 1778, and held that office, with the exception of one year, until his death in 1797.

## CHAPTER XXVII.

### THE HOUSE IN THE WOODS.

BY the end of July the House was done, and as August was to come in on Friday, Saturday, the second, was chosen as the great day of its dedication and introduction to the friends.

No lessons therefore were to be thought of that day. After early breakfast, the workmen departed to the scene of festivities. The girls were invited to arrive about eleven, in order to do their share in the preparations for the great feast which was to take place at one o'clock, in honor of the chief guests, Mr. and Mrs. Bruce. Alice's mother, and her father, Mr. Martin, were also invited in great form, but they declined the dinner part of it; the farmer saying that if he could manage to get round, he would bring Mrs. Martin up in the carriage in the course of the afternoon. Mrs. Martin was a little of an invalid, and seldom left the house, except for meeting on Sundays, — never on foot.

Accordingly, a little before eleven, Lucy and the carryall stood before the door, while Lavinia Mary and Belinda packed the latter with baskets containing the dinner. Augustine stood by the head of the horse, lest she should start, for form's sake, though Lucy had never been known to start, within the memory of the oldest inhabitant, before she had received many cluckings and jerks of the reins. Alice ran down from up-stairs with a large mysterious paper package, which she put carefully on the front seat, — for the girls too had their secret, — and Bessie appeared last, drawing on her gloves, and looking about her to see if she had forgotten anything.

"Guess you'll have a good day," said Lavinia Mary, shading her eyes with her hand to inspect the sky. "Mighty hot, though,—hot as mustard. Land's sakes!" Ending her sentence thus abruptly, she vanished into the kitchen by the back door, but returned in a min- ute with the mustard-

BARS AT THE END OF THE ROAD.

pot, which she was hastily doing up in a newspaper. "I'd as liked to as not forgot it, Miss Bessie," she said. "Some likes mor'n some, so I didn't put none on."

"Come on, Augustine," said Bessie. And Augustine climbed up on the front seat.

"Do not sit on the —" cried Alice, checking herself.

"What is it?" he asked, squeezing the bundle.

"You'll see!" replied Alice, smiling joyfully.

It was less than half a mile that they could go with the wagon, for the charm of the House was to be totally inaccessible to the world. The first part was along the village road, past the weather-worn homestead where an old lady, the last of her race, lived all by herself, and then turning off to a cart path through pastures to the entrance of the woods, where a pair of bars stopped their progress.

"Now, do you think it is safe to leave the horse here," asked Bessie, "till Augustine goes back for the Bruces?"

"Yes, indeed," replied Alice, "what could happen? My! what lots and lots of raspberries there are."

"Don't say 'my'! and take this basket, please," said Bessie.

THE WEATHER-WORN HOMESTEAD.

"What a pity not to have some at the feast. Look here, Augustine, suppose you stay here and pick all you can, instead of coming on with us, and then you can go back for the others."

Relentless Bessie! It was not a pleasing scheme for Augustine, who was wild to see the House, as it was now a fortnight since he had been near it.

"I have no basket," he urged, "and, besides, how should I know when it was time?"

"See, I will lend you my watch, only do not smash it; and you can have this basket that the bottles of milk and coffee are in. Now jump out, Augustine, that's a good boy. It's just eleven

FESTOONS OF CLEMATIS.

now, and you can start back by half-past twelve, or sooner if you have filled that basket."

Alice had taken down the bars, politely, for Bessie to get over.

"Just put them up, will you, Augustine?" she called out, and she and Bessie ran off, laughing, their hands full of parcels and baskets.

"The boys will be soon here to get the big things!" cried Bessie, and then they turned into the woods and Augustine was out of sight.

"Bessie, you were tyrannical to make him stay!" exclaimed Alice.

"Poor boy," said Bessie, "but, you see, I thought the boys would be gruff with him; they consider him so lazy about the House. If he brings a pail of berries it will serve as a propitiatory offering. Anyhow, I shall put it in that light. Where are they? Halloo!"

Answering voices told them to turn in at the blazed birch on their right, and a few moments brought them to the site of the House. The spot was chosen chiefly on account of the depth of the water there, affording good advantages for diving. The shores rose high above the pond, and a steep bank sloped down to its edge, so that from the top of the ridge a lovely view of the opposite shore and the sparkling blue surface of the water were to be seen through the thickly growing birch and oak-trees.

"How pretty!" cried both girls; "but where is the House?"

Tom and Ernest had come to meet them, hot, and with blazing faces, their hats pushed off their brows. They led their visitors two or three steps, and then they beheld the *House*, on a little natural opening in the thick woods, yet quite embowered with branches, which had been cut away sufficiently to admit the view of the pond.

The House was but a rude affair, but of course it was regarded by all as nothing less than a castle. Four trees, at convenient distances of about ten feet, had been chosen for the corners, and to these planks were nailed. The back was higher than the front, to allow a sloping roof; there was a "practicable" door of entrance, and opposite, a large opening by way of a window, admitting a draught and a pretty vista through the House.

"Where did you get this door?" demanded Bessie; "it seems more ancient than the rest of the architecture."

"Why! it's that door that was in the barn chamber at Alice's. Don't you know? we had it in the performance," said Tom.

"Come in," cried Hubert. He was inside the House, still occupied in putting up festoons of clematis brought from the woods.

There was a plank floor laid, and the interior decorations gave the charm to the House, which on the outside had but a bare, new look, that did not recommend it. However, every chip and shaving had been cleared away, so that it had already a settled look, and the battered paint on the old door lent respectability to the glare of the new bright boards of which the walls were made.

Inside there were tables and chairs, some of recent construction, others brought from garret and barn ; and everywhere flowers,— in ginger pots, flower pots, and knotholes in the boards. Colored prints from the *Graphic* adorned the walls.

"How nice you have made it look!" said Bessie, after some time had been occupied in admiring details. "Now, Alice, show them your surprise."

"Perhaps you will not like them," said Alice shyly, "but I wanted to make something for the House."

She was opening her paper parcel as she spoke, and now drew out of it a set of curtains for the window, made of delightful gay chintz with great roses spreading over it.

Strange to say, the curtains exactly fitted the window. They were all ready to put up, and just the size to stretch in gathered folds across the top, and parting in the middle, to fall to the ground. There were bright ribbons with which to loop up either side.

FINISHING TOUCHES.

"How did you know how to make them fit?" said Tom.

"How did you know there was a window?" asked Hubert.

"We made Augustine tell, and was it not clever of him, he knew the exact dimensions of the window."

"Where is Augustine?" then they asked, all of them.

The girls related how they left him gathering berries in the hot sun, and in compassion for such labors, the boys agreed to condone for good and all his abandoning work at the House.

"But all this time," exclaimed Bessie, "we ought to be setting the table, and somebody must get the baskets."

So the boys led the way to a short distance from the House, where, with planks left over from its construction, they had erected a table on legs driven down into the ground, a foot high, "suited," as they explained, "to the height of the seats," which were nothing else than the ground.

The tablecloth was in the parcel with the curtains, so that could be spread at once; and soon Ernest came panting back from the bars with two heavy baskets, one containing plates, and the other solid provisions.

He reported Augustine as making good progress with the raspberries, adding, "He wanted, though, to come on and leave me to go back for the others. I told him 'not much'!"

The feast was set, the guests arrived. They were as indulgent in praise as the girls had been, and indeed the place was very pretty. Augustine was honorably escorted to all points of interest, and made to feel that his raspberries were a valuable contribution to the occasion.

Bessie had been promised a chance to boil the kettle, if she would bring it, to make coffee, an accomplishment learned from Belinda; she was delighted with the preparations made for her,— three crossed sticks on which to suspend the kettle, gypsy fashion, and a little pile of dried branches all ready to light.

. The repast was excellent, and a soft breeze from the water tempered the heat. As soon as it was finished, they repaired to the House. One old rocking-chair was comfortable enough for Mrs. Bruce, who sat in it by the window, looking into the thick foliage. The professor put himself upon two chairs, and smoked his pipe, the others grouped themselves on the threshold or on the floor, reposing after arduous labor. They recited all their adventures and difficulties in building the House; and Tom explained how trifling had been the cost.

"I mean to have a cupboard, Bessie, up over your head there, where we can keep some cups and saucers, for we mean to live here a good deal." And they went on to plan other improvements.

Alice told how she put the finishing touches to the curtains the night before, after she went up to bed, with only one candle. "For," she said, "we wrote to New York for patterns, and they did not send the stuff till day before yesterday."

Mr. and Mrs. Martin did not come. The day ended in a swim for the boys in the cool water below their House.

# CHAPTER XXVIII.

## FRANKLIN AND LAFAYETTE.

THE boys now rested upon their laurels. They felt well satisfied with the happy end of their labors in housebuilding, and slept with the sense of being proprietors in real estate. The land, by the way, was supposed to be a part of the old woodland farm which had once been included in the original property of Mr. Horner's grandfather. Titles and boundaries were but vague in the outskirts of Utopia, and no one was likely to lay claim to the place; but Tom and Hubert scorned the imputation of being squatters.

The whole family rejoiced and sympathized with them in the well-earned possession of their country-seat. The next day, Sunday, which was truly a day of rest for them, the conversation chiefly turned upon the favorite subject. Plans were made for additional decoration, and internal improvement; and no other expeditions were thought of than those which should centre on the House. Many a fine name was proposed for the new acquisition: "Horner's Corner," "The Alhambra of the West," "Hole in the Woods," "Divers' Places," and many others, but all were rejected as unsuitable, and it never was called anything but The House.

They expected to enter at once upon a series of daily visits to the House, where they meant to pass all their leisure time; but alas! on Monday it began to rain in the course of the morning, and rained steadily for several days, as it sometimes does in August, though not often so early in the month. In the afternoon the storm was violent, so that not even Tom and Hubert cared to venture out so far. There was thunder and lightning; great crashes rattled round the sky, and it was almost dark in the middle of the afternoon. Every one thought it was going to clear up, but instead of that, the weather went from one disagreeable phase to another,—cold and chilly, or hot and muggy, but always wet.

These were trying times for Bessie and Alice. The boys, of course, did not stay in the house all day, but sallied forth in spite of the weather; but there were hours when time hung heavy on their hands, and they invaded the quiet of the room where Alice was trying to paint, and Augustine composing historical pictures.

OLD LIBERTY BELL.

"Do, Hubert, go away!" cried Alice. "If you sit on the edge of the table it shakes my drawing-block."

"Let me mix your colors for you," said he, taking a brush; "you ought to do the middle of that daisy with gamboge."

Alice leaned hastily forward to rescue her favorite brush. The water-bottle was upset and ran all over her careful drawing. An outcry was the consequence. Bessie came to the rescue with towels, but said impatiently:

"Tom, I think you might take the boys away from here!"

Tom was engaged in drawing a cannon for Augustine in the foreground of the battle of Bennington, in a realistic manner, using spools plucked from Bessie's work-box, to mark round the wheels. He looked up at the rain which was pouring in torrents.

"Where shall we go? Do you want us to be wet through? Come, fellows, let us go upstairs and rummage round in the garret."

HISTORICAL PICTURE.

Hubert, meanwhile, apologized humbly to Alice, and tried to dry her block with his handkerchief.

"No matter," she said, "I was going to wet it all over in a minute."

It might be supposed that this enforced suspension of out-door amusements would have made the boys turn willingly to their studying for occupation. But it did not work exactly in that way. They were restless and irritable, and less able to fix their attention to abstract subjects than when their daily toil in the woods had worked off their superfluous energy and animal spirits.

Still, however, the reading went on. Mr. Bruce employed different boys to look up different points of history concerning the men and times they were engaged upon.

The Federal Convention which brought about the new constitution was a remarkable body of men. Every State sent up in her delegation some one renowned as a statesman or a soldier of whose services she was justly proud, in the cause of freedom. A few of them, when the Revolution broke out, had raised regiments, hastened off to the army, fought through the war, and come home as distinguished and skilful officers. Some had been Governors of States, some were renowned as jurists and scholars, and others had year after year represented their States in Congress.

But the fame of no man was so splendid, or went back to so early a time, as that of Benjamin Franklin. His name was known to every learned society in Europe, when half the delegates to the convention were in the nursery, for he was born in 1706.

He was, in truth, the greatest American then living. His mind was one of the finest in an age not born of great minds, and among its diverse qualities was prominent that homely wisdom which had been well named "common sense."

The son of an English tallow-chandler, his early years were spent among the children of laborers and mechanics. When a boy, he stole away from his father's house, with a few pence in his pockets, and went forth to seek his fortunes.  He slept in cock-lofts and garrets, and had to endure poverty and want.  Before he was fifty, this low-born, friendless, self-taught Yankee had overcome every obstacle in his path, and raised himself to great reputation and position.  In his old age he stood before kings and Parlia-

BENJAMIN FRANKLIN.

ments, was the friend of powerful statesmen, and honored by men renowned in every walk of science and art.  From such training, which might have spoiled an inferior nature, he came forth a rounded and perfected man, the most kind-hearted, the most genial, the most unassuming of mortals, — a delightful companion and friend.

His popularity in France was great. When he walked the streets of Paris the people followed him in crowds. His portrait hung in the window of every print shop and over the fireplaces of men of fashion. Men of science did him honor, women of the world wrote him sonnets. Snuff-boxes and walking-sticks were *à la Franklin.* His maxims and sayings were printed in the newspapers and quoted everywhere.

The popularity of Franklin in France was matched by that of Lafayette on this side of the Atlantic. In 1776, he was a captain of dragoons in a French regiment. Hearing, one day, at a dinner, that the American colonies had declared their independence, he resolved at once to draw his sword in the cause of American liberty. He made the acquaintance in Paris of Franklin, and the other American agents there, and told them his intention. Even they themselves, as well as all his friends, endeavored to dissuade him, for this was at the darkest period of the Revolutionary War. But no persuasion turned him from his purpose.

FRANKLIN GARDENING.

He arrived in America with eleven officers, on the twenty-fifth of April, 1777; he was then about twenty years old.

The sensation produced by his appearance in this country was of course great, for it gave timely impulse to the disheartened Americans to find that there were men in the first rank of nobility in Europe who not only took an interest in the cause of liberty, but were willing to share its sufferings.

Lafayette landed in Charleston, S. C., and went to Philadelphia, where Congress was then in session.

He received a commission from Congress, which, however, was considered merely honorary, but it soon became evident that he meant to fight in earnest. From this time he served regularly in the army, became a warm friend to Washington, and received the command of important positions, in which he distinguished himself for his bravery.

After two years, his own country being at war, Lafayette considered it his duty to place himself at the disposal of his own government, and he returned home, to be received there with demonstrations of popular enthusiasm. He was untiring in his efforts for the cause of liberty with the French government, and it was mainly his efforts that caused French troops to be sent to America.

STATUE OF LAFAYETTE.

Fifteen months after leaving America, he re-crossed the Atlantic, and rejoined Washington at headquarters, inspiring the army whenever he came, with fresh hopes. For his services at the siege of Yorktown, he was publicly thanked by Washington on the day after the surrender of Cornwallis.  The campaign being over, he returned to France, but in 1784 he revisited the United States.

Everywhere he was heartily welcomed and entertained.  He landed on the fourth of August, and went directly to Mount Vernon, the home of Washington; on the fifteenth of October he reached Boston, where the presence of the distinguished Frenchman created no little excitement.  Three hundred of the most respectable of the citizens assembled in Faneuil Hall, where thirteen arches were put up, adorned with flowers, and made gay with bunting.  These arches grew smaller from the centre towards the ends of the room, and in the one immediately over the head of the Marquis was a *fleur-de-lys*.  Music was played during the dinner, and when the cloth had been removed, thirteen toasts were proposed; as each toast was drunk, thirteen cannon were discharged in the market-place, and three rounds of *clapping* were given, a new fashion of applause but lately come in.

No toast brought out such shouting as the toast of General Washington.  No sooner had the name of that well-beloved general been announced, than a curtain, which hung behind the Marquis, was rent asunder, displaying the picture of Washington, covered with flowers and laurels, and supported by the ensigns of America and France.  Lafayette quickly arose from his seat, his face beaming with pleasure and surprise.  He began to applaud, and was instantly joined by the assembled company.

Everywhere throughout the country he was received with enthusiasm.  On Christmas day he quitted New York for France.

Marie Jean Paul Roch Yves Gilbert Motier, Marquis de Lafayette, was born September 6, 1757, and died (in Paris) May 19, 1834.

"I begin to see," remarked Hubert, "what makes Faneuil Hall so important.  I wish I had looked at it more attentively.  You see, I took no interest, that first day, in the Cradle of Liberty."

"I wish we could go to Boston again," said Tom.  "I believe I never thought much about its historical interest before, myself."

# CHAPTER XXIX.



SOON after the Revolution, the growing commerce of the United States began to extend itself as far as the Mediterranean, and there, being entirely unprotected, it became an easy prey for the Barbary powers. Without any previous notice, and without any pretext other than that Congress had not purchased their friendship with a tribute, the Algerine corsairs, between the years 1785 and 1793, captured fifteen American vessels. The ships and cargoes were made prizes, and their officers and crews condemned to slavery in its worst forms.

There is scarcely anything in modern history so extraordinary as the existence for nearly three centuries of the private princedom of Algiers. A State which lived by robbery, and that of the worst and most cruel description; a stealer of souls, trafficking in human blood, it was a perpetual danger to every traveller whose duty or business led him across the Mediterranean.

The State was founded by the Moors on their expulsion from Spain by Ferdinand and Isabella, in 1492, and the Spanish authority was never established there. Charles the Fifth made an attempt to subjugate the Barbary powers, but it was a failure, and from that time forward there were unceasing hostilities between them and the Christians; thence sprang the system of piracy which made the corsairs so terrible in the Mediterranean, and which was so long submitted to by the Christian powers.

These Algerines lived upon exactions and plunder,—a nest of robbers, with few redeeming traits save those of courage and nautical

ONE TYPE OF PIRATE.

skill. Though their avowed religion was that of Mahomet, many of their leaders were renegades, — Greeks and Italians, fiercer and more bitter with their captives than any native Turk. With such a population, almost altogether dependent upon the robbery of the seas, the Algiers of that period presents a singular spectacle of the moral effect of the fear produced by the tortures of slavery, which made the sight of a corsair at sea appalling. One of the early authorities from which knowledge is gained of this strange community is Cervantes, the author of *Don Quixote*, who was a captive for five years in Algiers.

When a young man, he served with the Spanish army in the famous battle of Lepanto, one of the most important naval battles ever fought (October 7, 1671), as the first effective blow given to the power of the Turks who had hitherto been thought invincible at sea. Cervantes received two wounds, and lost the use of his left hand for life. Returning from Naples to Spain, the galley in which he was was taken by the pirates. It is hard to imagine, in this country, how a shipload of weary veterans coming home after an exhausting war, could be thus suddenly arrested upon their way and carried off to the most galling slavery.

"When the ship," says the early account, "arrived in the harbor of Algiers, all the oars were taken out and carried away, and not a single Turk was allowed to leave the ship until it was thus stripped bare, like a bird without wings; for a moment of forgetfulness would have given the captives time to seize the oars and escape. Having taken these precautions, the goods, slaves, and all the booty was landed, to the great joy of all the merchants and of the king. The captives were examined, and arranged in classes. The rich and noble represented money; they would pay a good ransom. The others were cruelly treated, and set to work at once, while the nobles were kept apart.

The masters were arbitrary and cruel; the captives were compelled to row the galleys, and do all sorts of menial work. When a new captive ship arrived, it was greeted with shouts of furious joy from the native population."

Such was the condition of the victims of the corsair in the sixteenth century. The strangest part of the story is, that such a state of things should have been allowed by Christian nations to last so long.

It was reserved for the United States to point the way to an abolition of this monstrous tyranny. As the young republic had no money, tribute to the Barbary States was especially galling. Negotiations were set on foot, and treaties at last made.

In the course of these negotiations, ambassadors were sent from America to the several Barbary States. Thomas Barclay, who was charged with the mission to Morocco, wrote home letters about what he saw, which were most eagerly read at that time (1786), when scarcely anything was known of the country. The emperor he declared to be a man possessed of many amiable qualities, but his private life was "disgusting and loathsome."

As for his subjects, they were fierce and lazy, delighting in cruelty, and avaricious to the last degree. Fear of God had made them put up some costly and beautiful mosques, but they had done nothing more. Their streets were despicable, and their houses a sight to behold.

His first audience with the emperor took place in the garden of the palace. His Majesty was on horseback; about him were a thousand attendants. He asked numberless questions about America, and the voyage from it: whether they grew in its forests timber fit for ships. When these questions were answered to his satisfaction, he said,

"Send your ships and trade with us. I will do anything you desire." Whereupon his people all cried out in a loud voice,

"Allah preserve the life of our master!"

Among the gifts brought to him by the Americans were an atlas and a watch. With the atlas he seemed familiar; the watch

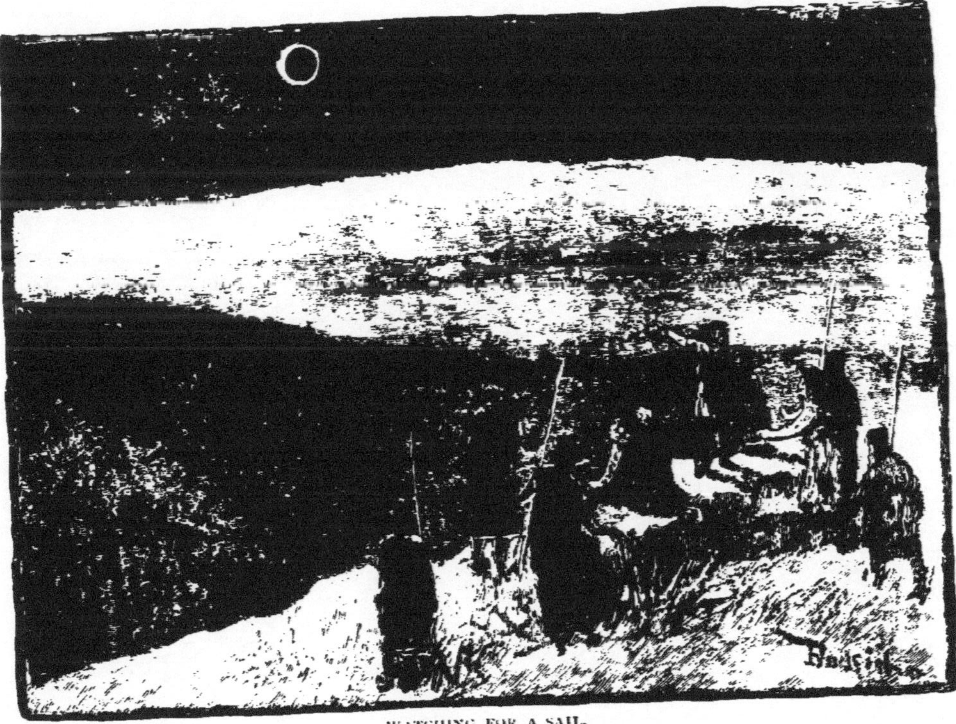

WATCHING FOR A SAIL.

he examined with much care, for it was an alarm watch, the first he had ever seen.

The result of Mr. Barclay's visit was a promise from the emperor, "on the first day of the blessed month Ramadan, 1200," of a lasting treaty with the United States. But it was not until 1817 that he prohibited piracy throughout his dominions.

The regency of Algiers was by far the most formidable of the

THE HOUSE FARED ILL DURING THE WET WEATHER.

Barbary powers. In 1815, Commodore Decatur, encountering an Algerine squadron, took a frigate and a brig, and sailed into the bay of Algiers, where he forced the dey to surrender all American prisoners, and to abandon all future claims for tribute. This bold example was followed by the English, but piracy was not suppressed. A long struggle between France and Algiers ended in the occupation of the country by the French, which has lasted to the present time. Since 1830, nothing has been heard of the system of Algerine piracy, a system which had been the terror of civilization since the days of the Conquest of Granada.

"So this was the career of your beloved Moors, Bessie, after they left Granada," said Hubert.

"It only shows," replied Bessie, "what a mistake it was to turn them out of Spain. If they had remained there, improving the land and developing their industries, the Alhambra would not now be a ruin, and the terrible system of piracy would not have been established.

Satan finds some mischief still
For idle hands to do,

you know," she added.

"That view should be taken with qualifications," remarked the professor, who was apt to take Bessie's bold generalizations

OLD SWORDS.

more seriously than she herself even cared to do.

"Many other elements entered into the traffic of the corsairs.

The Turk had as much to do with that warfare as the Moor."

"The Moors," remarked Bessie sententiously, "surrounded by Christians, were intelligent, peaceable and refined. Under the influence of the Turk, they became barbarous and cruel."

The boys, who cared nothing for such speculations, were willing to fill up a rainy day by imagining themselves Algerines and captives at the top of the house, making use of a collection of rusty swords and other weapons they found there. From the noise which shook the ceilings of the story below, it was imagined that the conflicts were of the most alarming nature. None complained, however. The girls were glad to be left alone; even Augustine deserted them for these contests, which proved to be not so severe a tax on his energies as carrying heavy planks up a hill in the hot sun.

The hearts of all were still with the House, and on the second day of the bad weather Tom and Hubert walked up over the road and through the woods, dripping with wet, to inspect it. On their return, the report was disheartening. "Everything is spoilt!" cried Hubert as he entered the house.

"There are your curtains," said Tom, throwing down on the hall floor a wet and shapeless mass.

"What a pity," said Bessie, who, with Alice, had come down to hear the tale. "I have thought of the curtains often since it began to rain. If it had only held up till you had the shutter made for the window."

"Shutter! held up!" exclaimed the boys together. "If you could see the House. It is a sort of swimming-bath inside. The water has streamed through the cracks, and run down the hill over the floor, and there is not a dry inch in the place."

"The pictures are all washed off the walls, and most of them are a kind of pulp. It is lucky we had nothing precious there."

"The box of crackers!" exclaimed Bessie.

"The box of crackers," said the boys, laughing, "was washed off the shelf, and fell open on the floor, and the crackers were all over the room, in different degrees of soak."

"Look here, Lavinia Mary," called Alice to that person, who was passing through the hall, "see my pretty curtains, all spoiled!"

"Land's sakes," she said, as she lifted them up, being the first one who had ventured to touch the wet heap. "Them will wash; don't you worry."

"Wash!" shouted Tom. "I should think they had been washed enough already; the question is, whether they will iron."

"Look, Miss Bessie," continued Lavinia Mary, not regarding his words. "It doesn't run one bit. Them colors is as sot as sot. I'll just rence them out and hang them up in the kitchen, and they will come out beautiful."

So saying, she dropped the curtains into an empty pail she had in her hand, and retired to the kitchen.

"Do you think you can make the House water-tight?" asked Alice.

"The thing is to tar and feather the roof," said Tom.

# CHAPTER XXX.

## TWO PAPAS.

SUMMER rains have an end sooner or later, and after the spell of bad weather the sun came out and dried up the roads, making every leaf and spray sparkle with light. Hot, "muggy" days succeeded, the flowers pressed forward with redoubled vigor, freshened by so much wet. Little humming-birds whirred about the bright blossoms of the honeysuckle that grew over the door, and darted in and out of its festoons. In the fields, golden-rod was gorgeous, its thirty-seven varieties being fairly represented at Utopia in quantities of each species. Bessie persuaded Augustine to take an interest in collecting as many different kinds as possible, and though he would not take the trouble to study the minute variations with the botany, through the aid of a microscope, he was quick to learn the various forms the plant assumes, and the soil they each effect. He knew where to find the slender one-sided plume of *nemoralis* growing thick by sandy roadsides, and in dry fields, while tall *canadensis*, sometimes six feet high, was only to be seen in the borders of the woods.

He and Bessie were very learned about the names, and joyously called to each other when they were walking to announce a *Virga-aurea* or an *altissima*. They were much delighted when Bessie's search in Grey's Botany was awarded by finding their very specimen attributed to "Rocky Banks in West Vermont."

This pursuit they had to themselves, getting no sympathy from their companions.

"It is all the same thing!" said Ernest one day pettishly.

SIDE DOORWAY.

"I do not see why you go grubbing after the ugly common stuff. It is all nothing but golden-rod."

"Let them amuse themselves," said Tom indulgently. "It makes them feel superior to have so many such learned names for the same thing. They will forget them all before next year, and then it will be all to do over again."

Botany contains a fund of enjoyment for those who attack it in earnest; it is, on the other hand, a source of irritation to outsiders, who are bored by the long names attached to their simple favorites, and who profess to regard it as a wanton destruction to pull the pretty flowers to pieces for the sake of classifying them.

The professor was delighted with the kindred soul of Bessie, and surprised at the skill with which she had drawn out of Augustine, whom he had been inclined to consider a dull and listless boy, tastes and sympathies of a refined character.

Every one was willing to bring home great bunches of the brilliant weed; and Alice had her hands full in arranging this

and the other splendors which came every day from the woods.
Each old jug, pail, plate that could be found, everything and
anything that would hold water, was put to service, and every
part of the large house was decorated, even to the side doorway
leading to the yard.

Meanwhile work was resumed upon the House. Not that Tom
ever hoped, or had hoped, to make it water-tight, but he had not
expected such a deluge as that it received on the very day after
its inauguration. Tar-
red paper was spread
upon the roof, and
that overlaid with ad-
ditional boards. An
ample cupboard. a
masterpiece of ama-
teur carpenter's work
which was really wa-
ter-tight, was made
and fastened up on
one side of the walls;
in this it was the
plan to keep whatever provisions were to stay there.
It had a lock and key, and
the key was kept by Tom.

After all, the enjoyment of
the House was in the building
of it. When it was done, the importance
of it subsided in the minds of the children. Alice's curtains were re-hung, and
the walls were ornamented again with

IN THE HONEYSUCKLE.

a fresh set of illustrations from the *Graphic* and the like. Bessie
suggested that statuary and plaster ornaments, as capable of standing

wet, were the proper ornaments for a house of this description, and she presented the establishment with a plaster cat which was in the collection of a wandering pedler who came round one day, even to that remote spot. Bessie talked Italian with him, and bought the cat. It was very ugly, with green and red spots splashed over it at irregular intervals. It was given a place of honor in the House, on a corner bracket made for it especially, and every one hoped that the first rain would wash it white.

As it happened, there was no more rain during the month of August. All the precautions taken too late for past mishaps, were unnecessary for the future. The cat remained the presiding genius of the House, and became a hero in consequence, often quoted as a living creature, and credited with strange experiences.

The boys dived and swam from their rock in the pond below their house. Alice often walked up there in the end of the afternoon, and stayed chatting with them till it was time to come home to tea. Bessie did not join them so often. Her favorite haunt was the brook, which babbled over the stones deliciously. It was always cool along its edge, and stepping from rock to rock, she discovered many treasures — flowers which delight in shade and dampness grew there, and there were ferns, even maiden-hair, to be found dipping their tips in the stream.

As she wandered along by herself, Bessie frequently thought how strange it was that the Horners, who so loved to be together, should be thus scattered about the world. Letters had come announcing the safe arrival of Philip and his mother at Bordeaux.

They had joined the Herveys, and now were all enjoying together the lovely scenery of Pau and its neighborhood. Summer is the *saison morte* there, but they did not find it very hot, and enjoyed the profound solitude of the town and the roadways. Mary was full of pleasure at having the society of her mother. Mr. Hervey was as cordial and energetic as ever; he and Philip were planning a little tour among the Lower Pyrénées on horseback. Nearer home, Mr. Horner wrote of long hot days in New York, varied by little trips to Newport, where Miss Lejeune had now established herself. She was very good in writing long letters

DASHING EQUIPACES.

to Bessie, describing the gayeties of the place, the fine clothes and the dashing equipages of the summer guests.

"It is pretty good fun to be here," wrote Miss Lejeune. "The Stuyvesants are here, and (you need not read this to the twins) are very splendid in their Paris costumes. Miss S. is decidedly popular; I think she has just about little enough to say to suit a place of this sort. I meet them at the Casino, and we exchange a few words about the twins. It is evident that I know more what they are doing than their relatives do, but it is not worth while to spend much time in telling them about your Utopian pursuits, for the mother's eyes are wandering in search of new toilets, and the daughter's for fresh admirers. For my part, I wish I were out of it all, and gathering orchis with you, dear Bessie, but Mrs. Wise will not hear of my cutting short my visit."

"So it would seem," mused Bessie, "that all of the family are greatly enjoying themselves except poor old Tom and me, while we are engaged in assisting Professor Bruce to instruct three cubs who have no sort of claim upon us." This strong way of putting the case made her laugh aloud, and the sight of a stately specimen of fringed orchis which she spied just before her, restored her equanimity at once.

BESSIE'S FAVORITE SPOT.

While she regained her equanimity she lost her equilibrium. A too hasty grasp at the orchis made her foot slip, and she found herself sitting on a flat stone, which was dry, luckily, while her feet were both in the water. She persevered in gathering her orchis, and made the best of her way home with boots full of water.

What a surprise! Sitting on the door-steps, in comfortable chairs, and puffing clouds of smoke before them, were her father and Mr. Stuyvesant, — good, jolly Mr. Stuyvesant, a little stouter and a shade grayer than when she saw him last. "Dear papa! what a surprise!" she exclaimed, springing forward.

"Mr. Stuyvesant thought it was time to be looking after his boys," said her father, "and we took the train for Burlington yesterday. We telegraphed, and here is the message," he added, drawing a yellow envelope from his pocket. "Mr. Brick received it at the telegraph office at East Utopia just before our train came in."

"That is the way we do things in the country, papa," said Bessie, smiling, as she took the telegram now more than twenty-four hours old, "but have you seen nobody?"

THE FRINGED ORCHIS.

"We have seen that vivacious, hospitable and voluble being you call Lavinia Mary," replied her father, "and she informs us that every living soul is out, just as sure as you are born."

"And I only came home early because I wet my feet. I am glad now I slipped into the brook!"

The joy of all the rest, as they arrived in groups, was great.

The professor and Mrs. Bruce appeared first, behind the·staid
Lucy whose jogging pace could not be hastened by the attractions
on the doorstep.  Soon after Alice and Augustine appeared, with
their arms full of plunder from the woods, and latest came the
other three boys, with hair sleek and wet from a recent bath,
and their towels stringing over their shoulders.  Then all talked at
once, and exclaimed and asked questions.

When tea-time came, it appeared that Lavinia Mary and
Belinda had outdone themselves in preparation.

Mr. Stuyvesant was well pleased.

"Madam," he said, "I hope you have another spare room, for
I should like to engage board here for the rest of my life, and
tuition as well from Dame Bessie," with a bow to the latter.

But this was only a joke, for the gentlemen returned to New
York the next day but one.

THE ROUND TOWER AT NEWPORT.

## CHAPTER XXXI.

### CONGRESS.

THE first Wednesday in January, 1789, was named as the day for choosing the Presidential electors, the first Wednesday in February for the meeting of the electors, and the first Wednesday in March for the assembling of the Senate and House of Representatives. This latter day happened, in the year 1798, to fall on the fourth of the month, and hence it was that three years later Congress decreed that each Presidential term should begin on the fourth of March next following the day on which the votes of the electors were cast. In obedience to this, the Presidents have ever since been sworn into office at noon, on the fourth of March, with the few exceptions when that day has fallen upon Sunday, and the times when, on account of the death of the President, the Vice-President has succeeded to the office out of the usual order of time.

To fix upon a date when the Constitution should become the law of the land was easier than to determine the place for the meeting of the officers of the Federal Government. Everybody agreed that it should be central, and that "central" should be understood to mean the Middle States; but these contained many large cities, and it was hard to say which had the best claim.

Great advantages would come to the city where the national government was seated and the national treasures kept. New York, on many accounts, was the most suitable place, but there was great opposition to giving it these privileges, for the State of New York had been reticent and disloyal in all the difficulties of the earlier Congress. Whenever the question came up, it was steadily resisted, but after a long time it was finally ordered that the new Congress should meet in New York, in the last session of the old, or Continental Congress, which held over till the new one was established.

Great preparations were made in New York to receive the distinguished body. The previous Congress had occupied rooms in

RECEIVING DISTINGUISHED GUESTS.

the City Hall, but the building was old and out of repair, and the rooms were thought to be too mean and shabby for the new one. The city was appealed to, but could do nothing, for its treasury was out of funds. Congress could do nothing, for the national coffers were empty. Some rich merchants took up the matter, and soon over thirty thousand dollars were collected by subscription. An army of carpenters, masons, and plasterers were employed to re-model the City Hall completely. So extensive were the changes, that when the fourth of March came, the place was still in the hands of the workmen. It was re-named Federal Hall. The day was ushered in with solemn ceremonies. As the sun went down on the third, some guns at the battery fired a farewell salute to the old Confederation. When the first gray streaks of dawn appeared, on the morning of the fourth, and again at noon, and at six in the evening, salutes were fired, and the bells of all the churches in the city rang out a welcome to the Constitution under which the United States has, in the course of a hundred years, become one of the rich and prosperous nations of the world.

However, on the morning of that day there were but eight Senators and thirteen Representatives in the city, and the New Government, from which so much was expected, could not go into operation. The distances were long, and, in those days, the roads were few and bad. Some of the delegates had pressing business to arrange, and could not leave home until it was settled. March was nearly over before the thirtieth representative arrived. There was now a quorum, and the House organized on the thirteenth of March (1789). But now a new delay arose. Nothing could be done till the Senate also had a quorum, and another week was impatiently passed in watching every stage-wagon that came to the city, and asking the name of every traveller. At last, on the morning of the sixth of April, a messenger knocked at the door of the House and informed the Speaker that the Senate was ready to count the electoral vote. The members hastened to the Senate Chamber, and the ballots were opened, read off, and recorded. The Houses then separated. When the Representatives were once more in their seats, the Speaker announced the result. George Washington had received sixty-nine, John Adams thirty-four votes. Thus were elected the first President and Vice-President of the United States.

FIRST PRAYER IN CONGRESS.

The two Houses of Congress had their hands full of other business at once, and advice of all kinds was showered upon them, especially upon the subject of the importation of British goods. It was said that if the country was to prosper, it must spend less on foreign goods, and learn to manufacture its own. It was plainly the duty of Congress to spare no pains to restrain importation and encourage home manufacture.

The advice was sound, and had begun already to be acted on by the people. In every great city societies for the encouragement of manufactures were flourishing. The members of the society in Delaware took a solemn pledge to appear on the first day of January, in each year, clothed in goods of American make.

The result of such resolves was a speedy return to old habits of simplicity and frugality. Young women wore plain clothes, and made haste to surpass their mothers in skill at the spinning-wheel. Young men were not ashamed to be seen in homespun stockings and home-made jeans. Politicians found the surest way to win the hearts of their constituents was to appear dressed in American broadcloth. The town of Hartford presented Vice-President Adams, when he passed

WOOL SPINNING.

through on his way to be inaugurated, with a roll of cloth from its own looms, and Washington himself stood forth to take the oath of office clad from head to foot in garments whose material was the product of American soil.

The selection of New York as a place of meeting for the new Congress was considered only a temporary one, and the end of the first session was occupied with a long and sharp debate on the question of a prominent place for the general Government. Every one of the fifty-nine members of the House had something to say. It seemed impossible to agree in defining the force of the word "central," the members from each part of the country finding good reasons for proving their own largest city the nearest to the central point. It is now curious and interesting to observe how the wisdom of the best statesmen of that day has been turned to foolishness by a long series of events of which they did not dream. Vast stretches of territory have since been added to the States, thickly settled by millions of inhabitants. The centre of population near which their Federal city was to stand, has been steadily moving westward ever since the beginning of this century; in ninety years, that centre, then thought so fixed that the permanent seat of Government was to be placed near it, had moved westward nearly five hundred miles.

This difficult matter was not settled until 1790, when an act was passed that certain territory on the River Potomac should be accepted for the permanent seat of Government. The same act provided that Congress should hold its sessions at Philadelphia until 1800, when the Government should remove to the new district. This district was named in honor of Christopher Columbus, and also with reference to the name Columbia as a poetical designation for the country. There the city of Washington has grown up.

"I think," said Hubert, "I do not clearly understand why they called everything 'Federal' in those days."

"It was a word which belonged naturally with the idea of a Confederation," explained Mr. Bruce; "in the dictionary I think you will find it defined 'belonging to a league or contract.' The patriots were leagued together to form the Constitution of the United States, and their success gave such glory to the word that

CAPITOL AT WASHINGTON.

they liked to give it to patriotic things. As different political parties begun to arise in the new State, one of them claiming to be peculiarly friendly to the Constitution, and to the *Federal* government, that is, the Government formed by a league or agreement, called themselves Federalists, and they called their opponents the Republicans, anti-Federalists, charging them with a sort of hostility to the Constitution and the course taken by Government. The Republicans, however, denied the truth of these charges. But in the early times of the Republic, the word Federal meant much the same as National does now, as a term of patriotic praise."

The word Federal was largely used. A dancing master advertised to teach the Federal minuet; horses were put up at Federal stables; a certain style of bonnet was named the Federal hat, and so on.

One of the difficult matters for the first Congress to settle was the question of what the officers of Government, and members, should be paid. There was little discussion over what the President's salary should be. Washington, indeed plainly said, in his Inaugural Address, that he would take none. But the Constitution had declared that the President should have a salary, and it was not to be supposed that all Presidents would show the same patriotism as the first. Twenty-five thousand dollars a year was agreed upon; the Vice-President was to receive five thousand a year; it was then declared that the members of the Senate and House should receive six dollars a day, and the speaker twelve, for every day of the session.

For such expenses, and many others, a full treasury was needed; revenue must be had. The whole subject of raising money had to be dealt with, and all the complicated questions relating to taxation. It is wonderful how, from such small beginnings, the prosperity of the country, and the general wisdom of its rulers, has brought the poor little empty treasury of one hundred years ago to be overflowing, so that the difficulty now pressing upon Congress is to decide what to do with the surplus revenue.

# CHAPTER XXXII.

## WASHINGTON'S INAUGURATION.

MANY of these things were not brought up in Congress until towards the end of the session of 1789. Meanwhile the inauguration of the President fell on the last day of April.

Washington left his home at Mount Vernon on the sixteenth of the month, and came by the most direct road through Baltimore and Philadelphia to New York. The journey, in spite of the bad state of the roads at that time of the year, might have been made in five days, but he was much delayed by the hearty receptions given him along the entire route. He was feasted and entertained everywhere. When he reached Philadelphia a grand reception was prepared.

The bridge over which he must cross the Schuylkill was hidden under cedars and laurel, flags and liberty-caps. Two triumphal arches were put up, and signals arranged to give warning of his coming.

About noon on the twentieth, the President was seen riding slowly down the hill, and under the first arch, where a laurel crown was let fall upon his head. The moment he entered the city limits the bells of all the churches were rung ; as he moved down Market street, every face seemed to say: " Long, long live George Washington ! "

At Trenton a still more pleasing reception awaited him. On the bridge over which twelve years before he had led his little army on the night before the battle of Princeton, the women of Trenton had put up a triumphal arch. Thirteen columns supported it,

ARCH ERECTED IN BOSTON AT WASHINGTON'S RECEPTION.

surmounted by a great dome adorned with a sunflower, and the inscription,—"To thee alone."

"Then it was not Oscar Wilde who invented the sunflower," remarked Tom, interrupting the reading.

"Do not be frivolous," said Bessie. "Go on, Ernest." Beyond the bridge was gathered a bevy of women and girls, who as the President passed under the dome, came forward to greet him, singing, and strewing the way with flowers.

Thus amid honors and salutes everywhere, Washington reached New York. He was received at the wharf by the Governor of New York, and by the Senators and Representatives, and escorted through lines of cheering citizens to the house made ready for his use. At night the sky was red with bonfires, and the streets full of an excited and joyous population.

This was the twenty-third of the month. But as a few finishing touches were yet to be given to Federal Hall, the inauguration was put off till the thirtieth. On the morning of that day, the people went in crowds to the churches to offer up prayers for the welfare of the new Government and the safety of the President. At noon, a procession which had been forming almost since sunrise, moved from Washington's house to Federal Hall. As the head of the line reached the building, the troops divided, and Washington was led through them to the Senate Chamber, where both Houses were formally introduced to him. When the members were seated, and the noise had subsided, Adams, who had already been inaugurated as Vice-President, informed the President that the time had come for the administration of the oath of office. Washington rose, and followed by the members of the two Houses, went out upon the balcony of Federal Hall, from which he could be seen far up and down the streets by the multitude that filled them. The Chancellor of New York tendered the oath, and when the ceremony was over, turning toward the people, cried out:

"Long live George Washington, President of the United States!"

The crowd took up the cry, and amid the joyous shouts of the citizens, and the roar of the cannon on the battery, Washington went back to the Senate Chamber and delivered his inaugural.

In framing an answer to the President's speech, the difficulty arose how to address him. Committees were appointed, conferences

EARLY NEW YORK.

held, and complete disagreement resulted. Should he be called His Highness, or his High Mightiness? The question has been settled in favor of the term, "His Excellency," as suited to the simplicity belonging to a republic.

While Congress was thus debating by what name the President should be called, Washington was troubled to know in what way he should behave. As he was the first of the long line of Presidents, he therefore had no precedents to guide him in matters of private and public etiquette. The place was one of great dignity, but just how much dignity was consistent with republican simplicity he did not know. It must be remembered that the stately etiquette of courts was then well understood to be a part of the dignity of Governments. Many of the people looked back with regret on the fine clothes, hosts of servants, the equipage and ceremonial of the royal Governors. These would gladly have seen the man whom they had raised to the chief place in the land, with a guard at his door, riding out followed by a train of menials, and would have gone on reception-days, with pride, through lines of liveried servants, to bow at the foot of some form of throne. But the anti-Federalists were bitterly opposed to all this, and begrudged him the fine house and furniture already given him by Congress.

Washington therefore drew up a set of questions as to his official conduct, which he submitted to Hamilton and Adams. Should he keep open house for all guests? Would one day in the week be sufficient to receive visits of compliment? What would be said if he were sometimes to be seen at quiet tea-parties? When Congress adjourned, should he make a bow?

These matters were all settled, and it was announced in the newspapers that the President would receive on Tuesdays and Fridays. On Saturdays the President might sometimes be seen driving through the outskirts of the city, or mounted on a fine Virginia horse, or seated in his box at the theatre.

On these occasions the "President's March" was always played. The air had a martial ring that caught the ear of the multitude. Later, Joseph Hopkinson wrote and adapted to it the well-known lines beginning "Hail Columbia," under which name, and not as the "President's March," it has become one of the most stirring of the national airs.

Shortly after the Houses rose, the President set forth to show himself to the people of the Eastern States. He went through Connecticut, passed a few days at Boston, rode thence to New Hampshire, and came back by another route from that by which he went. Everywhere he was received with a great show of Federal spirit. Bonfires were lighted, triumphal arches put up, feasts made ready, and odes written in his honor. The President returned to New York later in the fall, most favorably impressed with the state of feeling in New England.

At the time of Washington's tour, two stages and twelve horses sufficed to carry all the travellers and goods passing between New York and Boston. These conveyances were old and shaky, the beasts were ill-fed and worn to skeletons. On summer-days the stages usually made forty miles, but in winter, when the snow was deep, and the darkness came on early in the afternoon, rarely more than twenty-five. In the hot months the traveller was oppressed by heat and half choked with dust, while in cold weather

WASHINGTON ON HIS TOUR.

he could scarcely keep from freezing. One pair of horses usually dragged the stage some eighteen miles, when fresh ones were put in, and if no accident occurred, the traveller was put down at the inn about ten at night. Cramped and weary, he ate a frugal supper and betook himself to bed, to be called at three the next morning, then to rise, and make ready, by the light of a horn-lantern or a farthing candle for another ride of eighteen hours.

John Adams, the first Vice-President, had been one of the foremost of the patriots from the outbreak of the Revolution. He assisted in the framing of the Declaration of Independence, and was one of the ambassadors to make the treaty with France at the close of the Revolution; and in 1785 was sent as American minister to England, a difficult position for which he was well-fitted by nature and experience.

He became the second President of the United States after Washington, who served two terms, or eight years, and declined a re-election for a third term.

As they left the library one morning, the boys found Bessie in the hall, with the letters in her hand. She gave them to the several persons to whom they were addressed, and when she came to Tom, she said in a low tone:

"I want to consult you about something. I have a letter from papa."

"Come along, then, up the river," he replied. "There is a place where you have never been, Bess,— where the old road crosses the west branch."

Alice looked as if she would like to be invited, but instead, Bessie turned to her, saying, "Then I think, Alice, we will not have a painting lesson to-day. I want to talk to Tom."

When they had pulled up a mile or more, and turned off into the smaller stream, Bessie rested her oars, while Tom merely kept the boat up against the slow current.

"Papa," she began, "has to go to Boston about that business of Brown's; and he wants us to come to him there."

"When?" asked Tom.

"About the first of October," he says. "He suggests that we should make a little party of it, and 'do' Boston thoroughly. He thinks the Stuyvesants would like to have us keep the twins through October, as they will not leave Newport until late; and he says we may bring Alice if we like."

"How exactly like papa!" exclaimed Tom. "Does he mention the professor and Mrs. Bruce? Why not invite Billy Brick to join us!"

Billy Brick was the black sheep of Utopia, one of those boys always out of employment and in some scrape.

UP RIVER.

"Well, but, Tom, it is a good plan, and I am ready to leave here, are not you?"

"Well, yes," said he, "though we have had a jolly summer."

"It occurred to me," said Bessie, "that we might take one of the twins, only we should not agree which one it should be."

"No; you would want your beloved Augustine," said Tom.

"And you your henchman Ernest. But how about Alice?"

"If you take anybody, take Lavinia Mary!" replied Tom jestingly.

"O, Tom, do be serious!"

# CHAPTER XXXIII.

## SOUR GRAPES.

IN diligent reading, hard study for the little boys, and hard work and play outdoors for all, the summer was going fast with the Utopians,— so fast that September was on the wane before they knew it. Days were growing short, and evenings long. Grasshoppers made their zzz-ing noise in the fields, and crickets chirped louder through the evening.

The character of the flowers was wholly changed from that of the spring. Asters and golden-rod are made of stiffer material than the fragile anemone and columbine; more capable of existing through short days and cool nights. Bessie and Augustine had their hands full when they undertook to analyze and classify the great number of varieties they found of the aster tribe, the distinctions of which are very slight and hard to detect. In fact, it was so puzzling that Augustine lost his interest, and Bessie could not persuade him to care whether a specimen was a *ptarmicoides* or an *acuminatus*. But he gathered them all the same, and Alice arranged them.

"If you bring them with stems as long as their names, it is all I shall ask," she said.

"Come over to the orchard," said Hubert one day; "I met Billy Brick's brother at the well just now, and he says the ground is covered with apples that blew off last night."

Hubert was bringing a pail of water from the well to fill up Alice's flower-vases. Lessons were over for the day, and there was no especial plan laid out for the interval before dinner.

"All right," said Tom, who was sunning himself in the doorway, with his hands in his pockets. It was really cold. The night had been rainy, and the weather had cleared off in the morning,

BILLY BRICK'S BROTHER.

sharp and bright, with a piercing wind that blew the leaves off the trees and hustled them over the ground, while the sky was intensely blue, and the sunlight sparkling.

"Let us make the girls go too," he continued. "Bessie!" This was shouted up to her window from the outside of the house. The window, for a wonder, was shut. Tom threw a well-aimed pebble against the pane, and this caused it to be opened, when Bessie's head appeared.

"Come out for a walk," said Tom, "it is splendid out-doors, and too cold to stay in the house."

"It is cold as Greenland," replied Bessie, "so I had to shut the window. I will ask Alice."

Alice had just begun to draw her ginger pot full of asters, but she willingly put up her things, saying her hands were too stiff with cold for good work ; and the two girls soon came down, Bessie buttoning herself into a thick jacket as she ran quickly down the stairs.

"Don't wear that!" cried Tom, "you will roast if you do, as soon as you begin to walk."

"My dress is too thin for this weather," she replied. "I can take it off if it is too warm. Where are the twins."

"Yes, where are they?" asked Tom. "No matter, though, we can go without them."

"They darted off," said Hubert, "the minute school was over. Do not you know they did yesterday too, and we saw nothing of them all day?"

"Where can they be?" said Bessie; "Ernest, Augustine!"

"Oh, let them alone!" said Tom; "they are old enough to take care of themselves."

"Well, but it is so mysterious," persisted Bessie. "I am afraid that 'Satan' has found 'some mischief' for them to do."

"ERNEST!" shouted Tom at the top of his lungs, and Hubert imitated him with an appeal for "AUGUSTINE!"

These yells brought Lavinia Mary round the corner of the house, who said, "You needn't be hollering and bellering for them twins, Mr. Tom, for Belinda see them going up the wood-road the minute you was done

AN ARRANGEMENT BY ALICE.

school. They came and grabbed hot gingerbread, and was out through the back door."

"Hot gingerbread! We will have some too," said Hubert. This favorite luncheon-cake put the thought of the boys out of all their heads, and they started along without them towards the orchard.

This was an old overgrown place, which had once been a flourishing orchard, connected with a house long ago deserted and fallen into ruin; nothing but the cellar, dug into the ground and built of rough stones, remained. Weeds and nettles had sprung up within, and brambles and blackberry vines nearly hid the old wall. The neglected apple-trees were all run out, and bore no

THE ORCHARD.

fruit that was worth much; long untrimmed shoots had pushed upward from the branches, wasting the vigor of the trees. As the place belonged to nobody in particular, it was nobody's business to care for the fruit, and all the boys in the neighborhood felt at liberty to help themselves. On a plentiful year, like the present, the old trees blossomed fully in spite of old age and want of care, and the apples they bore, although not handsome nor large, had a wild, Bohemian sort of flavor, attractive, like all undisciplined things. Moreover, the trees stood on a southern slope, warm and sunny on an autumn day, with a pretty view off towards the winding river.

"Mushrooms!" cried Alice. "Just the day for them!" and she picked a shiny white ball, with pink folds on the under side.

"How do you know the good ones from toad-stools?" asked Bessie, who had never gathered mushrooms before. Alice explained to her the difference in shape and smell and color.

"Besides," she said, "they always grow in a pasture like this, and other kinds do not, except," she added, "that hateful puff," illustrating her words by kicking contemptuously a brownish puff-ball whose fault was not being a mushroom.

Soon they were all searching for mushrooms. They are likely to be found almost anywhere in New England in fields and pastures after a rain; and freshly gathered, and skilfully cooked with salt, pepper, and a little cream, are delicious.

Bessie's jacket had to come off, for it was warm enough, and too warm in the sun; so that by the time they reached the orchard, the shade was welcome of the old trees. They were by no means the first to enjoy the harvest. Two boys came towards them with a bushel basket well heaped with apples they had picked up or knocked down from the trees. A smaller boy followed.

"Hallo, Billy Brick!" cried Hubert. "Have you left any for us?"

"Plenty," replied these boys. "But you had better look out for the bull up there!"

"The bull!" exclaimed the two girls, coming to a full stop.

"He ain't there now, but he is sometimes," said the boys. "He comes over the fence from Jones' pasture when he feels like it."

"Let us go back!" said Alice.

"Oh, come along," cried Tom, "these boys only said it to frighten you." The boys were running off as fast as their legs, and the weight of their heavy baskets, would allow.

The Horners had no basket with them, as their intention was simply to try the apples, and refresh themselves while they rested under the trees. While they were thus reposing, and taking a bite here and there from the sunny sides of different apples, Alice showed them how to peel the mushrooms, and persuaded Bessie to taste one, just as it was, uncooked.

"What an odd taste," said Bessie.  "It is good, though; it seems like a pure essence of earth."

"Now, Alice, if you have given us the wrong things to eat, we shall all be poisoned," said Tom.

"Never fear," she replied, "I have known mushrooms all my life."

As they sat, apparently tranquil, leaning against the crooked trunks of the old trees, after the two boys had gathered a little

EARLY APPLES.

heap of apples, which lay between them, each of the girls was secretly a little anxious about the bull, though neither would mention it for fear of being laughed at by their braver companions. They had all been silent a little while, looking off on the sunny fields in the distance through which the river wound its way. Suddenly, from behind the tumble-down stone wall near them, there was heard a crackling of dried sticks, and then the unmistakable bellow of an animal of the bull species.  Without stopping to look behind them, the girls started and ran, dropping mushrooms, apples, and Bessie's jacket. They never paused till they reached the bottom of the hill, in spite of shouts from the boys telling them to come back.

Perhaps the boys would have liked to run too, but as this was not the manly part, they paused, though starting to their feet, to await some renewal of the noise. As none came, they cautiously approached the stone wall and looked over.

The only live thing to be seen was a red cow standing in a sort of tangle of bushes and briars. She had apparently squeezed herself into a place she did not like, for when she perceived the two boys she opened her mouth and produced a precise repetition of the fearful sound which had so alarmed them just before.

The boys burst out laughing.

SOUR GRAPES.

"See those wild grapes!" exclaimed Hubert, in almost the same minute. "I wonder if they are ripe!"

He began to climb the wall after them, while Tom went back

to reassure the girls, if possible. They were far down the hill, and still running. In vain he shouted after them, "Bessie! Alice! It was nothing but an old cow!" They did not turn round; probably they did not hear him. There was nothing for him to do but to pick up jacket, mushrooms and apples, and follow them, which he did in a frame of mind not altogether amiable.

He overtook the girls at the foot of the hill, for they had slackened their pace as soon as they thought themselves out of danger. Tom's wrath ceased after he had scolded them for their cowardice, and they all walked home together.

Hubert, meantime, scrambled through the tangled bushes on the cow's side of the wall, and reached home by a different route, about the same time the others did. He reported, however, that the grapes were sour.

VIGNETTE.

## CHAPTER XXXIV.

### A CATASTROPHE.

THE summer was really over, and October was drawing near, when the children arrived in their reading and talks at the point of American history where Washington was inaugurated as first President of the United States, on the thirtieth of April, 1789.

Here Professor Bruce decided it was best to stop, after consulting Bessie, whose interest in the subject was as great, and whose judgment he kindly considered as good as his own.

"We have gone over a good deal of ground, you see," he said, as he walked up and down the library, "and as much as young heads can well receive. Another time it would be satisfactory to take up the story of the youngest nation, and follow the first Presidents through the difficulties of their administrations, examine the causes of the War of 1812, watch the growing extent and prosperity of the country, and rising differences between North and South which led to the Civil War. But let that be," he continued, "for another year, when I hope I may see you all here again, my dear Miss Bessie, for, indeed, I shall be sorry to part with my charming group of young friends."

Bessie smiled, and said, "You have made us all so happy, dear professor, that it will seem very strange to go away and lose the associations of this place. How well the summer has turned out for all of us!"

Accordingly McMasters, and Gilman, and the other books of American authority, were put back upon their shelves, and the reading for the rest of the time was devoted to learning something of the condition of Continental Europe at the time that the new government brought repose to the American nation, — enjoyable to all.

In England, in 1789, George the Third was still on the throne, and consoling himself as best he might for the loss of his American colonies. The London public were not yet tired of amusing themselves with two new plays, *The Rivals*, and *The School for Scandal*, by a young man named Sheridan, which held the stage at the two theatres of London, Covent Garden and Drury Lane.

In France, in 1789, the first murmurs of the Revolution were making themselves heard. It was in this year, on the fourteenth

SUMMER WAS OVER.

of July, that a wild army of the populace attacked and destroyed the Bastille.

In Austria, Maria Theresa the Empress, was dead since 1780. Her son, Joseph the Second, was on the throne, full of good wishes meditating schemes of reform. The great enemy of his house, Frederick the Great, had died in 1786, an old man who survived most of those who had shared his triumphs and defeats. His mind remained active to the last, and he never lost his interest in affairs of State. He was succeeded by his nephew, Frederick William the Second, who was reigning in Prussia in 1789.

In Spain, in 1789, Charles the Fourth was on the throne, the weak and pitiful grandson of Philip the Fifth, who afterward played so mean a part toward his country at the dictates of Napoleon.

THALER OF PRUSSIA.

The frightful convulsions were still to come of the French Reign of Terror; and Napoleon, in 1789, was, as yet, unheard of in the annals of Europe.

The end of September was wet, with frequent rains, clearing off at intervals with cold, windy weather, which settled back again into a chilly drizzle.

"Summer is over, I think," said Bessie, as she shivered over the stove one morning.

"It is very often like this in the end of September," said Mrs. Bruce, "and then we have mild, soft weather again. October is a lovely month here. I know you will enjoy it."

"I am sure we shall," replied Bessie, but in her secret heart she was thinking that they had had about enough of the country, and that it was time to be making some decision about the Boston visit and their return to New York. She longed to see her father and Miss Lejeune, also to see shops and pretty autumn clothes, and even to visit *Huyler's* and refresh herself with a pound of candy.

"Come, Alice, let us go for a walk, instead of baking before the stove," she said, and they started off, returning in an hour much blown and draggled, but with their arms full of long trails of clematis gone to seed, covered with bunches of the pretty feathery seed-vessels, besides bright streamers of Virginia creeper which had already turned scarlet.

"Here is autumn for you!" they called out as they entered

the house. "Now we are going to decorate the sitting-room."

"Where is Augustine?" asked Alice; "he will get the steps for us to fasten this round the cornice."

"Where is Augustine?" repeated Bessie. "I am worried about the twins; they are always off by themselves now."

"I think they have taken to playing with Billy Brick," replied Alice; "I see them together a good deal."

"The fact is, Tom and Hubert are tired of them," said Bessie. "I must speak to Tom about it; if the twins are left to themselves they are sure to get into some scrape."

This remark was thought of afterwards as prophetic, for the words were hardly out of her mouth, than Bessie, who was near the open door, saw Augustine alone, running with all his might towards the house.

"Where's Tom?" he called out, panting. "Oh, come, everybody!"

"Land's sakes! what is the matter?" exclaimed Lavinia Mary, appearing at that moment.

"O, Bessie!" he continued, seizing her by both hands, "the House is burnt up!"

"The House! our House! what do you mean!" exclaimed Bessie, giving him a shake in her amazement.

"I don't know,—we don't know how it happened," and here he began to cry. "We went there and went in, and it is all black and dreadful."

"How could you go in if it is burnt down?" said Bessie sternly.

"I said burnt up! Boo-hoo!" sobbed Augustine, and delivered himself up to loud grief.

Bessie was wild with impatience. "Do tell us what you mean. Is Tom there? Where's Hubert?"

"No-oo! I don't know," bellowed Augustine. "Billy Brick and Ernest are there. They made me come and tell you!"

"I see Master Tom and Hubert, Miss, a-going down in the other

CLEMATIS AND CREEPER.

direction. I think they were going over the mountain to meet the mail," interposed Lavinia Mary.

"Come, Alice, we must go up to the House," said Bessie, "and see what this is all about. Come, Augustine."

"I don't mind if I step and meet the young gents," said Lavinia Mary, whose curiosity was aroused. "But I'll lock up front and rear, as there's no soul in the house, except the cat," she added as she walked off to her seat, "and she don't count."

The professor and his wife were away for the day.

As they hurried along the way to the upper end of the pond, Bessie succeeded in extracting more light from Augustine. It appeared that the twins, in company with their new acquaintance, Billy Brick, had taken up the habit of going by themselves to the House for amusement. Nobody thought of forbidding them, for the key of the House was in Tom's pocket; and it was taken for granted that he had the control of the premises. Something clandestine about climbing in by the window, a perfectly easy feat, made the whole charm of the practice, apparently, for there was nothing particular to do inside.

THE POND.

"Only," said Augustine, whose compassion came out in jerks, "the last time, we thought it would be good fun to roast some corn."

"In the House!" ejaculated Bessie.

"No; in your kitchen." This was the place where a sort of fireplace had been arranged to boil the kettle.

"We roasted it, and then we went back inside to eat it, and we played we were pirates."

"Where did you get the corn?" demanded Bessie sternly.

"In Farmer Martin's second field. It's ripe there."

"Did you ask his leave?"

"No. Billy Brick said we had better not."

Bessie groaned. "Well, go on."

They reached the premises, however, before his story was finished, where they found Ernest sitting on the ledge of the window with his legs hanging out, alone, Billy Brick having fled.

The House indeed was standing, but on looking in, the girls perceived that the interior was all charred and blackened, a large hole burned through the floor, pictures and everything of a slight nature destroyed, while Alice's curtains, scorched to tinder, hung in shreds and tatters.

LAVINIA MARY.

The boys explained that this feast of stolen corn had taken place two days before. The afternoon had been chill and cloudy, and they recollected that as they were coming home it had begun to rain. It poured sheets during the night, and rained steadily all the next day, to which circumstance was owing the preservation of the House, and also of the woods around it.

"You naughty little boys!" said Bessie. "You might have destroyed the whole of these woods."

Meanwhile, Tom and Hubert, on their way back from East Utopia, were amazed to see Lavinia Mary blowing along the road, against the sunset light, toward them.

She announced the disaster, and they started on the run for the scene of it, so that while Bessie was still holding her inquisition, they arrived. The door was unlocked, a careful search made, and sure enough, the round top of a wooden box of matches was found, which, having rolled off under the flooring, was not burned up, and remained to tell the tale.

"So you had a box of matches?" remarked Tom dryly.

Ernest started, and felt in his pocket. "Yes; they are gone. I must have left them here."

"And stepped on them, probably, just before leaving," said Tom, still more severely. "Well, come on, it is done now."

He shoved the boys out of the House, and with a bitter laugh, turned the key once more in the door. Tom was so angry he did not trust himself to speak. Hubert, bursting with wrath, followed his chief's example. Silently, they all turned homeward. The little boys, on arriving at the bars where the road began, started to run on ahead.

"None of that!" commanded Tom. "Walk behind us." And so they did. Not a word was spoken by any of the party.

## CHAPTER XXXV.

### LAST DAYS AT UTOPIA.

IT was well that the catastrophe of the burning of the House took place so late in the summer, for the breaking up of the Utopia party gave a ready solution to the question, What to do about it?

Tom expended his displeasure by a full account of the matter contained in a long letter to his father. He was not, perhaps, wholly surprised to receive in the answer strong reproof to himself for his want of attention to the boys who had been in a measure placed in his charge. Tom was half inclined to resent, half inclined to acknowledge its justice.

This letter of Mr. Horner's was immediately followed by another to Bessie, further unfolding plans for a fortnight in Boston, and the discussion of these plans occupied all minds.

Professor Bruce was obliged to go to New York on business, and offered to take with him the Stuyvesant boys. Tom, who was tired of the fight, and longed to see the last of them, rejoiced at the proposal, but Bessie thought kindness and politeness required that they should be asked to join the Boston trip, as it came within the time which they had been expected to spend in Vermont. Their mother and sister were to stay at Newport till the fifteenth of October or later, and there was no place for the boys to go. Tom yielded with reluctance to Bessie's view, but he and Hubert were relieved when Ernest promptly declined the invitation.

"I'm tired of improving my mind!" he exclaimed sullenly when the project was explained. "I want to go home. I don't want to know any more about the Revolution. I have not had any soda water all summer."

This was true, although the statement appeared to have but little connection with the subject in hand.

There was complete silence after he said this. Tom went on whittling a stick; Hubert pulled the cat's tail, and Bessie even did not dare to ex-press commonplace regrets at Ernest's decision. Augustine made no remark on either side of the question. He looked out of the window, and fidgeted with the curtain tassel. The

LAST DAYS.

position of the twins had been uncomfortable for the last days; they felt themselves to be tolerated, but not desired by the others.

The situation was relieved by the entrance of Alice, who came in breathless at the front door, saying:

"Mamma says I may go to Boston! She says it is very kind in you to ask me, only I have not a proper dress for autumn, but she says perhaps we can buy it there."

While Bessie assured her that this could be easily affected, Ernest slipped out of the room.

"Then I suppose it is all settled," said Tom. "Come, Hubert, let us go off up the river."

Thus Augustine was left with the two girls, and Bessie, with a significant glance at Alice, went over and sat by the window where he was standing. Alice picked up the cat and ran out of the room.

"Augustine," said Bessie, "I think you had better go with us to Boston. I hope you will. Papa says there need be no limit to the party, and you know you are not 'sick of the Revolution'!"

"No, I am not," said Augustine in a low tone, "but — but" —

"Well," said Bessie kindly, and with a smile, "but what?"

"You all hate us," he broke out, "and you want to get rid of us; and it was not my fault, but you never give me a chance to tell about Billy Brick!"

He spoke violently now, his face grew red, and he was on the point of crying.

"We do not hate you, and we do not think it was all your fault, and we do not want to hear about Billy Brick," said Bessie firmly and quietly. "We all feel sorry about the burning of the House, but Tom and I think it was partly our fault too. It does no good discussing it, and laying the blame about on different people, and so we do not like to talk about it. I think the best thing for you to do, Augustine, is to go with us, and show how nice and pleasant and intelligent you really

THE HOUSE CAT.

are, and so make everybody forget about the House."

Augustine had pulled out a not very creditable pocket handkerchief and had begun to bite the corner of it.

"Ernest won't go," he said gloomily.

"Well," said Bessie, "that makes it all the easier; if he really does not wish to go, and prefers to return to New York with Mr. Bruce, there is nothing to prevent your going with us."

"But we are twins!" said Augustine, with a kind of stare. The two boys had never been separated.

"You are not Siamese!" said Bessie, laughing gayly; "there is no law, either, to compel you to stay together."

"But you do not want me, you only"—said Augustine, beginning to whine again.

Bessie looked annoyed. "Come, Augustine, I should not invite you if I did not wish you to come with us. As for Tom, he told me I had better ask you; and it is for you to win his friendship and Hubert's by being nice. Do not you think that is more manly than running away from us?"

Thus it was settled. Bessie's greater work was persuading Tom and Hubert to relax from their sternness toward Augustine. Ernest departed for New York with Mr. Bruce,

MISS LEJEUNE AGAIN.

rejoicing, with some bravado, in the prospect of staying at the Fifth Avenue Hotel with his father till the ladies of his family came to town. It was inferred, however, by his letters to Augustine, that his reception by Mr. Stuyvesant was not altogether satisfactory, since Mr. Horner had felt obliged to communicate to that gentleman the escapade of the House-burning.

As time passed on, all the children felt they had attached too much importance to what, after all, was an accident, and one which might have been much worse. In looking back upon the summer at Utopia, all unpleasant features were forgotten, and each individual of the party will regard it as one of the pleasantest periods of his life. The good professor and Mrs. Bruce keep up a lively interest in the children, and are always hoping for another summer just like this one.

Meanwhile, Miss Lejeune devoted herself to working up the Boston plan. She wrote to Bessie:

Everything is arranged. I have invented a new cousin for you, who is the one ingredient wanting in our combination, as Mrs. Sherwood says about pepper and salt, on cantelope melons. Do you remember your aunt Turner? Dear me, of course you do not; she died before you were born. Besides, she was not your aunt, any more than I am, nor half so much, because she was not so agreeable. Her son is in a banking house in Boston; he inherits his father's passion for genealogy and numismatics, history, ancient and modern. The children here think him a prig and a bore; he does turn out his feet rather too much, and I wish he would not say "marm" to me quite so often. Still, he would be invaluable as a guide and escort, and was immensely pleased when I invited him, as I made bold to do, to join us all at the Vendôme, and help you to *do* Boston. He is all ready to "call cousins" with you Horners, and will explain to you, root and branch, where he comes in on the Horner tree. It seems there was a Horner who married a Turner,— but I will spare you till you meet him.

Tom and Hubert groaned at the picture. "Oh, why did she thrust him upon us!" cried Tom; "that is exactly like aunt Dut, —she always wants to have an extra man around."

"Oh, well," replied Bessie cheerfully, "in that case, she will take care of him herself; and we need not trouble ourselves about him except to tap him for information whenever we need it."

The work of packing went on. Mr. Brick and his wagons were summoned from East Utopia. Poor Mrs. Bruce was to be left all alone, for Belinda and Lavinia Mary were to retire like bears and turtles to hibernate, after the summer work was ended.

"Land sakes!" exclaimed the latter, as she ran backward and forward, with her apron tied round her head. "Just to think, the

summer is over so quick, when it ain't mor'n half begun. Them
chickens shows it, though; sh! sh! They was eggs when you
come, Miss Bessie. Sh! sh!" she continued, addressing this part
of the sentence to a number of well-grown fowls.

The travellers climbed into the great wagon, the packages were
put under the seats. Alice leaned forward and waved her handkerchief to her mother, who could be discerned at the window of
her sitting-room, in the distant house.

The four young people made a merry journey through Vermont,
passing Rutland, Bellows Falls and Keene, and crossing Massachusetts, reached Boston, after dark, of the short October day. The
foliage all along the route was superb, the brilliant reds and yel-
lows of maple and birch contrasting with the still unchanged
dark green of the oaks.

Mr. Horner met them at the station, and at the Vendôme
they found, just arrived and awaiting them, Miss Lejeune. After
dinner, for he could not come sooner, they were joined by Mr.
Turner, who was now presented to his new cousins, and as they
sat over their coffee and dessert, enhanced by the addition of
bright red apples from Utopia, they allowed their guest to mount
his hobby, by turning the subject to the landmarks of Boston.

It was wet and drizzling, but not unpromising for the morrow.

APPLES FROM UTOPIA.

## CHAPTER XXXVI.

### THE FIRST DAY IN BOSTON.

"YOU see," said Mr. Turner, who was a little conceited as to the merits of his "poking about" in one and another corner, "you see, the absolute original landmarks of Boston are gone, or as much altered as they could be. When the first people came here, old John Blackstone, and even Winthrop and Dudley, of course it was not called Boston. It was called Trimountain, or Tremont, I suppose by the people in the fishing ships, because at the top of Beacon Hill there were three hummocks, like this,"—and the speaker cut a bit of bread into the shape he meant,— "two protuberances in the side of a hill a little higher."

"Oh, yes! Fort Hill, and Copp's Hill, and Beacon Hill," said Bessie, not unwilling to show that she also knew something.

"Not quite yet, Miss Bessie," said Mr. Turner, modestly enough. "Most people think so. And I think most Boston people would tell you so, but they would be wrong. The three hummocks were all on Beacon Hill,—that's where the State House is now. Oddly enough, they are all gone. They dug down the highest, where the beacon was, part of it when they built the State House, and the rest afterward, to fill up the old mill pond. And the others were so steep that they had to be dug down for streets. But when I take you to the State House, and over Mount Vernon and Somerset streets, you will have tramped over them all.

"I really think, Miss Lejeune," he added, "that at least the boys had better go to the top of the State House with me, first of all. You know Dean Stanley did."

It is true that when Doctor Stanley came to Boston, true to the principles of Arnold's school of history, he wished, first of all, to understand the precise topography of all he was to see. His first visit, therefore, was to the top of the State House, and his last, after his short stay, was to the same observatory, t h a t h e might be sure he had rightly placed all that he had seen.

In our case it need not be said that all the children shouted at the idea of Miss Lejeune's consenting to climb two hundred and twenty stairs, more or less, for the sake of instruction or amusement; but while she took Alice with her for some shopping, at the request of Alice's mother, while Mr. Horner w e n t d o w n town upon business, Mr. Turner was permitted, to his solid satisfaction, to take the young people to the top of the State House, to the Common, and anywhere else he chose. "And we will get our lunch where we do our work," he said.

BOSTON COMMON.

"Cousin Nathan," said his new friend Bessie,— who was no more his cousin than you are, as you already know, but after learning the genealogy of the families Bessie concluded to call him such,—" be sure that I see a ship, a real three-master, before we go away. Steamships I don't care for." And he promised.

Bessie had crossed the ocean in a steamer, ascended the Nile in a dahabieh, and passed over a part of the Gulf of Lyons in a clumsy boat with a lateen-sail, but she had never seen, except afar off from the deck of a Cunarder, any of the three-masted schooners which ply between Boston and the coast of Maine.

A street car brought the party to the head of Winter street, and here Nathan brought them out of it upon what he called the Lower Mall, on the eastern side of Boston Common. Here he put the girls upon a seat, while the boys grouped around him, and with his stick, he drew a rough map on the ground.

"We may get parted from each other. But if any one is lost while you are in Boston, the streets are just as easy to understand as those of Philadelphia or Chicago, after you once know the law of the instrument.

"This hill we are on is the east slope of Beacon Hill. If we had followed in the car we could have ridden it to Cambridge, in this open horseshoe which I draw.

"North of us, quite at the north of the town, is Copp's Hill. We will see that another day. The streets around that are in curves also.

"Off here on the southeast was Fort Hill. The streets there bent to follow the curve. But that is all dug down.

"Then, of course, in a seaboard town, from every wharf or pier, there ran up streets into the town. If you took a fan, and put the centre at the Post Office Square, the sticks would be Water street, Milk street, Pearl street, Federal street, and so on. Now all this is just as much according to rule as if you made a checker-board. Only you must know what the rule is."

"I think it is a great deal nicer," said Bessie.

"The rule in practice is said to be, Find out where the place is to which you go, and take a horse car running the other way."

"Is it, really?" asked Hubert, still literal, although he had been so long with Americans.

" No.  That is a joke," said Bessie.

"Now we will go up to the State House."  So they slowly pulled up the Park Street walk, up the high steps between the two bronze statues, stopped in the Doric Hall to see the statues and the battle flags, and then slowly mounted the long stairways

THE STATE HOUSE, BEACON STREET.

which led to the "lantern" above the dome.  Fortunately the Legislature was not sitting.  When the House is in session visits to the lantern are not permitted, lest the trampling on the stairs above the Representatives' Hall might disturb the hearers.

When they had regained their breath, they looked round on the magnificent panorama which sweeps a circle of forty miles in diameter, and Nathan lectured. His lecture must not be reported here in detail. But the main points of it shall be stated, because they give the clew to the expeditions which the party made afterwards.

They were so high that all the rest of the city was quite below them. Nathan was able to point out almost in a group, Faneuil Hall, the Old State House, and the Old South Meeting House of Revolutionary times.

"We will do those," he said, "to-morrow, and then you can see where the tea was thrown over, and the scene of the Boston Massacre. That will be a good Revolutionary day."

To the north, with a strip of water between, so narrow, and bridged so often that it hardly seemed a deep river, half a mile wide, was the monument on Bunker Hill. The summit was the only point near them as high as they were. We will go there, perhaps," said Nathan, "day after to-morrow. And that same day we can see Copp's Hill, which is the north headland of Old Boston, and we can go to the Navy Yard, and Bessie shall see her ship with three masts.                                    •

"Saturday,—I don't know what Mr. Horner will say,—but I vote that we go down the harbor. We will see Nahant, which is a rocky peninsula ten miles northeast, or Hull, which is about as far southeast; they make the headlands of Boston Bay." And he tried to make out both these points. He did show them the outer light-house and the great forts between. Bessie, Tom and Hubert were delighted with their first view of Boston Harbor.

"Then Sunday," continued Nathan, calculating his scheme prudently, "some of us can go to Christ Church, where the sexton showed the lantern."

"And can not we see the church with the cannon ball?" asked Hubert.

Which bears on her bosom as a bride might do,
The iron breastpin that the rebels threw.

"No," said Mr. Turner sadly. "We were barbarians, and pulled that church down." And he added savagely, "And no good came to the society that did it.

"That will leave next week for a good tramp over Dorchester Heights, and another day, if you are not tired, we will go to Cambridge, and see Harvard College."

"Hubert," said Bessie, aside, "how did you come to be quoting poetry,—or is it original?"

"No," replied Hubert, "it is Doctor Holmes'. Miss Augusta showed it to me, in a book, this morning."

Meantime, Nathan Turner was showing how high the Dorchester Heights, now in South Boston, rose, and how completely they commanded the harbor; so that when Washington seized them the English army and navy had to go. He also showed them Cambridge and the college buildings, lying quite near them, westward, but on the other side of the Charles River.

The party spent a long time in the cupola of the State House, going from window to window, and asking all sorts of questions of their guide, who showed himself steady on all points. Bessie took a sincere liking to the young man, or rather boy, who, in spite of a preciseness of manner which made him appear absurd, at first, knew so thoroughly well what he was talking about.

As Nathan took them home from the State House he led them down Beacon street. This is a beautiful street, making the north side of Boston Common. Where the Common ends, Charles street crosses Beacon street nearly at right angles. Near this corner, on land now built upon, or perhaps crossed by some street, was the cottage of Blackstone, who lived in Boston for six or seven years before Governor Winthrop and the settlers of 1630 arrived.

They made their first settlement at Charlestown, on the other side of the river. The records of Charlestown say: " Mr. Blackstone, dwelling on the other side of Charles River, alone, at a place called by the Indians, Shawmut, where he had a cottage at, or not far from, the place called Blackstone Point, came and acquainted the Governor of an excellent spring, inviting and soliciting him thither."

Blackstone's house, or cottage, in which he lived, together with the nature of his improvements, was such as to authorize the belief that he had resided there some seven or eight years. How he became possessed of his lands here is not known; but it is certain he held a good title to them, which was acknowledged by the settlers under Winthrop, who, in course of time, bought his

DORCHESTER HEIGHTS AND THE HARBOR.

lands of him, and he removed out of the jurisdiction of Massachusetts, to the valley of the Blackstone River.

Of Blackstone's personal history, Mr. Charles F. Adams makes this note:

"He was in no respect an ordinary man. His presence in the peninsula of Shawmut, in 1630, was made additionally inexplicable from the fact that he was about the last person one would ever have expected to find there. He was not a fisherman, nor a trader.

nor a refugee : he was a student, an observer, and a recluse. A graduate of Emmanuel College, Cambridge, he had received Episcopal ordination in England. In 1631 he was in his thirty-fifth year. Probability would strongly point to him as Winthrop's authority where Winthrop, in 1631, speaks of a species of weather record going back seven years since this bay was planted by Englishmen."

THE RECLUSE IN THE NEW TOWN OF PROVIDENCE.

## CHAPTER XXXVII.

### THE SECOND DAY.

MEANWHILE Alice and Miss Lejeune passed the day very pleasantly going from one large shop to another, the results of which were visible in a pretty walking suit of dark flannel bought ready-made and fitting admirably. Alice was impatient to put it on as soon as it came home, and as it arrived before six o'clock, and as the sight-seers came in late, she was already dressed in it, and waiting for Bessie's approval. A new hat, gloves, boots and umbrella were added also.

That evening a certain plan was laid out for the next day, in which every one agreed to join. It was settled that they should lunch down town with the gentlemen, and should take the elevator at the "Equitable" Insurance Company, so that Alice and Miss Lejeune might have something to substitute for the view the children had had from the State House. This view is not as sweeping on the west as that from the State House. But on other sides it is equally satisfactory. And you can go up by steam,—a great matter if you happen to have passed forty years.

"It is a pity," said Miss Lejeune, "that they have given up the restaurant at the top of the Equitable. I remember lunching there on a warm day one summer, and it was delicious to sit in a cool breeze, looking off upon the lovely harbor, and the little sails coming and going far below, while we ate our soft-shell crabs and ice-cream."

They went instead to Young's, where, in the pretty and quietly ordered dining-room, their large party had a merry lunch. "Do, papa," said Tom, "order oysters on the shell; there is an R in the month, and Hubert has not seen any."

"Is it possible?" said Mr. Horner. "To be sure, there has been no R in the month since he came."

"What do you mean?" asked the English boy.

" Oysters are supposed not to be good in summer, and as all the summer months are spelled without an R, that makes a rule for not eating them." Large New York oysters on the half-shell were brought, surprising Hubert greatly by their size.

After lunch Nathan took them to the head of State street, to the "Old State House."

"This," said he, "is what the Philadelphia girl called the State street Meeting-house."

He had brought them in a horse car, so that they saw the building from the southern side. The lion on one side and the unicorn

ALICE MARTIN IN BOSTON.

on the other, dance on their hind legs at the top, with the roof
to part them. Nathan was careful to show Tom and the rest that
as they looked up on the beasts they stood themselves on the very
ground of the "Boston Massacre" of March 5, 1770. The English troops were in a little semicircle on the north side of the
street. Attucks, the mulatto, and the rest of the mob who stoned
the troops and snowballed them, were in the street, or on the
southern side. There were, then, no sidewalks.

The lower part of the "Old State House" is now used for
public offices. But the upper chambers are restored to much the
condition in which they were when Sam Adams defied the Governor there, and when Otis made his plea in the "Writs of Assistance cases."

"Then and there," said John Adams, afterwards, " American independence was born."

"The Bostonian Society" occupies these halls, simply that they
may be open to all visitors, and here the party found many curious mementoes of Revolutionary and of older days, and were able
to prepare themselves for their later excursions.

Before the " Town House " was built, this spot was occupied as
the market place, being the earliest in the town. The first town
house was erected between 1657 and 1659, of wood. It was destroyed in the great fire of 1711. In the following year, 1712, a
brick edifice was erected on the same spot. This the fire of 1747
consumed, and with it many valuable records were lost. The present Old State House was erected the following year, 1748, but it
has undergone many interior changes, the exterior, however, pre-
senting nearly the same appearance as when first erected. From
1750 to 1830 Faneuil Hall was used as a town house, and the
first city government was organized there. In 1830 the city government removed to the Old State House, which was, on September 17, dedicated as City Hall. But the City Hall has since been
removed to School street.

Leaving the Old State House they passed down State street, where they had a chance to see the merchants who were "on 'change," and to look in at the Merchants' Exchange, and by a short street leading north, came into the square between Faneuil Hall, "the cradle of liberty," as Boston people liked to call it, and Faneuil Hall Market.

Peter Faneuil, a rich merchant of Huguenot origin, told the town that he would build a market house on this spot if they would accept the gift for that purpose, and maintain it forever. "The town," by which is meant the town meeting, looked a gift-horse in the mouth, and made some diffi-culty. At the end of a stormy meeting, his

EQUITABLE BUILDING.

proposal was accepted by a majority of only seven votes in a vote of seven hundred and twenty-seven.

Mr. Faneuil set to work at once on the building, which, by the original plan, was to be but one-story high. But he added an-other story for the town hall, which has made his name famous to all New Englanders. The original hall accommodated only one thousand persons, being but half the size of that now standing. He died, himself, just as the building was completed, on the third of March, 1743, and it was first opened to public use on the fourteenth of March of that year. The whole interior was destroyed by fire in January, 1763, and rebuilt by the town and State. In 1806 it was enlarged to its present size.

Nathan made them look at the grasshopper, which is the weathercock, which is selected in memory of the Athenian cicada. The Athenian people selected this as their emblem because they believed they sprang from the ground, and they supposed the grasshoppers did.

The people of Boston long since provided themselves with a much larger market house than Peter Faneuil's. When they did so, they gave up the market in Faneuil Hall, and used the basement for other purposes. But their lawyers, after a while, recollected that stirring town meeting, and the promise of the town to maintain the market "forever." Clearly enough, if the town meant to keep the hall, it must maintain the market. So the butchers and fruit men were brought back again ; and Miss Lejeune did not fail to buy some bananas for the party in the market, that they might keep Peter Faneuil well in their memory.

The Historic Hall is over the market, and always open to visitors, and here the party spent half an hour in looking at the pictures. Mr. Horner told them of the last and only time when he heard Wendell Phillips there. It is not the largest hall in Boston, but it is still the favorite hall for any public meeting about some public interest, where people are not expecting to sit down.

The gentlemen joined the party by appointment here, and they all went to lunch together. They then went up the Equitable elevator and mounted the tower, so that the ladies might see the sea view. And they finished the day's excursion by going into the Old South Meeting House.

This old meeting house was twice as big as Faneuil Hall of the Revolution, so that the crowded town meetings of those days often adjourned to the Old South. As the patriots called Faneuil

CITY HALL, BOSTON.

Hall the "cradle of liberty," Governor Gage called the Old South the "nursery of rebellion." The religious society which formerly occupied it built, a few years ago, a new church in the western part of Boston, and sold this meeting-house to an association which wished to preserve it as a memorial of the history of Boston. The sellers did not wish to have any opposition church established in the old building; they therefore put a provision in the deed, that for twenty years it should not be used for public religious purposes. It is probably the only spot in the United States where, by the expressed wish of a church, public worship is forbidden.

The travellers found a great deal to interest them in the meeting house,— relics of the past there preserved. The boys, indefatigable, obtained leave to climb up the spire, from which it is said that the English governor, Gage, saw the embarkation of his troops for Bunker Hill, and what he could see of the battle.

The next day proved favorable for Nathan's plans, which involved a visit to Bunker Hill Monument and the Navy Yard.

"I should like," he said to the girls, "to begin by taking you out to Concord, that you might see the bridge over the Concord River, and the scene of what we call Concord Fight. But if the day prove hot, it would have been tiresome, as we have the Monument to climb. For that expedition one needs half a day, or better, a day. You know you would want to see Mr. Emerson's house and Mr. Hawthorne's."

They started later, therefore, than the Concord plan would have required. A transfer at Scollay Square, the very heart of active Boston, put them in a Charlestown car. In Scollay Square stands very properly a statue of Winthrop, the founder of Boston. and its first Governor; as at the foot of the street stands Sam Adams.

Nathan explained to the girls, when they came to river and bridge, that at the time of Bunker Hill battle there was no bridge. The English army, when it attacked the hill, had to cross in boats, and he showed them on the east, the line the boats took, landing where the Navy Yard now is. The forces landed there and waited through a hot day before the attack. The battle was fought on a hot June afternoon.

After they came to Charlestown, a short walk brought them to the top of the hill, where a large green park takes in all the ground of the historic Redoubt. A bronze statute of Prescott seems to welcome the visitor.

By an ascent even longer than that they made at the State House, they climbed the Monument, and earned their sight of the panorama from its top.

The party had given them a note to introduce them to the commander at the Navy Yard on their return. It proved that he was absent. But they needed no pass nor introduction. They were very courteously received; and as there happened to be a ship fitting out with stores for the Mediterranean Station, Bessie had her chance

PULPIT WINDOW IN THE OLD SOUTH CHURCH.

to see "a three-masted ship," nearly ready for sea.

"But after all," she said, when Nathan very kindly attracted her attention to the craft, "this is not what I mean. Papa, we have seen plenty of these passing at sea!"

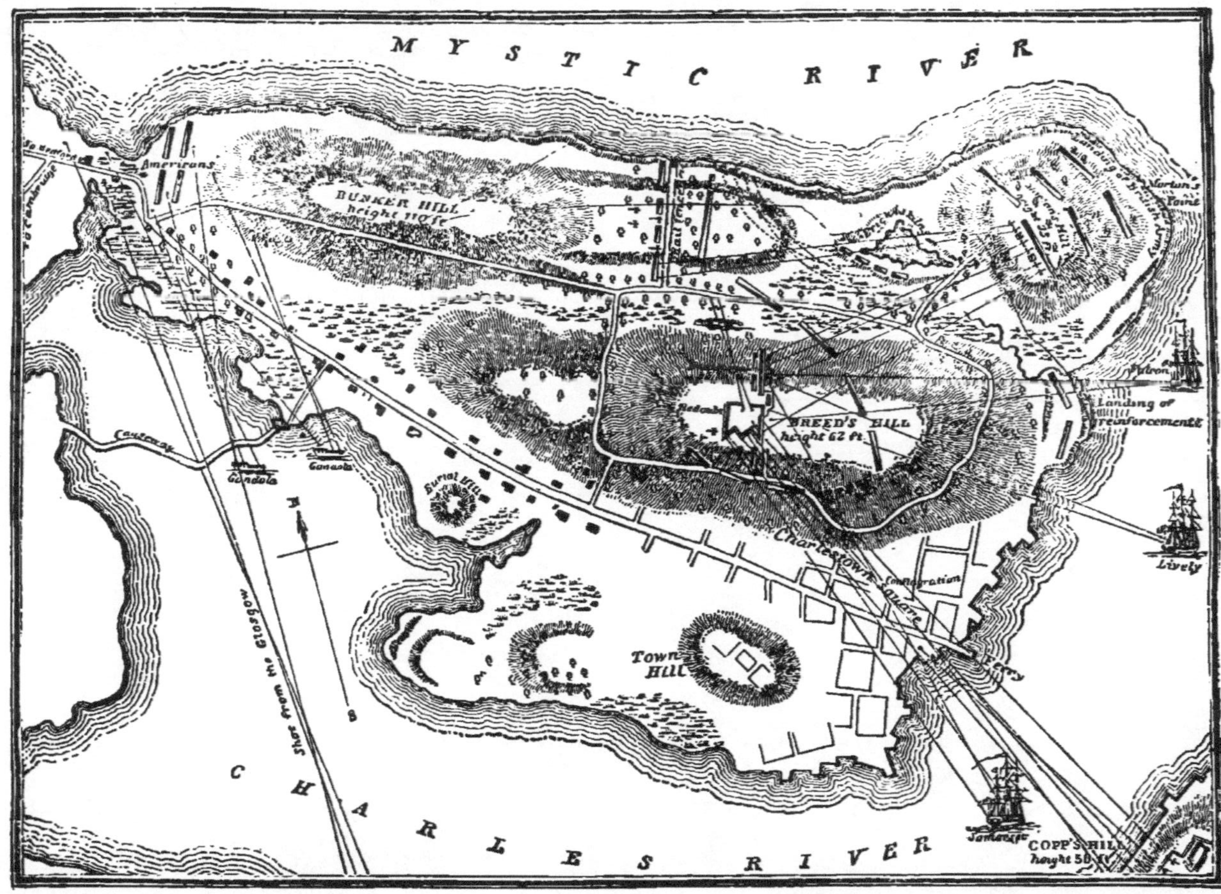
MYSTIC RIVER
CHARLES RIVER
BUNKER HILL height 110 ft
BREED'S HILL height 62 ft
COPP'S HILL height 50 ft
Town Hill
Burial Hill
Redoubt
Rail fence
Americans
Causeway
Gondola
Gondola
Charlestown
Conflagration of Charlestown
Shot from the Glasgow
Landing of reinforcements
Moulton's Point
Falcon
Lively
Somerset
N
S
E
C

Mr. Horner found that Nathan Turner was thinking of one thing, and Bessie of another.

"A three-masted schooner," he explained, "is like any other schooner, with the addition of a third mast. They are, I believe, steadier with the third mast, and better fitted to carry the loads of stone and lumber which Maine furnishes to the other States."

NEAR THE WHARVES.

## CHAPTER XXXVIII.

### NAHANT.

SATURDAY proved to be a warm day, and it was proposed at breakfast that they should carry out Nathan's plan, and that all hands should go to Nahant, the rocky peninsula which bounds the outer harbor on the northeastern side.

So they took the horse car and "transferred" at Summer street for the ferry-boat, which would take them to the Lynn Railroad. They could have taken the Eastern Railroad, but the Narrow Guage Road (so called) runs along the water's edge, and the sail is more attractive.

Miss Lejeune begged off from this expedition. She had made a visit to Nahant during the summer, where she had hosts of friends. "I shall be sure to meet some of them," she said, "and in that case, every one at Nahant is so hospitable, they will insist upon lunching or dining you all. You will have better fun incog."

So the young people had their first sniff of sea air from the boat which crosses from Old Boston to East Boston, where the railroad begins. Bessie had chances enough to see "ships with three masts," brigs, schooners, sloops, barks, brigantines and barkantines, all which the learned Nathan explained to her. After a voyage of a mile or two they took the Narrow Guage Railway and flew along Chelsea Beach, which gave a fine ocean view, and more of the glory of the infinite sea than the steamboat had done. At Lynn they found public carriages waiting for the drive to Nahant.

Mr. Horner, with unwonted extravagance, said that Nahant looked like the open hand of a giant who had been struck down in the sea, and that Nahant Beach was his arm. A very thin arm he had, — a mere thread-paper arm, — for a big hand. For the beach is only a strip of sand and gravel about two miles long, washed by the ocean on both sides. At the southern end rise, abrupt and bold, the rocks of Nahant. They are mostly of trap-rock, which has been forced by some volcanic effect of the fiery times, up through the hissing sea. They have a reddish color, with stripes of black stone, even harder than the rest. And the perpetual washing of the sea has worn out clefts and chasms of every strange outline and form.

One of these is the Swallow's Cave, a long passage through wet rocks, covered above by rocks, through which at low tides adventurers can clamber. Another is the Spouting Horn, where, at half-tide, a sea heavily thrown in by a stiff eastern gale, bounds back in spray and water, as if indeed a sea-god had thrown it up in a great fountain. But the glory of Nahant is not in any one of these sights.

SAMUEL ADAMS' STATUE, WASHINGTON STREET.

It is the glory of the infinite ocean. Southeast and west you have the sea, and it is no wonder that in this perfect sea-climate so many people are glad to make a summer home.

Mr. Horner met, by accident, a Boston friend, after they had crossed the beach, who husbanded their time for them in visiting different points, and before the afternoon closed, asked them to come back to town in his yacht.

This they accepted with delight, especially as the steamboat which usually plys between Nahant and Boston was not running. So, after all, the party were indebted to the hospitalities of Nahant, to the amusement of Miss Augusta, when she heard of it.

From the deck of the *Sylph*, its owner showed them that nearly south of them, a string of little islands shielded the harbor, in a measure, from eastern gales. Of these the three most important are the three Brewsters, on one of which is the outer light-house. The yacht first ran by these. Then she turned inland, and he pointed out to them the villages of Hull, which on the southeast protects the bay, as Nahant on the northeast. He bade the helmsman bring the vessel up at Fort Warren, and the young people had then a chance to see the arrangements which a great fort makes to repel an enemy. And then, as the

GOV. JOHN WINTHROP, SCOLLAY SQUARE.

sun went down, down, they ran swiftly up to Boston, saw the State House and Bunker Hill Monument against the evening glow, and landed after a day of thorough satisfaction and variety.

Mr. Turner left the party at the door of the Vendôme, to return home for the night. He had been with them hitherto at the hotel, but he lived out of town, and felt that he must report to his family.

"Be sure you come to-morrow!" called Bessie, as he turned the corner from the hotel, flourishing his cane at a street car.

"How sleepy I am!" said Bessie, after dinner, as she threw herself on a sofa in their parlor.

"I am more tired than sleepy," said Alice, "my feet ache so. The sidewalks are so hard."

"This is the first time, then, Alice," said Miss Lejeune, "that you have been in Boston?"

"The first time I was anywhere except East Utopia," replied Alice.

The arrival on the scene of the Horner family was an event of importance to Alice. The country girl had suddenly been introduced to a series of experiences wholly different from the quiet tenor of her life.

The next day was Sunday. So much chance was there for a day of rest. But at breakfast it proved that there were one or two ecclesiastical landmarks which were to be counted in with the others, and that, with perfect gravity and reverence, the young people had arranged to unite their sight-seeing with the religious services of the day. The party all together made an addition not unacceptable to congregations not yet crowded; for although it was October, summer wanderers had not yet returned.

The first point was King's Chapel.

> The chapel, last of sublunary things
> That shocks our senses with the name of King's.

Such is Doctor Holmes' description. It is in the very heart of active Boston. After the Revolution it was long called "The Stone Chapel," for in those early days stone churches were rare, and nothing bore the name of King. Royal biscuit was then called "President's biscuit." But after people were sure that no King George would return, the Chapel people, who were no longer in the habit of praying for the royal family, returned to "King's Chapel" as the historical name of their church, and found again

CHRIST CHURCH, SALEM STREET.

the neglected gilded crown and mitre, which had once adorned the organ, and restored them to the places from which they had been removed. After the service, which interested all the young people, they remained in the church to look at the curious old monuments. They were specially interested in that of Mrs. Shirley, the lovely wife of Governor Shirley. She died just as he was fortifying Boston against the largest fleet which France ever sent across the seas. This is the fleet of Longfellow's ballad:

> For the admiral D'Anville
> Had sworn by cross and crown,
> To ravage with fire and steel
> Our luckless Boston Town.

While Shirley had the whole army of Massachusetts on Boston Common, and was bringing every resource to bear to resist the enemy, his heart was wrung day by day by the sickness and the death of the young bride, whose bust the children saw, and whose epitaph they translated.

Mr. Horner told them that when the King's Chapel was built there had been no quarries of stone opened in New England. The stones for this building were split and hewed from bowlders.

By the time it was finished it was currently said and believed that there was not stone enough in the province for another church as big. He took them to the back of the church and showed them, on a little green, Franklin's statue, placed in what was the yard of the schoolhouse where he studied as a boy.

King's Chapel was not popular with the Puritan inhabitants of Boston. And, because the lower windows are square, and look like port holes, the street boys of a century and a quarter ago nicknamed it "Christ's Frigate," somewhat irreverently. On the other side of the street was once the schoolhouse where John Hancock and Sam Adams studied. And Nathan showed them where the "coast" was in winter, which was obstructed by the English officer whom the schoolboys called to account for his violation of their inalienable rights.

They went to church with a friend whom they had met on the yacht coming from Nahant the day before, in the morning, and in the afternoon Bessie and Mr. Turner went to Christ Church, which is the oldest church building in Boston now standing on the ground where it was built. It was the second Episcopalian church erected in Boston, and was built in 1723, several years

KING'S CHAPEL, TREMONT STREET.

before the present Old South. It is a brick edifice, and has long been known as the "North End Church." In its day was con sidered one of the chief architectural ornaments of the North End. The old steeple was blown down in the great gale of 1804, falling upon an old wooden building at the corner of Tileston street, through which it crushed, to the consternation of the tenants, who, however, escaped injury. The steeple was replaced from a design by Charles Bulfinch, which carefully preserved the proportion of the original. Its chime was the first in New England, and began to play its charming tunes in 1744.

The Bible, prayer books and silver now in use were given, in 1733, by King George the First. The figures of cherubim in front of the organ were taken from a French vessel by the privateer *Queen of Hungary*, and presented to the church in 1746. There is an interesting bust of Washington in the church.

From the steeple of this church the historic sexton hung out the lanterns which warned the patriots on the other side of the river that an expedition was starting from the English camp, against Concord.

"One if by land, — two if by sea," says Mr. Longfellow, whose history of those days is more likely to be remembered well than any other. That steeple, as has been said, was blown down in 1804.

As they walked to the car, which was to take them home. Nathan led Bessie through the Copp's Hill burying ground. Copp's Hill has never been cut away. Fort Hill is wholly leveled, and Beacon Hill partly so. These were the three hills which were the landmarks of old Boston.

# CHAPTER XXXIX.

## A SEA BATH.

THE next day, Monday, was deliciously warm, one of those left over from summer, which drop down sometimes even late in October.

Bessie, ever since her first glance at the ocean from the top of the State House, had been longing for a salt bath, and Alice, who had never bathed in the sea, shared the longing, for she had begun to swim already in fresh water, and everybody told her that salt water was more bouyant, making it much easier.

But the way was beset with difficulties, and if Bessie had not laid her plan before speaking of it, she would have found it difficult to resist the objections which were raised when she broached the subject at the breakfast table.

"Bathe after the first of October!" exclaimed a wiry little old lady who sat at the same table. She was a Boston woman, and the incarnation of conventionality. "We never think of such a thing," she said.

"I think we can manage it," said Bessie. "We know our way about so well now. Alice and I can take the Narrow Guage Railway, and stop at one of those little stations on —— Beach. I saw bathing-houses to let at every one of them, as we passed the other day, and we have our bathing dresses."

As she said this a smile of intelligence passed between her and Alice, for there had been a little doubt on the part of Alice's mother about the wisdom of packing Alice's bathing-dress.

"My dear," Bessie had said, "you just put it in. It is always safest to have it. And I should take mine to Siberia in January."

So there was no difficulty on this score. But old Mrs. Fletcher raised her hands and eyes. "——— Beach, — but, my dear Miss

FROM THE FERRY-BOAT.

Horner, nobody bathes there. In fact, I have been told that the railway itself is terribly vulgar. Is it not narrower than common?"

Bessie bit her lip, more with vexation at herself for broaching the subject in such company, than with amusement at the question. Opposition from this quarter, however, brought her an unexpected ally, for Miss Lejeune said suddenly:

"My dear Mrs. Fletcher, you are quite mistaken; Miss Swimmer, whose mother was a Claveridge, you know, one of the William P. Claveridges, goes there on purpose, every summer, just for one bath. Of course, you know, one would not stay there; but especially at this season, when the crowd has left, —"

"At this season, — well, yes, it might do," mumbled the old lady, and retired vanquished from the field.

The Horners had a good laugh, and the girls had their bath, passing the whole morning in the expedition. Miss Lejeune went with them and watched them from the piazza of a deserted hotel. The tide was high, the waves came creaming along the shallow beach, the water was cold, but delicious. Alice thought she had never enjoyed anything so much in her life. The occasion was always afterwards referred to as Mrs. Fletcher's bath.

Nathan Turner's expedition arranged for the day was to Dorchester Heights, to see the view of the harbor from that point. The party were scattered all the morning, and had agreed to lunch solidly, or dine, in the middle of the day, at any place where they happened to be, and to assemble at some central point late in the day.

Accordingly, about five o'clock, they started for South Boston. "Take any car for City Point," was Nathan's final direction as the party separated. "Ask for the Reservoir, and we will meet there."

"Dorchester Heights" is simply the name which only old-fashioned people would understand, of the hills in what is now "South Boston," now surmounted by the "Blind Institution," and a public park, in which is one of the city reservoirs.

From the hill they enjoyed the spectacle of the harbor, white with the sails of hundreds of yachts, and all alive with the movements of the steamers as they went out, just before sunset, on their voyages to every port of the seaboard, not to say of the world.

These high hills completely command the harbor, in a military sense. Why the English generals did not take possession before Washington did, no one ever knew. That was the sort of imbecility George the Third got by appointing men to office because they were his relations. When, at last, the winter of 1775–76 broke up, and no ice had formed strong enough for an attack on Boston over the ice, Washington seized these hills. By the road now called Dorchester Avenue, which Nathan Turner showed his friends, he sent from the camp in Roxbury the men and munitions. It was all done by night. On the morning of the fifth of March the Americans had built a fortification which surprised the English officers in Boston as that on Bunker Hill had surprised them nine months before. "It is like Aladdin's lamp," wrote one of them.

General Howe's first plan was to assault the works, as Gage had assaulted those at Bunker Hill. Howe sent an attacking force to the fort held by him on the island. But a storm made this attack impossible. Ward, the commander of the American right wing, strengthened his ranks. Thomas, the general in command on the Heights, asked nothing better than an attack. But Howe, at the last, saw that the venture was madness. He entered into negotiations with Washington, and, a fortnight after, withdrew fleet and army. For several months there was not an English soldier on American soil.

Before they left the park, which now takes the place of the fortification, they looked at the tablet of stone which commemorates

THE BEACH.

the history. They found the name of the mayor who put it up, but no allusion to General Ward who planned the work, or General Thomas who carried it out. Such, alas, is fame!

Nathan Turner was surprised to find Hubert, and even Augustine, well versed in the cause of these historical events. He was not called upon to tell the story, but only to point out places, to an intelligent and interested audience.

"I wish I had been in Utopia with you," he said. "You must have had first-rate books of reference."

THE HOME OF LONGFELLOW.

"We had Professor Bruce," replied Hubert, "and he is better than a whole library."

When they left the hill the sun was going down, in a red mist, promising another hot day. The evening was so soft and warm that they lingered until bedtime in the public garden, sitting upon benches where they could watch the people who walked about in crowds under the electric light, and the boats gliding about on the water.

When they told Mrs. Fletcher, the next morning, how they had spent the evening, and how pretty it was, she said, "Ah, indeed? but nobody does it, you know." Alice thought there must be a great many nobodies in Boston, if all the happy people she had seen in the garden counted for nothing.

The next day, when they visited the Historical Society, Nathan showed his cousins the original gold medal which Congress gave to Washington in honor of this victory. It was designed by a French artist, and struck in Paris. It represents Washington seated on his horse, on Dorchester Heights, as the squadron retires. It bears the proud motto:

*"Hostibus primo Fugatis,"*

which may be translated: "The first Flight of the Enemy."

Nathan's programme would have been incomplete without a trip to Cambridge. Bessie and Miss Lejeune had both made visits to Philip, in his college room at Harvard, but Tom had not seen it. "What a pity," said he, "that Philip is away, so that we cannot go to his room."

"How soon he will be back, now," Bessie replied; "only three days more." They supposed he was already upon the water, having sailed the week before.

At the station of the Providence road they found a street car waiting to take them from Park Square to Harvard Square. The ride takes a short half-hour. At Harvard Square they were on one side of the College Yard, as the region is called, which in colleges of more pretence would be named the *campus*. Buildings of all ages and all aspects fill it, from the venerable brick of old Massachusetts, built near two centuries ago, down to the last devices of modern architecture.

First of all, Nathan led them to the Library, where they looked at some of the curiosities; and here they met a classmate of Philip's, who recognized Mr. Horner, and did the honors of his room; so they saw a little of the college life of the students.

Next they went to Memorial Hall, where are the portraits of the old worthies of the State and college, the trophies of many base ball victories, and, most interesting of all, if you go at a meal time, some five hundred of the young men of to-day, eating with a good appetite; and then to the Agassiz Museum, which is so skilfully arranged that they will all date back to that hour's visit a clearer knowledge of the great classifications of natural science.

The young people declared that they were not tired even then. So 'after lunch, they went up to the Botanic Garden, stopped at the Observatory, and crossed to see the house which was lately the home of Longfellow, and in the Revolution, that of Washington.

As they all returned to town in a horse car, Mr. Horner said to Miss Lejeune, " I fancy, Augusta, you have never done Boston in this sight-seeing fashion."

" No, indeed," she replied, "and I dare say half the people in Boston have not themselves. "If," she added, "I should ever go abroad again, I shall be able to converse with more credit to myself about the landmarks of Boston."

"If you ever go abroad again!" exclaimed Tom. "You know, aunt Dut, you are saving up now for your next excursion."

At this they all smiled.

Hubert was silent. He knew that he was soon to return to Europe, and for him to cross the ocean again, separated anew from friends who had become very dear to him, was no attractive prospect.

## CHAPTER XL.

### SCATTERING.

IT was quarter of eleven o'clock, before noon, and Nathan Turner and Alice Martin were walking up and down the sidewalk outside the Boston & Albany station.

"It is to be hoped they will not be late," remarked Mr. Turner, in his precise way, looking very carefully at his watch. "Exactly fifteen minutes to eleven; I always allow a quarter of an hour at the station for the regulation of baggage."

"I do not believe they will be late," replied Alice. "Mr. Horner is an excellent traveller."

"Still, it is well to be accurate," he said, adding, "and so you are to remain in Boston, Miss Martin?"

"Yes; is it not wonderful? Miss Lejeune has so kindly arranged everything for me. It has been the dream of my life to spend a winter in Boston, at school, and now it has come to pass!"

"Have you friends in Boston?" he inquired.

"Not one; but I am to board with some pleasant people, and I hope I shall make friends,— but here they are!"

Two carriages drove up to the end of the station where baggage is received. All the party were there, and all the parcels.

"Ah, you arrived before us," said Mr. Horner, shaking hands with Nathan. "Thank you, again, for taking care of Alice, and for all your kindness to us. Tom, if you will look after the ladies, I will buy the tickets."

"Had not I better see about drawing-room seats?" asked Tom.

"Yes, that will be better; and, Hubert, take,—ah! you have it,—Miss Lejeune's bag."

"Your umbrella, papa," said Bessie, handing it to him.

They all passed into the handsome new station, and after a few moments, through the gate to the train, Alice following them, though she was to be left behind. Now that the moment of parting had come, she began to be frightened at the prospect.

BOSTON AND ALBANY DEPOT, KNEELAND STREET.

"Keep up a good heart, Alice," whispered Bessie, who had come to be very fond of the girl, "and be sure and write me about everything."

"Good-by, Mr. Turner," Tom was saying, and, "Good-by, Nathan," said Miss Lejeune; "our little scheme has worked admirably, has it not?"

"I thank you most sincerely," he replied, turning out his toes more than ever, "for the great favor I have enjoyed in making the acquaintance of Mr. Horner and his family."

"Well, Alice," said Hubert, "I hope we shall meet again some time. Will you keep this to remember our quarrels by?" To her surprise, he pushed a long narrow box into her hand. She found it afterward to contain a pretty little pin in the shape of a dagger, which, with Miss Lejeune's assistance, and Mr. Horner's approval, he had bought for a parting gift.

. The car was cleared of all but passengers, and the train rolled out of the station. As the party settled themselves in their comfortable turning seats, Mr. Horner said:

"Here is all our mail. We were lucky not to miss it, for it has the foreign letters."

There was something for every one, even Augustine, and for some time all were absorbed in the contents of their respective envelopes. Then a few comments were exchanged, and the letters passed from one to another, that each might read every one.

When Bessie had done hers, and saw that her father also had finished the last flimsy sheet, she came and sat down by his side on one of the low carpet foot-stools which accompany the chairs.

"You see, papa, what mamma says in her letter?"

"Yes, my dear."

"And may I tell you my plan?" she asked.

"I long to hear it, Bessie," he replied.

She glanced at Miss Lejeune as if to summon her aid, and that lady leaned a little forward, the better to join the discussion.

"Aunt Dut and I, papa, think we had all better go over at once, to be with the rest of them. I long to see Mary," she went on, while tears came in her eyes, "and there is no need for mamma to come home. And then, do not you see, we can take Hubert along with us, as far as we go?"

Her father looked at her for a moment with no expression on his face but a half-smile, then he said,

"Now, Bessie, may I tell you my plan?"

"I long to hear it, papa," she said, repeating his own words with stronger emphasis.

"It is precisely the same as yours."

The boys all looked up at the sound of laughter and approval which followed this remark, and Tom came from his remote seat to find out what was going on.

"There is only one difficulty,—and that is Tom, what shall we do with him"—Bessie was saying as he came up.

SCENERY BY THE WAY.

"Do not allow Tom to be a difficulty," said he. "I know very well what you were talking about. Tom will stay in New York and study his lessons like a good boy, while the rest of you go to mamma and Mary."

"And I will stay at home," said Miss Lejeune, "and take care of Tom."

"Now that, aunt Augusta, is out of the question," said Bessie; "for you must come with us."

"You must go with them," said Tom. "I shall do very well.

Philip will be at Cambridge, and we can meet whenever we feel solitary."

"Never mind, then, about me, now," said Miss Lejeune; "that can be settled later."

Hubert was looking eagerly from one to another while this talk was going on, without half understanding it. The rapidity with which this American family formed a plan for crossing the Atlantic was something to which he never became familiar. The present one brought a wonderful hope to his heart, and he exclaimed, in a joyful manner,

"Then I shall not have to cross alone!"

"No, my dear boy," said Mr. Horner, "I have been hoping for some time that we could manage to spare you that."

By and by they all subsided into silence, each one behind the pretence of a book, revolving sunny schemes for the future opened by the new arrangement.

Tom was the only one whose prospects were not of the *couleur de rose;* his mind was at leisure enough to allow him to talk with Augustine Stuyvesant, that he might not feel shut out of the general joy.

"Well, old fellow," said Tom to him, "we have had a pretty good summer, have we not?"

"Yes, indeed," said Augustine; "I hate to go back. I wonder what will become of us all winter."

To everybody's surprise, while the train was stopping at Springfield, Mr. Stuyvesant stepped into the car. The meeting was a purely accidental one, for he had missed Mr. Horner's letter telling him at what time to expect Augustine in New York.

"I came up from Newport to Boston," he said, "and should have looked you up, but this boy did not give us the name of your hotel in his letter. I was hastening back to New York, in order to be on hand when my goods were returned to me," he continued, smiling at his son; "I have been in one of the rear cars all the way; they told me I could have a drawing-room seat in this one at Springfield, but not sooner."

His arrival was most opportune, as he could now join the family counsels.

"Tom, my boy, spend the winter with us," he cried; "we will

ALONG THE SOUND.

take the best of care of you. We have just engaged a furnished house for the winter." And he went on to detail the street and number of it.

Close upon Mr. Stuyvesant, entered the porter with straw-baskets containing a plentiful lunch previously ordered by telegraph.

Little tables were put up between the chairs, a cloth spread upon each; and forth came from the baskets knives, forks, napkins, tumblers, pickles, and the food for a substantial meal. Hubert was pleased with this feature of American travel.

The journey between Boston and New York is very pleasant, by the road and the train which the Horners had chosen. The scenery is pretty all the way, especially along the Sound, and in the end of October, as they saw it, was brilliant with rich tints of autumn foliage. After crossing the Connecticut River the road follows its banks for a time.

"Only think!" cried Hubert, "that this is our river we have been swimming in and rowing on all summer."

"Is it?" exclaimed Augustine, amazed; "it is much bigger here!"

"And so are you much bigger than when I saw you last," said his father. Augustine had grown in every way wonderfully through the summer, and was now a stout-looking boy.

They arrived in New York about six o'clock, after dark, and drove at once to the hotel which always served as a home for them when their own house was closed. As they tumbled out on the broad sidewalk, light as day with the white glare of electric lamps, a tall young gentleman ran to meet them. It was Philip,

IN CONNECTICUT.

who, after one of the wonderfully short passages often promised and sometimes made by modern steamers, had just arrived.

"Why, Philip, you here?" they all exclaimed. "We did not dream of expecting you before to-morrow!"

"How long have you been here?" asked his father.

"About a couple of hours. They told me in the office here you were coming by this train."

Then when they were all assembled in the public parlor waiting for their rooms, Philip said:

"And here, sir, is a telegram which had just come for you. I ventured to open it."

He was smiling. Mr. Horner pulled out the long, narrow strip of paper from its yellow envelope and read aloud, while they all gathered about him:

PAU, *October* 20, 18—

Mary Horner Hervey, æt. sixty minutes, sends her love to grandpapa.

CLARENCE HERVEY.